Chill

By: Naomi Charles

First paperback edition August 2021
Second paperback edition August 2023

Cover art and design by OkayCreations

ISBN 978-1-7352292-7-0

Prologue

The sun lights the sunset sky, begging for us to remember her before she retires for the day. There's no doubt that we will. I'm enthralled by the fierce oranges and pinks she casts across the sky when I notice the music playing from the car stereo is turned down to a measly hum. I look over my shoulder, and I see Dad glancing at me before his eyes stare out on the road again.

It's the last day of summer vacation, and Dad's driving the pick-up back from our camping trip. It was our tradition at the end of every summer, and this year is no different. He was always busy with work, but he always made time for our trips. My favorite was our camping trip. We would fish, hike, and look at cool animals. More than anything, this is one of the trips that Mom never went on. She never liked the outdoors if it didn't involve the beach.

"What are you thinking about?" Dad nudges me from his driver's seat.

"School. I don't want to go." I shrug.

His face goes into a smirk, and he narrows his green eyes at me from under his cap. I shake my head in response. Here comes some lame conversation about middle school being cool or something. I'm not amused.

"Middle school is so much more fun than elementary school. It's brutal sometimes, but it has its upsides too," he says.

"Like what?" I ask.

"I met your mother when I was in middle school," he replies like that's actually a good answer.

I look up at him with the same smirk and narrowed eyes he gave me before. If him meeting Mom — a girl — was his answer as to why middle school would be great, then he had failed this argument. He could've at least mentioned meeting someone that I was actually a fan of.

"Amazing," I deadpanned.

"Be nice." He raises his eyebrow.

"*I'm just saying*, a girl is not going to make anything better," I say.

"One day, you'll find someone who will," he says, and I know there is no possible way he could be speaking about Mom. There was no way that a guy like Dad would think someone like Mom would make things better, but I stay silent.

"Promise me something," he says, glancing over at me again.

"Yeah?"

"If you do find her, don't let her go. Ever."

Chapter 1

Let's get a few things straight. First, I am not a pansy. Just because I did not want to take part in my mother's abysmal ventures did not mean I was weak. It meant that I had a moral compass. After Dad died, I felt like I was the only one in our circle that did. That was until I finally reconnected with Eliza. She had just gotten sent home due to some boarding school scandal, and it soon became clear that it was us versus all the adults in our lives who had forgotten what being a good person was — especially my mother.

Anyway, I'll speak more about that later. The second thing you should know is that I will never, ever love someone as much as I love Nicole Aaliyah Smith, and, if anything had ever happened to her, I know my life would be significantly less. After all, I'm sure one would know if part of their soul went missing.

I'm getting sidetracked. The reason I brought that up was to explain exactly how worried I was on our way to Williamsburg the night of the call, the night everything as far as I knew it changed. This was the second time my life had changed a crap-ton. The first was on my sixteenth birthday.

***

I groaned at the sound of my alarm sounding from my phone. I picked it up and turned off the worst sound known to man. I looked through my notifications and tapped on the one with Nicole's name on it. She sent me a birthday message at midnight. She always stayed up late to post and send messages for the birthdays of her friends and family.

Nicole Smith: Happy Birthday Noah! I'm so happy I get to celebrate an angel being born today (that's you). I love you so much and can't wait to celebrate later. I hope you survive whatever business stuff your mom is making you do today. Actually, you better because I don't think I would really like it much without you around. Okay, this is enough gushiness for now. I'll save the rest for later.

I read the message twice with probably the dumbest grin on my face. I finally replied.

Noah Crawford: Thanks, baby. I'm sure today is going to be a lot, but I'll survive for you. Love you. Talk later.

I walked downstairs to the kitchen a half-hour later with a suit on and my hair situated. My mother was sitting at the table behind a newspaper. She already had her heels on and was ready to go. Our maid, Lora, had set my breakfast on the table and went back to her quarters. I sat down and started eating. Tracey had not moved to acknowledge me. This was not unusual for her, but I decided to entertain the idea that she would care about it being the day I entered the world rather than the business aspect of whatever the day was supposed to be.

"Good morning, Mom," I said after a few bites of my Belgian waffle.

"Morning," she said.

"You know what today is," I said, overly excited.

"Yes. Happy birthday," she said from behind the newspaper.

I knew that was most likely all I would get, so I started to look at my phone. I wanted to see all the birthday wishes on my page, especially the one from my girlfriend, who liked to post the most embarrassing pictures of me. I scrolled until I saw a picture of us in school. She was in her cheer uniform and I was in my varsity jacket for a homecoming event. The caption said, "It's this stud's birthday today."

"Who are you talking to?" my mother asked, finally folding her newspaper.

"No one. Why?"

"You're smiling ridiculously at the screen like you do when you speak to *her*," she said, and I was pretty sure her eyes were trying their best to shoot lasers at me.

She walked over and looked at the phone screen. She wrinkled her nose at the sight of Nicole.

"Stop staring at it and hurry up," she said, walking out of the room.

We drove downtown to the CCT building. As soon as Tracey walked through the glass doors, two of her assistants came up to her. They were frantically updating her on meetings and the paperwork that needed to be done. She ignored them as if they had said nothing. It was odd, but, unfortunately, not out of character for my mother.

"Clear my schedule until noon. I need to do something with my son," she said when we stopped at the elevators.

"Yes, Ms. Crawford," the woman said, tapping on her tablet.

"Can I get you anything else, Ms. Crawford?" the guy asked.

"No, Eric. That's all," my mother said before the elevator doors opened.

"It's Ethan," he hesitated.

"Close enough," my mother replied before the doors closed.

She typed on the elevator's keypad and pressed on a button that brought us down to what seemed to be the basement. We walked out into a clean, white hallway. It was the type of clean that made you almost uncomfortable. There didn't seem to be any doors along the shiny walls.

"Where are we going?" I asked.

"You'll see," she said, tapping the wall, which made a door slide to the side.

The revealed room seemed super dark, and I hesitated at first. My mother walked through the door and greeted two guys that I hadn't noticed there until she said something. I questioned why they would sit in the shadows the way they did, but I slowly followed. The men stood as we walked through the doorway. The room was small, with one dim chandelier above a large, shiny wooden table. It was oval-like in shape, but more flat on the longer sides. My mother took a seat at the center of one of the flat sides.

"Take a seat," she said, pointing to the seat directly across from hers.

I nodded and sat down. The two men in the room stayed silent and sat down once I did. The door slid close and it was even darker. The black walls made it feel like a cave.

"As you gentlemen know, today is my son's sixteenth birthday. It's a big day," she said with what sounded like humor in her voice.

"A big day indeed," a man with snow-white hair agreed.

"The older he gets, the more he looks like Carter," the other man said, playing with his waxed mustache.

"Where's Daniel?" my mother asked dryly, purposely disregarding their comments.

"Elizabeth got into some trouble up at Westover again. He had to take a call," Bow Tie answered.

"Well, I guess we'll just get started without him," my mother said, running a hand through her hair.

"Start what? Can I know what's happening now?" I asked.

My mother and the two men looked at each other with wry smiles before looking at me again.

"Welcome to The Table, son," White Hair said.

I looked down at the table we were sitting at and back up at them confused. What was so special about this table?

"What," was all I could say at that moment. I wanted to laugh because he sounded like he was welcoming me to some camp or something stupid, but I kept a straight face.

"Your father and I agreed that you would become part of The Table when you turned sixteen." Tracey smiled.

"Oh… okay. What does that mean?" I asked, wondering what Dad had to do with my mother being a weirdo.

"Twenty-two years ago, your father and Daniel established The Table. It started out as a network of a few close friends and colleagues who wanted to ensure their business ventures would always result in success. It soon grew, and we are now the glue that ensures that power stays where it belongs," my mother said.

Have you ever wished you could have seen yourself react in a situation? When things happen you don't get to see your face. You don't get to see your natural reactions unless someone is recording them. My point is that I wished I could have seen what my face looked like when my mother started to explain what The Table was.

"Um… alright and how do you make sure that happens? You invest or something?" I asked, sitting back in my chair.

My mother rolled her eyes before looking at the guy with the bow tie. It had no effect on me anymore — the look I mean. I was used to that at this point. My mother never took anything that I said with any value. I was more concerned about what this guy was about to say.

"We're fixers. We ensure our investments prosper. We do whatever needs to be done to make sure that happens," he said.

"And what do you mean by *needs to be done*?" I asked, concerned because this sounded way too similar to *The Godfather*.

"Whatever needs to occur will occur," my mother said, folding her hands on the table.

Her eyes looked intense, and it sent shivers down my spine. Whatever she meant was not something I wanted to be part of. I knew my mother definitely had to be up to something sometimes, but I never imagined this. I didn't know what it was, but I immediately felt a weird feeling in my stomach.

"I don't want to be involved in this." I stood up.

"You don't have a choice." White Hair gave me an incredulous look.

"Sit down, Noah," my mother said.

I struggled, but then I finally sat down. Bow Tie slid over a folder. I looked at it before giving them a questioning look.

"What is it?" I asked.

"It's what you need to know before you start," my mother replied.

"*Woah woah woah!* Start what? I'm not starting anything," I said.

"Noah Carter Crawford, if you do not do as I say and open that folder… you will not get your gift," my mother said through her teeth.

I didn't care about the gift at that point. I listened in hopes that I would be able to get out of there as soon as possible. I opened the folder and scanned the words. There was a page titled "Issues" with a bunch of names. Most of them had the word "resolved" at the end of the paragraph. I scanned on and noticed these were names that had been in car accidents. Some of them had died.

"These people were in car accidents… What happened?" I asked.

Not a word was said and that was enough for my suspicions to be confirmed. I looked through some more and saw people who had "immunity" and were listed as "alliances."

"What do immunities and alliances do?" I asked.

"Those are people who are known to have our best interests in mind. They have taken care of us. They are untouchable," Bow Tie said.

All of a sudden, the doors opened, and a tall bald man that looked vaguely familiar walked in with a shorter younger guy behind him. The young guy had a face of slight discomfort. The bald guy gave me a small smile.

"You made it," my mother said to the bald man.

They touched cheeks before he sat down next to Bow Tie. The younger guy sat at the end of the table near the door.

"I had to deal with some business with family. You know how Eliza can be," the bald man sighed.

"Yes, well… Today is Noah's big day," my mother said, looking back at me.

The bald man looked over to me and extended his hand. I took it and shook it.

"You probably don't remember me much. I'm Daniel… Daniel Craig. Your father and I were business partners," he said.

"Hi, Mr. Craig," I said.

"Daniel is fine. Do you have any questions for me?"

"Yeah… Why do I have to do this on my birthday? Couldn't this have waited?" I asked, checking my watch that read almost eleven in the morning.

"What do you have planned today? Something with *that girl*?" my mother asked.

"My girlfriend's name is Nicole. Please, not today, mother," I sighed.

My mother hated that Nicole and I were together. She told me that I could do better. She said Nicole was weak and I would regret wasting time on her one day, that she would betray me. I knew that would never happen. Nicole was a gentle being, but that didn't mean she lacked strength. She was so bright, and I was a mere fly attracted to her light.

"Your father and I agreed that on the sixteenth birthday of our children, we would have them get involved in our business… It's more of a gift. We can grant you one request," Daniel said.

"What type of gift?" I asked.

"Virtually anything," Daniel answered with a shrug.

"Examples?" I asked.

"If you wanted a car, an internship at a good business, power on a social media platform… we could give it to you," White Hair said.

"So, let's say I wanted a bunch of strippers to come to my room tonight. You would do that?" I asked.

"That's what you want?" My mother seemed more amused than concerned, and

I found yet another reason to be disappointed in her.

"No. Of course not. I'm just curious," I said.

"Yes," she said.

I thought for a moment. I didn't actually want anything. I looked down at the paper in front of me with the list of people who were immune and safe from whatever dangers of this organization that one could come across. My phone vibrated. I slid it out of my pocket quickly to see Nicole's name on the screen. She probably was checking in. She always worried about me.

"Phone away. You can't talk to her right now," my mother said when I smiled.

I slid the phone back and looked back up at the four of them staring at me. I looked over to the younger guy, who was looking at me with a look I couldn't read. I was always intrigued by those who I couldn't read like a picture book.

"What's your name?" I asked.

"Who?" my mother asked.

"My name is Gregory Nelson. You can call me Greg," he answered nervously.

"Nice to meet you, Greg," I said.

"Likewise, Mr. Crawford," Greg said.

"Anyway," my mother interrupted.

"So can anyone be harmed by you guys? Is anyone off limits?" I asked.

"No one over sixteen is off limits unless specified with granted immunity," Bow Tie said.

"So I can grant someone immunity?" I asked.

"Yes. I mean, your wife and children get automatic immunity, but you don't have any of those yet, so yes, you can," Daniel said.

"Then I want to grant immunity to my girlfriend, Nicole Smith," I said.

My mother's face wrinkled with disgust. Daniel didn't show emotion. Instead, he silently turned to my mother.

"Pick something else," she said.

"Why?" I asked.

"Until you are fully inducted, you cannot give more than one person immunity. This would be your only one to grant," Daniel said.

"Okay, I still choose Nicole," I said.

"No," Tracey said.

"Why not? Why shouldn't she have it? Do you want something to happen to her?" I asked.

She didn't answer immediately, and I felt like I could've cried. I didn't though. I hated how much she hated Nicole.

"Don't answer that. Nicole gets immunity. She turns sixteen in a few months, and I want her to be safe. I don't care if you don't like it, Mother," I said.

"Alright then. Put that in the system, Greg," Daniel said.

"Yes sir." Greg fumbled around to get his laptop out of his briefcase.

Mother crossed her arms as we watched him open the laptop and press a button, which made the screen show up from a projector. Greg asked me how to spell her name and I told him. He typed it in.

"You're impossible sometimes, Noah. You're acting like your father," my mother spat.

What I wanted to say was "better than being just like you," but I kept my mouth shut. I exhaled and looked over at Daniel. He had a forced, politician's smile on his face. Bow Tie and White Hair looked just as uncomfortable.

***

In an hour, that day would have been exactly three years ago. It's crazy how time could heal wounds, but create them just the same.

Nicole stared at her feet as the train ride went on. She was silent, but she was breathing as if she had just run a marathon. I put my hand on her shoulder and she jumped. She was deep in her thoughts. It was like she had forgotten I was there.

"Sorry," I said, giving her shoulder a squeeze.

"It's ok. I'm fine," she said, rubbing her hands together.

She was not fine. She was visibly suffering, and I'm sure the inside of her head was worse. I felt terrible. It was all my fault. I was the reason all of this was happening. My family was crazy, and I knew my life would never be the way it was before any of this happened. Part of me regretted not breaking up with her when it had crossed my mind. I was in love and it made me selfish.

Nicole pulled herself up to stand with one of the metal bars. It broke my concentration and I looked at her.

"This is Grand Street," the automated voice on the L train said.

The train started to slow to a stop. It was almost midnight, and the platform looked pretty empty except for a few people scattered around. Nicole walked over to the door and looked at me from over her shoulder.

"You ready?" she asked.

"Um… yeah," I said.

I was not ready at all.

Chapter 2

We walked in silence as Nicole followed her phone's directions to the warehouse. It was silent, but the quiet was extremely loud and frightening. The only sound I could hear was the occasional scratching sound when one of us would drag our feet across the sidewalk. There were hardly any people around, but I felt like I was being watched. Whenever I looked over my shoulder, all I could see was a poorly lit neighborhood.

"I thought Williamsburg was supposed to be up-and-coming and… fun," Nicole said dryly.

"Not this part," I said, getting closer to her as we reached an area with more warehouses and fewer apartments.

"It says we're almost there," she said. I could hear the shakiness of her voice.

"We don't have to do this."

Nicole stopped walking, and I finally stopped a few steps ahead of her. She looked furious.

"And just leave Jason there? *I'm not like you.* I care about what happens to him and other people, for that matter. He didn't do anything. The person said I had to come here so he… so something wouldn't happen to him," she said, and I decided to not remind her that he, in fact, *did* do something. Although, it didn't warrant what was probably happening to him.

"You think I don't?" I asked without really thinking. I already knew the answer.

"These are your people. The people you and your family choose to associate with, Noah," she said as she pointed her finger and stuck it into the chest of my coat.

I already knew that, but it wasn't the best thing to hear. I didn't choose this, and it still didn't matter. In her eyes, I was one of them.

"I don't want to leave him, Nikki. I don't like him, but I would never want this for him. That being said, what's more important to me is your safety," I said softly.

Nicole scowled at me and kept walking. She sighed and said something underneath her breath.

"We can't leave him," she finally said, loud enough for me to hear this time.

"But Nikki, who knows what they want you for," I pleaded.

"I know that Noah, but he's my friend, and I care about him. Whatever he did… he doesn't deserve this," she said.

I continued to follow her. She silently followed the phone directions. After a few moments, we stopped in front of a very old warehouse. The bricks looked worn. The windows were dirty and cracked. It looked dark inside. It was the opposite of inviting. Nicole looked around before knocking on the door.

"Are you sure about this?" I asked.

"Yeah… you should not be here. They asked for me to be alone," she said in a small voice.

"Are you *insane*? I'm not leaving you alone."

"Just wait out here," she sighed.

"No," I demanded.

"Look, Noah, Jason is in there, okay? I fucking hate this, but you know what? I'm doing this for him. I feel partially responsible for this. Do both of us a favor and hide for ten minutes," she said.

"And what if you're not out in ten minutes?"

"Then come looking for me," she said.

I nodded reluctantly and backed away. The door started to unlock on the other side. I jogged over to a car and hid behind it. I was still able to see through its windows. The door to the warehouse opened and a man who looked like he was just a little shorter than me answered the door. His silhouette showed he was jacked. It was definitely someone from security. Nicole walked in and the door closed behind her.

I kept my kneeling position behind the car. The cold started to seep through my jeans and it made me shiver. I pulled out my phone to check the time, but instead, it started to vibrate with Rachel's name on it. She was probably wondering what was going on with her sister. She was not alone.

"Hello," I whispered.

"Nicole won't answer her phone. Where is she?" she asked.

"We're in Williamsburg," I said, preparing my ears for the killing they were about to endure.

"Why *the hell* are you there?" she asked.

"Because she got a phone call saying to come here or something could happen to Jason."

"And you let her? Are you insane?" she screamed.

For the next two minutes, I held the phone away from my ear. Rachel continued to scream and say things along the lines of me being an asshole and how this was all my fault. I wish I had reason to retort the claims, but I didn't at that moment.

"I'm heading back to you," she said when I brought the phone back to my ear.

"*No*, you're not," I demanded.

"*Yes, I am*. You're clearly incapable of keeping her safe, so I'll just have to do it myself," she said.

"It's not safe, Rachel," I sighed.

"Right, but someone important to the both of us is not safe… I'll be there in less than an hour," she said before hanging up.

I rested my face in my palm for a moment before I looked up at my phone screen again. Ten minutes was just a few seconds away, and I wondered what was happening inside. What were they saying to her? I stood up and walked up to the door. I was about to knock, but then stopped myself. I wasn't supposed to be here. I looked around and saw an old fire escape going up the side of the building. I found myself staring at it longer than I needed to. I hated heights, but then I thought about what could be happening to Nicole. I took a deep breath before I jumped and grabbed onto the bottom of the ladder.

I pulled myself up and started to climb up to the first small platform. The metal was so cold that it stung my fingers. I rubbed them together when my feet met the platform. I looked in the dusty windows of the floor I was parallel to, but there was nothing in there. I held on tight as I walked up to the next level. I leaned into a window that seemed to be lit up by a dim light.

I rubbed my sleeve against the glass in an attempt to see more and the difference was minimal. The windows opened inward and I froze, unsure of how I would get in. I pushed on the window with a small amount of pressure to see if it would move. It did a little without any noise. I pushed it again and it squeaked slightly. I held my breath for a moment before I looked in. Nicole was standing very still as my mother spoke animatedly. Jason was tied to a chair with his mouth taped shut. He looked like he took a few hits.

I scanned the rest of the room. A few jacked guys were watching from a far corner. This was not something I could handle on my own. I called Eliza as I shuffled carefully on the fire escape away from the window. The phone rang twice before she answered.

"I thought you said you were heading to Nicole's for the night. Why are you calling me?" Eliza sighed tiredly.

"Because I thought she was in trouble," I said, matching her tone.

"You don't have to explain to me out of guilt anymore. It's getting old. Anyway, why are you calling me?"

"Nicole and… *Jason* are in trouble. I need some backup. Can you send a couple of guys over to my location? I'm sending it to you now," I said as I sent my coordinates to her.

"Why are we helping Jason? He's a pretentious dick," she said, and I could hear her sitting up in bed.

"Yes, but he doesn't deserve to die. We're better than that. We're not our parents," I said.

Eliza was silent for a while. She knew what I meant. Over the past couple of years, we had learned some things about our parents that I'm sure we both wished we could erase from memory. *One day, I would make things better*, I thought, be the guy I at least thought my father was. I wanted to be the guy I thought he was when I was growing up.

"Whatever Crawford," she exhaled.

"Does that mean yes?"

The phone beeped, and the call was over. She hung up. I sighed and walked back over to the window. This time it was open, and I could hear what was happening.

"As I said, you've caused trouble for this family since the moment my son realized you were the girl of his dreams, or whatever he said that night he called me crying about *finding the woman he wanted to marry*," my mother went on. I wasn't sure what I felt more at that moment: embarrassment or fear for the… woman I wanted to marry.

"Ms. Crawford, with all due respect, I think you got this all wrong," Nicole said, and I could hear the incredulity with a mix of fear in her voice.

"And how is that?" my mother asked, crossing her arms as she paced nearby.

"I never wanted to take Noah away from The Table. To be honest with you, I had no idea it existed until a few days ago," Nicole said.

"You didn't have to want to. All you had to do was play the little good girl act and convince him that your values were more important than what I told him."

"There's no act. There was no intention," Nicole said.

"Right, because you're boring and lack all the things I'd want for my son," my mother said, and the tone even stung me from outside.

Nicole was silent for a moment. I knew immediately that my mother's words had hit a soft spot. When there was no quick-witted response, something was wrong. Regardless of what things were in that moment, anyone in their right mind knew Nicole had sacrificed a lot for me. She would forever be different because of what I put her through.

"Well, I don't want your son anymore."

Ouch. I knew that, but still.

"Lovely, then you won't mind doing me a favor and signing the papers we spoke about," my mother said, pointing to the papers on the table.

"Why can't I tell Noah about this?" Nicole asked.

"It's against our agreement," my mother said.

"Then I need time to read it."

"Then I will take that time to make sure your little friend doesn't see tomorrow," my mother answered without missing a beat. Oh no.

Nicole gasped. She looked over at Jason, and he made noises behind his covered mouth. One of the jacked guys in suits punched him in the face, and, even muffled, his scream was painful to hear. I felt bad for the guy, even if his being there was partially his fault.

"Please don't hurt him," Nicole choked.

"Too late, but you can take him out of here *alive* if you sign."

"Can you at least tell me what I'm signing?"

"I already said you're signing over your immunity and rights in our community," my mother said, and my blood started to boil.

I knew she wanted Nicole's safety to be out of the equation to hold over my head. I hated that I knew that, but I immediately did. Tracey's goal wasn't to hurt Nicole, but I knew she could have easily changed her mind.

"No!" I shouted, making everyone jump in the room as my voice boomed against all the metal.

My mother looked up with a smile that made my skin crawl, and, all of a sudden, I felt something cold held against my temple. I was being grabbed away from the window. I tried to fight, but that's when everything went black.

Everything started to come back into focus. Nicole was holding my face in her hands. Her look told me whatever happened to me looked bad. I grimaced at the thought and tried to look around. I swung my head around quickly as I scanned the space around me. Jason was still tied in his seat looking at me with sympathetic eyes. Okay, if *he* was looking at *me* like that, I knew I looked horrific. My mother's face looked unbothered, like I was some injured roach. She was sitting in a chair, and she almost looked bored. I stared right into her eyes. She stared back like she dared me to be upset about this, like I didn't have a right. My blood boiled even more.

"Enough. Bring her back," she said, and two men pulled Nicole back to the table. She didn't fight, so they weren't rough.

"Time is up. Sign the papers, or that's it for your friend," my mother threatened.

Nicole just stared at me for a long moment before she grabbed the pen on the table. Her hand shook as she looked at the paper. My body immediately felt all the weight of the stress I was feeling. It was like it took double the effort to breathe. She clicked the pen before she brought it to the paper. Before she could write anything, three shots were heard. Nicole froze, and I was scared she had been shot. She hadn't. I sighed in relief before I looked around. Walking through a hollow window frame was Eliza.

"Oh good. Eliza is here. Someone who actually shows promise," Tracey said.

Eliza climbed down a metal contraption that looked like scaffolding and walked past me. She looked at the paper on the table and wrinkled her nose.

"Eliza, make sure she signs it," my mother said.

"No, you vapid bitch," Eliza said to her before grabbing the pen out of Nicole's hand.

Eliza threw it across the room, and I heard the ping when it hit the concrete ground. She mouthed something to Nicole before turning to Tracey, who had a shocked expression on her face.

"What's going on?" my mother asked, standing up.

"She's not signing that contract, Tracey," Eliza said, pointing the gun at her.

"Miles, do something!" my mother screamed.

"I can't do anything to her, ma'am. Only if her father ordered it. He's still on the board," Miles responded with a scared look.

My mother stood up and sauntered over to Eliza who was tapping the side of the gun on her thigh. She was so comfortable with it, like it was nothing. My eyes went over to Nicole, who was looking at the weapon with wide eyes. All I wanted to do was get her out of here.

"I suggest you stop while you're ahead," my mother said coldly.

"I suggest you let the guy go," Eliza said, pointing the tip of her gun to Jason.

Jason made a muffled scream from under the duct tape. Miles pushed his face to the side to keep him quiet. All of a sudden, I heard the gun go off, and I froze. Nicole screamed, and my mother's face looked shocked for a moment before her cold look returned. I looked back at Miles, and he was on the ground holding his arm.

"Let him go," Eliza said.

Jason's eyes were wide, and he was frozen. He looked over at me as he trembled in his restraints. I tried to pull at my arms that were being held tightly by the two guards at my sides. They just held on tighter, and they made it hurt this time. I cursed underneath my breath.

"I will let him go once Nicole signs our little agreement," my mother said, crossing her arms and looking at me smugly.

"No! I'm not going to let you do this," I yelled, trying to pull free only to fail.

A guard came up and tried to grab Eliza by surprise, but she shot him in the foot. I shook my head in shock. I mean, she hardly *looked*. That was badass. I started to wonder if she even called backup. Eliza always thought it was better to do things herself. She looked at me with sad eyes before my mother spoke again.

"It's either that, or... you give up your position to me at The Table," my mother said.

"Why?" I asked.

"It's clear that this position is more fit for me. Once I got your father out of the way, and I saw how much of a pansy you were, I knew I was the one who was supposed to make this continue… the right way. My title as Head needs to be permanent," she said as if what she had said was normal.

Everything around me got cold. I felt like the air had been taken out of my lungs, and I couldn't catch myself. She was doing this for a title. She was hurting a bunch of pretty-much-kids for power.

"Mom? How could you?" I asked, and the words had a hard time getting out my throat.

"Now you want to call me Mom? Oh, please. You're pathetic. You thought you were fit to run this business?"

I felt tears running down my face. I couldn't wipe them away so I looked down. It had already been such an emotional night. I was almost too tired to fully react. It's not like I wanted to be part of The Table — not what it currently was, at least. I wanted to make it better. It would make Dad proud.

"Oh honey, not in front of the love of your life," she taunted me.

I felt a hand on my shoulder. Eliza's red ponytail swung into my view when she knelt next to me.

"I'm sorry… We'll make this right," she whispered.

I heard the sound of heels clicking on the concrete floor. I heard my mother's voice, and then Nicole's. Eliza left my side for a moment before I heard Eliza respond to them. I was in my head for a moment, and it all sounded so far away. At the moment, I was just trying to process everything that I now knew in that moment.

"Hey," Eliza said loudly in warning.

That pulled me back into the present before I heard a gunshot. The sound made my ears ring a little. I looked up quickly to see who shot who. I was a little scared to see who it was, because no option would be great. Jason getting hurt would mean that we lost. My mother getting hurt would mean war. Eliza getting hurt would mean our only source of safety was gone. Nicole getting hurt would mean the pain that would follow would be unimaginable.

"Miles! Miles, I've been shot," my mother cried as her personal security guard ran over, which meant one of my arms was let go.

I was jerked to the side, and the other guard that was still holding my arm reached for his back pocket. Two more shots went off, and he let my arm let go before letting out a guttural yelp. I turned to him, and our eyes met while he was on his way down. Standing behind him was Nicole with the gun that he had probably been looking for. *Holy shit.* I couldn't find the words fast enough.

"She took his gun," Miles said to the guard who had been standing by Jason.

Nicole's whole body shook as she looked at me ashamed. There was fear in her eyes. I looked down at the fallen guard. He wasn't dead. He was just hurt. She hit him in the thigh. He would be ok.

"Is he..." she started to ask in a whisper.

"No. He's not. Hand that over, Nikki," I said softly.

She handed it over and looked down ashamed. I wiped it off with my shirt and then put it in my back pocket.

"You always have my back," I said.

"Whether I like it or not, it seems," she sighed.

Another shot went off. I looked around, and Eliza had just shot a guard who was trying to stand up and charge toward us. Nicole ran over to Jason and used her keys to poke at the ropes he was tied up with. I went over and took out the switchblade in my pocket. Nicole's eyes looked at it quizzically as I cut the ropes off of Jason. She was about to say something when Jason pulled the tape off his mouth and pulled out whatever the hell was in his mouth.

"We should call the cops," he breathed.

Before I could tell him how much of an absolute idiot he was, more gunshots sounded. We all looked over to Eliza, who had her gun pointed toward the ceiling. She was looking at Jason as if she wished he would drop dead on the spot.

"You're actually a waste of space. We are not calling *anyone*," she screamed.

My phone began to ring in my pocket. All eyes were on me now. Rachel's name lit up on the screen.

"Are you here?" I asked.

"Why would Rachel be here? What the hell is going on?" Nicole asked, pushing me.

"Yeah. Should I come out of the car?" Rachel asked.

"No, we're coming to you," I said softly, just in case any of my mother's minions were listening. I gave an apologetic look to Nicole. I knew I would hear an earful about this later.

"Let's go," Eliza said, walking toward the exit.

"Don't you move another muscle or I will make sure you regret it," my mother screamed, and I could hear the pain in her voice.

I looked behind my shoulder, and I saw her reaching for something in her pocket. Eliza's eyebrow raised.

"Run," Eliza said, pushing a slow moving Jason forward.

Tracey lifted a little ball of something. I couldn't tell what it was, but I didn't want to know what would happen if she threw it. I pulled Nicole, who was staring at my mother. We pushed through the door first. Eliza and Jason followed. I heard a sizzling sound behind us. I looked over my shoulder before the doors closed and saw the room beginning to fill with steam. Miles was running through the cloud and would be running through the doors within seconds.

I looked ahead of me and I had fallen behind. I was in the back. Nicole, Jason, and Eliza filled in the back row of the white SUV parked in front of the building. I opened the front passenger door and hopped in. We all screamed at once for Rachel to drive, and she did not disappoint. We flew through the streets at a speed that was nothing less than twenty miles over the speed limit.

"Where am I going?" she asked, and I could hear the fear in her voice.

"Long Island," Eliza chimed in.

"If they're looking for us, they'll go there first. I know somewhere where we can go. Make a right at the light," I said.

Chapter 3

We were making our way upstate. It had only been twenty minutes, but it felt like twenty hours. Either way, I knew I was about to kick Jason's ass into the East River.

"I'm not going anywhere until you tell me where we're going," Jason yelled from the back seat.

"You idiot, we are literally driving there regardless of what you say," I spat.

"Guess you're a kidnapper too. Makes sense," Jason shot back.

"What are you talking about?" I asked, looking to the back middle seat. It was dark, but the street lights passing by temporarily illuminated his face. He looked like he wanted to kill me. Ditto.

"Jason, do not act like most of this isn't your fault. You were problematic and made us all risk our lives to save your ass. You had to keep pushing," Rachel chimed in from the driver's seat.

"Yeah, why *did* you keep pushing this? There are other cases you could've used for your nerd fetish," Eliza finally added.

"Noah knows why," Jason said pointedly.

We all looked at Jason with a questioning look. Even Nicole broke her concentration from out the window and looked at him with drawn eyebrows. He took in all our expressions before he spoke.

"Your father knew where my brother went. You knew if I dug deep enough I would reveal some human trafficking ring or some other sick dealings your family is part of," he said, and if it weren't for his tone, I would've thought he was kidding. The Table has revealed itself to be deplorable in the past few years that I've known about it, but children were always off limits. I didn't have a lot of things that allowed me to sleep at night anymore, but I was certain that was one of them.

"There is no human trafficking ring. I saw that you have a missing brother, but that wasn't us," I said.

Nicole narrowed her eyes at me quizzically. She was dating the guy, and she was in the dark too. I wondered why he wouldn't have told her about something as big as his brother going missing. Regardless, from what I had seen in the files, there was not a lot of information about it to share.

"What are you talking about?" she asked calmly, but I could almost hear the wheels turning in her head.

"My brother went missing when I was three. They never found him, but I did some digging and... things pointed to Noah's dad. He knew something, and Noah probably does, too," he said.

"When you were three, I was also three, almost four, and living in Queens," I scoffed.

"I'm sure he put a lot of work into that one as a toddler," Eliza chimed in.

"*Good one*," he looked over at Eliza with disgust before looking at me, "you didn't start The Table, but you are at the center of it now. I know you know something, Crawford."

"I don't know anything about your brother. I'm sorry," I said softly. I hated the guy, and I didn't have any siblings myself, but I knew the situation must've hurt him. I wondered why he thought my dad would know anything about it. Dad had done some questionable things in his day, but he would never hurt a kid. He had the biggest soft spot for children.

"Where do I go next?" Rachel asked.

"Go straight, for now… You sure you don't want me to drive?" I asked.

"There's no way you're touching this wheel, white man." She glanced at me before doing a neck roll to look back at the road.

"Just offering," I sighed.

"I know your father knew something. That asshole ruined my life," Jason pressed.

I sighed before running my hand over my face. Before I spoke, I reminded myself that Nicole had feelings for this guy, so I couldn't rock him for calling Dad an asshole. I turned around to look at him, but I saw Nicole looking at me pointedly. She knew that would piss me off.

"Okay, why do you think Noah's dad had something to do with your brother going missing? That doesn't fit anything else you dug up. Plus, the increase of suspected crimes occurred after he died," Nicole said softly, and I realized my jaw dropped in shock.

"He was a suspect in the investigation. He was seen visiting my neighborhood many times before my brother disappeared," Jason said.

"They clearly didn't find anything," I said.

"Just like how you evade authority constantly. Way to follow in Daddy's footsteps," Jason said.

Before I realized what I was doing, I unbuckled my seatbelt and turned around to reach in the back. Eliza called for me to stop. Then Nicole did, but all I could pay attention to were loud sirens going off in my head. I didn't react to much, but making fun of my Dad was one of them. Nicole took off her seatbelt, reached up on the ceiling of the car, and turned on the light. She put herself in the middle of us.

"Jason, I swear to God just shut up. You've done enough. He doesn't know where your brother is, regardless of what the investigation said. I'm sorry. Noah, please sit down and put back on your seatbelt. Please, everyone just chill out. Just stop already," Nicole said loudly, and I could hear all the frustration in her voice.

Our eyes met for a moment. They were tired, and she looked disappointed. Lately, I had been used to her not being thrilled with me, but the last time she looked at me like how she did tonight was when she thought I killed Reggie. The shadows of the world crossed over her face as the car continued to drive into the night. Even then, I wanted to continue looking at her. The privilege was short-lived, though. She gave a quiet huff before she turned to look out the window once again.

It ate at me that Nicole and Jason dated. Maybe they hadn't broken up yet. I didn't know. I did know that I was clearly struggling with the idea of them. She could do so much better. He was making our lives miserable, and she didn't need that.

***

I could feel the sanity drain from my body as I looked across the room. Jason Westbrook was kissing Nicole. My Nicole. It had been two years since we dated, or since I had a right to stake any claim over her, but it still burned just the same. I still burned *for her* just the same. She was betraying me — at least, that's how I felt. Before I knew it, I was charging in their direction. My initial goal wasn't to deck Westbrook in the face but to stop whatever was happening from happening. This stupid jerk was kissing Nicole, and if she was not going to be with me, she should've at least done better than Jason. I didn't know how much I would stand by that statement in the following weeks. I punched Jason in the face, knocking him to the ground.

"You fucking idiot," I said.

"What the hell man," he said, finally looking up at me before getting up.

"Don't you touch her," I said, pushing him again.

"She's not your girl anymore. Relax," he said before pushing me a few feet back. I caught myself before I fell.

I was going to obliterate him. Screw the fact that Nicole wasn't mine anymore. I knew I should've considered what would've happened if Nicole did eventually date someone else. It wasn't fair to think it would never happen. She stood between us, and I found myself even more pissed that she wanted to protect this loser.

"Nikki, get out the way," I breathed, keeping my glare on Jason.

All I could hear was the blood pumping through my ears. A firm hand pulled me back. I looked over, and it was Greg. I had forgotten he was there. He was worried about my safety since he had noticed that there was some activity surrounding someone looking into the case of my uncle's unsolved murder. *Gee*, wonder who it was.

"You can't just beat up a guy for wanting Nicole. You know what that's like," Greg reasoned with me back at my dorm.

"Not him," I murmured. My face was buried in my hands.

"Why not? Don't you want her to be happy?"

"Yes," I said.

I wanted nothing more than for Nikki to be happy. It was just hard for me to imagine her with someone else. My chest hurt at the thought.

"Not to be a dick, but here's a suggestion. If you want to reconcile any type of relationship with her, you have to not do this. You're not her boyfriend. Don't be stupid. Before you hate this kid, give him a chance like she is," he said.

Ha, look where that fucking brought us.

***

We drove in mostly silence after that episode. Rachel and I only spoke occasionally about directions or her declining my offers to drive. It wasn't that I didn't think she could do it, Rachel was a great driver, but I knew she had to be tired. Nevertheless, she was alert the whole time. Maybe it was the adrenaline, or just the strong two parts of a soul the Smith girls possessed.

"Not to be a pain," Jason began.

"Too late," Nicole retorted before I could, and I felt a smile creep up on my lips.

Jason gave her an exasperated look, but was smart enough to not say anything smart back. I think he knew there was a conversation that awaited him when we reached our destination. Nicole barely got angry, but when she did, it was scary. The past few weeks had been slowly pushing her to the edge. Jason completely deserved what was coming for him, but I didn't want Nicole to suffer for it to happen.

"How much longer? I need a bathroom break," Jason said.

"A while," I sighed.

"How long is that?" he asked, and I didn't answer.

"Yeah, how long?" Nicole asked after a moment of silence.

"Probably a little more than an hour," I answered her immediately.

I looked at the screen of the car stereo. It was 3:35am in the morning. We had been driving for almost two hours. I felt my eyes getting heavy, but I had to give directions. Sleep was not going to be in my immediate future. I felt frustrated with my desire to sleep, but the will to make it to a known safe haven was stronger. I watched the thick darkness created by the trees pass by as we drove.

"So are we pulling up to a rest stop or what?" Jason asked after a few minutes.

"Is it really that much of an emergency, or are you insistent on being the human equivalent of a wet sock?" Rachel asked, glaring at him through the rearview mirror. I heard Eliza chuckle behind me and saw Nicole try to hide her smirk. The only person who did not appreciate her words was Jason, who, I could tell, was being mindful of what he would say to the sister of the woman he *supposedly* had feelings for.

"Yes, Rachel, it's an emergency," he breathed.

We were in the middle of nowhere, and it took awhile for us to find a rest stop, but Jason kept quiet until we arrived. We decided to split up into two groups. While one group would make sure the coast was clear, the other would take care of their business. The plan was for Eliza and Jason to go, but when Rachel realized she was left in the car with Nicole and myself, she left the car and caught up with them.

I turned around to look at Nicole sitting in the back seat. Her arms were crossed, and she was looking past me out the windshield. It was clear that it was on purpose. She didn't want to look at me. I didn't blame her. If I were in her place, I wouldn't want to speak to me either.

"Hey," I said because I couldn't help myself.

"Hi," she said softly.

She didn't say anything else. We sat in some more dark silence. Rachel forgot to leave the keys with us, and the car started to feel cold. Decembers upstate were brutal, and this night was no exception.

"What's on your mind?" I asked.

"Everything. This night feels like three put together. I'm just processing," she said softly. Her voice always soothed me. Even when she got on my nerves. Even when she was upset with me. Even when the world was on fire, like it was in that moment.

"I'm sorry."

"For what, exactly? We have your mother being absolutely insane. We have you not telling us exactly where we're going. Oh yeah, we also have you dropping an emotional bomb on me," she listed.

I had forgotten that I told Nicole that I loved her earlier that night. I had beaten myself up about it the first time I left her apartment, but when Rachel called and said Nicole could be in trouble, I forgot about it. There were so many other pressing matters to think about. I was surprised that she had the capacity to think about that with the night we were having.

"Sorry," I said again, because I didn't know what else to say. "I shouldn't have said that."

"So… you didn't mean it," she said, as if she had come to that conclusion and no longer needed my input on it.

"I do, but I probably should have waited for a better time to tell you."

"Noah…" she sighed before we heard Jason yelp from across the parking lot.

Nicole leaned forward into my row of seats to get a better look through the fogging glass of the car. I took the sleeve of my fleece to wipe the window and give us a better view. Rachel was speaking very loudly to Jason who was holding the left side of his face. Eliza walked behind them with a smirk on her face. Eventually she surpassed them and got in the back of the car next to Nicole.

"What the fuck?" I asked, looking at Eliza, who sat down and looked at her phone like chaos was not ensuing outside.

"What?" Eliza asked nonchalantly.

Nicole scowled at her and exited the car. I followed. At that point, Jason and Rachel were only a few feet away. Rachel was rubbing her knuckles with a look of satisfaction. Jason continued to rub his face.

"What happened?" Nicole asked, looking back and forth between the both of them.

"Ask her," Jason said through his teeth.

Nicole looked over at Rachel with a raised eyebrow. Rachel rolled her eyes before huffing out a big sigh. Her expression was as if her sister's question was ridiculous. I held in my smirk.

"He was in my way. You mess with my sister, you mouth off to me, and you get in my way? I did something about it," she said, clenching her knuckles and releasing over and over again.

"Does it hurt?" I asked, looking at her hand.

"Yes," Jason's self-absorbed ass answered.

"He wasn't talking to you, you expired coupon," Rachel snapped.

I let out a laugh, and Nicole elbowed me in the side. I looked over at her, and she gave me that look that was supposed to make me feel guilty. I shrugged apologetically. She never liked when I would entertain Rachel's "antics," but there were times I couldn't help it. Sometimes she would say things that were so funny, you would laugh before you could stop yourself.

"Okay guys. Get in the car. Rachel, are you okay enough to drive?" I asked, unable to mask how amused I was.

"Yeah, I'm fine," Rachel said.

"Are you sure you don't want me to drive?" Nicole asked, reaching out to look at her sister's hand.

"I'm sure. I'd rather be in pain than sit next to him," Rachel replied.

"Fair enough. Let's go," I said.

Chapter 4

It was really difficult to see in the night once we made it up to the Catskills. It was as if there was a sheet of darkness over the sky. The only light we had was the SUV headlights, which were only so helpful. To say I was stressed would be an understatement, but I kept following the directions on my phone. At least I knew we were close. When we turned off a paved road and drove on a dirt and gravel one, everyone was alert. I said a little prayer, asking for us to make it to our destination in one piece. I couldn't handle something else happening at my own hands. We took a turn onto yet another dirt road, and that's when I saw the faint light of the second floor of a house. We made it.

"Is this it?" Rachel asked, coming to a slow.

"Yeah," I said.

"Whose house is this?" Nicole asked.

"Mine," I answered.

I got out of the car and heard everyone behind me follow suit. The frigid air went right through my shirt, and I pulled my zipper up on my fleece. It was extremely hard to see where I was going. I knew I was going toward the house, but every time my foot reached the ground, it looked like it was disappearing into a sea of darkness. That was until a flash of light cascaded over the area surrounding the house. I heard the sound of movement behind me. I looked over my shoulder to see Nicole and Rachel holding each other. Jason held onto himself, which was fitting considering that he didn't care about anybody else, but I knew it was because he knew no one else wanted to. I considered feeling bad for him for a moment, but then I remembered he was the asshole who almost got us killed.

Eliza reached for the gun that was stuffed in her boot. I put my hand out to put her at ease. There were sensors. The security system sensed movement. I slowly walked to the front door. There was a keypad with a thumb-pad. I typed in the code — my birthday backwards — and put my thumb on the pad. The sound of a slow hum came before a click, and the sound of a bell signaled the door was unlocked.

I turned the knob of the front door that opened up to a dimly lit foyer. On the right of us was the entrance to the living room. The left was the entrance to a white and grey kitchen. Farther down was the entrance to an office. In the forefront, there was a grand staircase that led to the second floor.

Everyone seemed to be relieved for the protection from the bitter cold of the dark woods. I turned to the kitchen and a middle-aged man came walking from a doorway that opened up from the other side of the kitchen. His hair was peppered and almost matched the colors of the kitchen. He gave me a familiar smile before giving me a nod.

"Mr. Noah," he said with a faint accent. His voice sounded familiar and kind. I wished I could remember who he was.

"Hi," I said.

"Who are you?" Rachel asked.

"My name is Caesar. I am the main butler here at Soteria." He smiled and nodded again.

"Soteria?" Nicole asked from behind me, her eyebrows furrowed.

"Yes! That's the name of the property, named after the Greek goddess of safety. What are your names?" Caesar asked with a smile.

Everyone shared their names and Caesar kept up with a smile on his face, despite the wild hour of the morning it was. It had to be no later than 4:30 in the morning. He told us he would set up five bedrooms for us and went off to get to work. We were alone again.

We found ourselves sitting in the living room with cups of tea and hot chocolate. At first, it was quiet. We were exhausted, scared, and in shock from the recent events of the night. I watched the chocolate swirl around in my cup in a tired trance before I looked over at Nicole, who seemed to be doing her tired trance on my face. She finally noticed and looked back over at the gas fireplace burning in the corner.

The closest to the fireplace was Eliza. The flames reflected off her auburn hair. She noticed me looking her way immediately and gave me an exasperated glare. I sighed. The moment of peace was over.

"What?" I asked.

"Literally everything, that's what," Eliza said.

"What was I supposed to do?" I sighed.

Eliza stood up and pointed to Nicole, who immediately raised an eyebrow at her. *Oh boy*. Jason watched intently behind his mug, probably happy to not be the topic of ridicule. Rachel looked bored with all of us.

"The plan was to keep her away from Williamsburg. Then we find out that the kid and smartass over here are in Williamsburg. Literally what the fuck happened?" Eliza crossed her arms with a cold, tired look directed at me.

"I didn't know any of this was going to happen," I said, irritated.

"Jason going to Williamsburg was his own stupid idea. I went to Williamsburg to follow Jason to see what he was up to because things were getting out of hand. Nicole was going to stay right where she was until the leader of your cult called her and said Jason would pretty much die if she didn't do something. I'm sorry you feel as if your family's criminal antics are our fault. Also, Eliza, I suggest you don't refer to me as "the kid" again. The least you could do is call me by my name," Rachel said, giving Eliza a challenging look.

Eliza took a moment to look at Rachel. She was not used to anyone speaking to her like that. She always got what she wanted, and that was law in her world. Nicole, who was rubbing her temples, sighed and stood up. She gave me a tired look before addressing the mess ensuing in front of us.

"Look, no one is happy with what's happening here. We all had something to do with how things went wrong tonight, but fighting or blaming anyone is not going to make it any better," Nicole said. I smiled inwardly at how calm and soothing she sounded, even in a time like this.

"Oh, how nice. Clearly you know what's best, right," Eliza taunted her.

"Eliza, stop," I warned her.

"You almost got killed tonight over a guy who was only dating you for his personal purposes of getting at your ex, who used you to get out of jail. Honey, do you really think you're the one who knows jackshit?" Eliza asked, slowly walking up to her with a couple inches over her in height.

Nicole crossed her arms and stood her ground. I thought I saw her eyes get glossy for a moment, but she blinked it away. At that moment, I felt so sorry for her. My chest hurt when I heard what happened being described in that way. I had no choice. I didn't want Nicole to be killed. An act of betrayal like telling the cops could have gotten her status of immunity revoked. I had to think fast. It wasn't only for me, it was mostly for her.

"Back up, Eliza," Nicole said firmly, hardly moving. Hardly breathing.

"Or what? You're going to send someone to handle me because you can't do it yourself — because you're weak? Who should I be waiting for? Your sister?"

"It's not my fault you couldn't get the only thing you ever been denied in your life. Get over it. He doesn't want you," Nicole said in her same firm tone.

Eliza took a step back and looked at her as if she couldn't believe what she had just heard. Nicole was still. Eliza picked up her arm and, before I could react, Rachel did.

"I swear, Eliza, if you don't back up, I will rock your ass this fine morning," Rachel screamed.

I stood up and gave Eliza an exasperated look as I stepped forward. She gave a fiery glare before looking at Nicole as if she was the worst person to walk the Earth. I looked up, asking God, or whoever was up there, for patience. I knew she wasn't done.

"Guess I was right. Little sister to the rescue." Eliza laughed before it was immediately stopped by brown liquid cascading over her face.

Nicole gasped and turned to Rachel in shock. Eliza shrilled. I felt my arm get wet as I saw brown dots across the arm of my white shirt. I gave Rachel a reprimanding look. She shrugged with a look of victory. I couldn't blame her. Eliza pushed it really far. My eyes went to Nicole, who was looking at the fire in a trance. Great, she was upset, too. I patted her shoulder before I grabbed Eliza's arm to usher her out the room. She was dripping chocolate onto the dark wood floors. I wondered if Caesar, or anyone else who worked here, would be smiling at us now.

"Guys, chill out! Seriously. Nicole is right. This isn't going to help anything," I raised my voice.

"Of course you choose her side," Eliza said, running her hands over her face and splashing the liquid in my direction.

I turned to leave the living room with a livid Eliza in my possession when I noticed him by the door. A guy with light brown skin and a head of curls that resembled Jason's. He was in pajama pants and a white tank top. He rubbed his eyes and looked at all of us in confusion. We had all noticed him now and silently stared back.

"Who are you?" Rachel asked.

The guy's eyebrows furrowed further, as if it were such a crazy question to ask. His eyes scanned over all of us before he answered.

"I'm Josh… Who are you?" he asked.

"Josh who?" I asked.

"Joshua A. Crawford," he said.

"Are you Reggie's kid?" Eliza asked him as she pulled away from my grasp.

"No. Who's Reggie? My father's name was Carter," the guy answered.

"Woah… That's definitely not Tracey's kid," Jason added from the other side of the room. Of all the things to choose to reenter the conversation with, he chose the most stupid and obvious.

I walked over to the wall and flipped the three switches in the room to turn the lights on. I wanted to look at this guy more than what the dark shadows allowed.

"Carter Crawford is your dad? Are you sure?" I asked.

"Yeah, well, he adopted me," Josh said.

The room went quiet. I couldn't help but feel like I had seen him before. His eyes met mine and his eyes looked similar to mine. I couldn't find words.

"He adopted you? You look a little like Noah… but you also kind of look like Jason, now that I think about it," Rachel said, walking past me to look at him.

"You said you were adopted. Do you know how long ago?" Nicole asked.

"Well, I'm twenty now, so around fifteen years ago," Josh answered.

"So, you were five. Do you remember your last name? Carter had a family, so why would he adopt you unless he knew your parents or something? That sounds messed up. I mean, like, why would he adopt you and not tell anyone?" Rachel asked.

"My last name was Westbrook. My family died and Carter adopted me. He knew my mom," Josh said.

I heard a shattering noise behind me, and I turned around to see Jason's mug broken on the ground by his feet. More hot chocolate was splattered around, and I made a mental note to give everyone who worked at this house a bonus for all our dysfunctional messes to come. Jason took a step forward. His mouth was open and his eyes were glossy.

"Did you have a brother named Jason?" Jason asked in a shaky voice.

"Yeah," Josh answered with a scared look.

"Were your parents named Erica and Derek?" Jason asked.

"Yeah, but how do you know that? Who are you?" Josh asked, taking a step back.

"I'm your brother," Jason said with a weary smile.

"No, you're not. My brother died." Josh took another step back.

"We're all alive," Jason said, grabbing his phone from his pocket to show him a picture.

Josh looked sick. This probably was too much to take in at once.

"Jason, maybe let's not overwhelm the guy," I said.

Jason shot me a nasty look.

"Your father kept us apart for fifteen years. I knew it," Jason said.

"I don't know what's going on," I said slowly as I tried to sort through all the new information in my head.

"Bro, your family is so screwed," Jason said.

I decided not to dispute that statement. If we were going to look at things objectively, my family was nothing short of screwed up. There was no need to deny it. What I did know was that Carter would never hurt a kid. If he told Josh that his family died, it had to be for a reason. He wouldn't want to keep a child away from his family. There was most likely no way he would gain from that.

"But even if Carter did do this for The Table, it would be documented. There's nothing, besides the fact that Jason's brother went missing," Eliza said.

"So pleased to know that you read up all about me, Elizabeth." Jason snorted.

"Don't ever call me Elizabeth again," Eliza said.

"See? Names are important," Rachel chimed in.

Eliza shot Rachel a look. I shot Eliza a warning look, as well. I didn't need Nicole being mad at me if Eliza touched her sister. I knew she would be, and I also knew I wouldn't be able to handle it. I already had a lot to be sorry for.

I zoned back into the conversation taking place with Josh. His eyes danced along all our faces as if he was trying to take all of us in at once.

"So… you're Jason, and you might be my long-lost undead brother. That's cool, I guess. Who are the rest of you? Are you kind of my brother, too?" Josh asked, looking at me with a wary look.

"I'm Noah. Noah Crawford, so yeah, I guess you are my adopted brother," I said.

Nicole walked up closer to Josh and studied his face. She circled around him and, instead of being uncomfortable, it was clear he did not mind getting a closer look at her. *Absolutely not.* That was not going to happen. I'd rather die.

"What's your name?" Josh asked with a smirk.

"Nicole," she answered, not noticing his expression.

"Nicole what?" he asked.

"Smith." She smiled at him before looking over to me.

"So, Nicole Smith, what was the deep analysis for?" he asked.

"You definitely look a little like both Jason and Noah," she remarked, glancing between the both of us.

"That's what I said," Rachel said.

"And who are you?" Josh asked, looking over at Rachel and then back at Nicole.

"Rachel Smith," Rachel said.

"So you're sisters," he confirmed.

"Yes we are." Nicole returned to her sister's side. I swore they looked so alike sometimes.

"Since you didn't ask, I'm Eliza Craig." Eliza gave one wave with a forced smile.

Josh mirrored her wave before looking around the room once again. He nodded before looking at the white digital watch on his wrist. The sky was a dark blue now, but it was nowhere close to sunrise yet.

"So, why are you guys here? I mean, this is probably your house, too, Noah, but it's also like five in the morning," Josh said.

Everyone in the room looked over at me to come up with an explanation. It probably wasn't a good idea to tell him about his crazy stepmother and the organization that made everyone in the room's lives crazy.

"We needed a place to crash. We were in the area." I shrugged.

Just then, we heard light footsteps before Caesar joined us. His smile faltered for a moment when he saw the mess Eliza sported on her clothes and in her hair. Then he saw the dropped mug and chocolate further into the living room. He looked at us with questioning eyes.

"Hi Caesar. We were a little clumsy this morning," Nicole said, looking at Rachel, Eliza, and then me.

"I see that, Ms. Nicole. I will make sure that this is all cleaned up shortly. Your rooms are set up. I left some loungewear, robes, and slippers for you all to use. If you need more, feel free to tell me. Follow me so I can show you the rooms," he said, leading the way toward the stairs.

I threw myself onto my bed and stared at the ceiling. I was so tired, yet my heart was going a mile a minute. I needed to figure out what my mother's next move was going to be and beat her to the punch. I had to make sure everybody was going to be safe when we went back home. Christmas was in a couple of days, and there was no way anyone would be cool with us staying up here. Just because I didn't have a family to worry about me didn't mean they didn't. We could only hold off the questions for so long.

I decided to call Greg. Greg had become my personal lawyer, assistant, and fixer when I became of age in The Table. He was not one of them. He was nice and drastically different from the rest of the people in this organization. I think we always got each other because of that. Papers were mixed up and, somehow, he got called for a law internship with The Table. He was great at what he did, but they had to keep him to make sure their secrets were never revealed. He was getting paid lovely because of it.

"Noah… It's very early in the morning," Greg answered his phone with a groggy voice.

"Hey Greg. I'm in a bit of trouble. I need your help. Can you come up to Soteria?" I asked.

"What do you mean by trouble?"

"Trouble as in Tracey wants all of us dead right now, so myself, Nicole, her sister, Jason, and Eliza are all hiding out up here. Also, please look up any documents you can find about my apparent adopted brother," I responded, and it was met with a few moments of silence.

"I will get there as soon as possible. Do not leave the house. No one leaves that house," he said, and I could hear movement.

"Will do," I said.

Chapter 5

I woke up to Eliza standing over me, tapping my arm. I tried to push her away, but I knew it wasn't going to work. I finally sat up and looked at the digital clock on the nightstand. It was ten in the morning. My room was filled with light seeping through the light curtains.

"What?" I asked a now clean Eliza, who was sitting on my bed looking at me.

"Greg is downstairs," she said.

"Okay." I stretched as I looked for my shirt to put on.

I looked over to my open doorway to see Nicole watching from the hallway. I gave her a small smile because the world was on fire, but her face was enough to brighten my day like the sun did to my room. She gave me a weary smile before she looked over at Eliza and kept walking.

"Wait, where are you going Nikki?" I asked in a voice loud enough for her to hear me.

"To go see who this Greg guy is," she said, taking a couple steps backwards for her to be seen.

"Wait up," I said, launching myself from the bed as I put my shirt on.

"I didn't want to interrupt," she whispered, not looking at me.

I looked at Eliza, who was following far behind us. She was typing away on her phone.

"There was nothing to interrupt. She came to wake me up," I said.

"Okay," she said as if she didn't fully believe me, but didn't want to talk about it anymore.

We walked into the office where Rachel and Josh were already sitting down on a loveseat. When he saw Nicole, he stood up and offered her a seat. His excuse was that she might want to sit next to her sister. I rolled my eyes and gave Greg a dap. He looked put together, like I didn't wake him up before sunrise. He gave me a smile and shook his head. My life was insane, and Greg would never admit to it, but he would watch in amusement a lot of times.

"So, the whole crew is here," Greg said in a low tone, glancing at everyone.

"I guess so," I said.

"At least your girl is here." He elbowed me in the arm.

"She's not my girl," I whispered back.

"Right," he said, clearly not convinced.

I took a seat on the edge of the desk next to Greg. Everyone was talking amongst themselves. Greg cleared his throat loudly, and everyone looked over at him.

"Greg, this is everyone. Everyone, this is Greg. He's cool," I said.

Everyone said hey in their own way, and Greg nodded curtly with a smile.

"Hey man," Josh said.

"What's up, J," Greg said back casually.

It was so casual that I knew for a fact that they knew each other — and well. Greg's eyes met mine, and he gave me a wary look before looking at everyone else.

"So, I heard you guys had a rough past few hours." Greg chuckled politely.

"We almost died, but I'll take 'rough' as a summary for it all," Jason said.

Greg caught me rolling my eyes. He nodded in recognition. Greg had gone with me to that party a couple months earlier and had talked me out of leaving permanent damage to Jason's face.

"You must be Jason," Greg said dryly.

Eliza snorted and Jason's shoulders sank a little. Josh looked at all of our silent exchanges with curiosity. He had no idea what he was in for. I wondered what his full story was. Why was he here? He was twenty years old with, I was sure, a fat bank account. If there was one thing my family was good for, it was that. He could be anywhere in the world, but he was here in a house nestled in the middle of nowhere upstate New York.

"You almost died? I thought you were just in the area," Josh finally said.

We all looked away. None of us wanted the responsibility of thinking of a response for that. Greg cleared his throat and I was happy a real adult was here to handle this.

"You know why you stay here? They are here because they want to be safe, too," Greg said.

I wondered why Josh would need to think about safety and made a mental note to ask Greg more about it later. I also wanted to know why he would've kept a secret like that from me. Greg was like family. He knew how lonely my childhood had been. I wondered if the same reason Greg kept him from me was the same reason Dad did.

"Any leads on Tracey?" Eliza asked Greg.

"She's currently waiting for surgery. She has four bullets stuck in her feet and legs," Greg said to her with a raised eyebrow.

"It was either that, or Nicole died or some shit. Then Noah would be more dramatic and sad than ever. No one needs that," Eliza said, looking at her nails.

"Well, the board issued a statement on my way here," Greg said sadly before he handed me a piece of paper with a lot of words.

I started scanning the page. The first part spoke about the incident that occurred. Then, they spoke about their plan of action. Because of Nicole's actions, they claimed she had proven herself to be a threat to The Table, and would no longer hold the status of immunity. I shut my eyes for a moment to keep my cool. I exhaled deeply and kept reading. Jason was also tagged as a threat to the organization, which, come on, that was no surprise. He probably was a threat to himself with how stupid he was. Eliza's future position on the board was in question. The board was also deciding to investigate my mental state, as well as question whether I was fit to be the next Head of The Table. Happy birthday to me.

Without thinking, I turned around and, with one swoop, cleared the desk. Everything came down with various, undesirable sounds. I tried to gasp for air, and, before I could, I felt Greg pull me away from the desk and into the hallway. I looked up and saw Nicole stand with fear in her eyes. All I could hear was ringing. I felt like I was floating, but in the worst way possible — without control. It was as if I had no control of what I was doing at all. I was having an episode. It had been a long time since I had had one.

"Listen, chill out. We will figure this out. You don't do this anymore," Greg said, finally letting me go when we were some feet from the office.

"She's going to ruin everything," I said, wiping the tears before they could roll down my face.

"We will figure this out. Noah, look at me," he said.

I looked up at him, trying not to shake. I was exhausted and scared. He put his hands on my shoulders and sighed inwardly. His blue eyes looked at me with concern.

"Give me a couple hours. I will figure this out. I'm going to need you guys to stay here until I do. It's safe here. They don't know this place exists," Greg said.

"I can't let this happen. This could be so bad," I said, trying to catch my breath.

Greg opened his mouth to speak until he looked behind me. He was hesitant before he tried to fake a smile.

"Am I going to die or something? What does this mean, Noah?" Nicole's voice sounded, and I turned around to look at her immediately.

Her eyes were glossy and her voice shook a little. Her eyes shot back and forth between Greg and myself. She wanted answers, and none of us could give those to her — not really. There was no telling what would happen.

"Nothing is going to happen to you here. I need to find more information and find some answers. I will have more to tell you after lunch," Greg said, pausing to look at both of us. Then he disappeared down a hallway.

Nicole looked up at me with a mixture of emotions. I felt helpless. I felt angry. I didn't want this for her. I took a step forward, pulling her in for a hug. She didn't hug me back, but instead cried into my chest. It was a deep cry —

one when you knew there was really something to cry about. There was.

Chapter 6

Caesar had told us lunch was ready and we gathered in the dining room in silence. At this point, it was clear everyone had read the statement. Josh was confused and probably didn't understand everything that was happening, but he looked upset too.

I uncovered my plate of penne alla vodka — my favorite — but I couldn't enjoy it the same way. As I ate, I realized that the last meal I had was about twenty hours ago. I needed this meal more than I had thought. I looked up at Nicole, who was sitting across from me leaning on Rachel's shoulder. She had hardly touched her food.

"You should eat something, Nikki," I said softly.

"I don't feel like it," she said.

"When was the last time you ate something?"

"Before Jason ruined everything yesterday afternoon," she said as her eyes cut to him. It was one of the first things she had said to him since we had gotten to the house.

Jason sighed inwardly and pushed his pasta around on his plate. Josh looked over at Jason with a raised eyebrow.

"Okay, Jason, what did you do?" Josh asked.

"Nothing," Jason had the audacity to say.

Everyone did their fair share of groans to that.

"Nothing? Where do I begin? First, you used my sister. You acted like you wanted to date her, but that was to just gain leads on the case of Reggie Crawford, Noah's uncle who died. Then, The Table, this cult, mob thingy that Noah and Eliza's dads made up, found out and started following Nicole around. Then, Jason found out that we were trying to throw him off his trail, got angry, and decided to go to Williamsburg. To do what? I have no clue. Anyway, I went to follow him, and while I did that, someone tried to poison Nicole. Then, she got a call from probably Noah's mother with some voice distortion shit. She told her if Nicole didn't go to Williamsburg, Jason would die. So, she risked her life for him, even though he went there in the first place. Now we're here, and her life is at risk because Jason doesn't know how to just drop shit," Rachel said.

"If your sister went missing, Rachel, you're telling me that you wouldn't do what it took to save her?" Jason asked through his teeth.

"I would find a way to make sure that nobody else would be in danger. Literally all of us are in trouble. Nicole would never want that, and I would do good by her. I'm sure Josh wouldn't want this for us," Rachel said.

Josh looked at Rachel mortified. His mouth parted and he looked over at Jason slowly.

"As someone who always has something to say in her sister's defense, who is always trying to speak for her sister, and wants to protect her at all costs, I expect you to understand where I'm coming from," Jason said to Rachel.

Nicole sprang up, making her chair fall back. She walked over to Jason's chair and stood there silently until he stood up. Everyone watched without moving a single muscle. I was sure I wasn't the only one not breathing.

"So, at all costs, meaning you never wanted to date me. You wanted to find your brother and you never cared about hurting me," Nicole said, as if she knew this for a fact.

"Nicole… It wasn't really like that—" he began, but, before he could finish, Nicole smacked him hard across the face. And I mean hard. The sound was extraordinary.

"That is a load of bs and you know it. Try again," her voice bellowed.

"I do like you, Nicole. I've liked you since the first time I saw you. I really didn't mean to get you involved. It just happened, and I felt like I was so close… I couldn't stop. I'm sorry," Jason said. I could hear the genuine sympathy and fear in his voice.

Nicole just stared at him. She didn't move. She didn't say a word. I felt myself on edge, too, so kudos to

Jason for not dying, or something, at that moment. I would have.

"Please don't hit me again. You and your sister must have a mean swing in your bloodline or something," he said, rubbing his face that was already bruised from the previous events of the night before.

"I'm tired of being used. Both of you used me for your own personal benefit. It's not happening ever again," Nicole said, looking between Jason and myself before disappearing into the foyer.

Greg finally gathered all of us back into the office. I was the last one to make it. I was busy sulking around in my room and had no intention of stopping anytime soon. I sat down on the office chair that was behind the desk Greg was leaning on. All the other seats were taken, and I didn't feel like standing.

"I spoke to the board," Greg said, and it came out so much more cheerful than it should've.

"Hope it was a lovely chit-chat," Eliza spat.

"Never, but anyway, I issued a request that no actions can be taken until Tracey Crawford can be present in front of the board. She is about to be taken in for surgery, so I'm guessing that'll give you until after New Years' since the board does not start meeting again until after that," Greg said.

"So, we get to spend one last Christmas alive," Jason deadpanned.

"Right, because if I'm not immune and Noah is voted off this episode of Big Brother, then essentially that's it. They'll kill me," Nicole said sassily, and I knew Greg wanted to laugh at the Big Brother comment, but he didn't.

"There has to be something. You guys are all annoying, but I don't want you dead. Even Nicole," Eliza said.

"How nice," Nicole deadpanned, not even bothering to look Eliza's way.

"There is a plan, right? Noah pays you to actually help, right?" Rachel looked at Greg expectantly.

"Well," Greg trailed off, and looked over his shoulder at me apologetically.

I sat up and sighed. *The past twenty-four hours have been filled with nothing but bad news, so he might as well just come out with it*, I thought. I was already starting to feel numb. My body was done feeling emotions for the day.

"What?" I sighed.

"There is only one loophole," Greg breathed.

"Great. Make it happen. I will pay you extra if it takes up a lot of time or something," I said.

"Even if it did, I would say it's on me," Greg said.

"What is it?" Nicole asked.

"The rule since the beginning was that wives get untouchable immunity. So, uh, well, an option we have is marriage," Greg said.

It might've been from exhaustion, but we all erupted into laughter. There was no way he was going to ask two teenagers to get married. Don't get me wrong, I had been dreaming of convincing Nicole to marry me for some years, but I didn't want it to be this way. She would be miserable, and I'd rather feel the pain of her absence than have her feel that way.

"I'm not kidding guys," Greg said, clasping his hands in his lap.

I pushed myself off the desk so I could get a better look at Nicole. Her mouth was open, and she was looking at us with a look that was nothing less than mortified. I'm sure my face wasn't that different.

"I can't marry him," she said, pointing at me.

"Greg, dude, this can't be our only option," I said.

"I am not going to sign off my life to a Crawford. Don't you guys think I already gave up enough?" Nicole asked.

"It wouldn't be forever, guys. It would just have to be after the board meets. You guys can be all done by around Valentine's Day," Greg said cheerfully, trying to make things sound better, but failing.

"*Amazing*. The answer is no. Marrying him is the last thing I want to do, and I don't want a divorce before I turn nineteen," Nicole exclaimed.

Greg looked over to me for support. I had no idea what he wanted me to do. I had nothing to say. I shook my head. Greg shook his head back. This was useless and, whatever was happening, I was losing. I rolled my eyes and looked at Nicole. It was as if she knew what I was thinking because her eyes narrowed at me.

"Was this your plan the entire time? Get me tangled in your mess so I'd be forced to be with you?" she asked. *Ouch*.

"No! There's literally no way I could've orchestrated this, Nikki," I said.

"I know it's your birthday and everything, but screw you," she said and walked out. I heard the front door slam close. Rachel ran out after her.

"There has to be another option," Jason said.

"There isn't. I'm sorry," Greg sighed.

An hour had passed and I was tired of being told by Greg in a thousand ways that I had no choice but to get married to the girl of my dreams in the worst pretenses known to man. I left the office and went to look for everyone else. They had left the room soon after Nicole had. I walked into the living room. Rachel and Josh were there looking at TV with sad, blank stares. I looked out the window and saw Nicole sitting there, looking at the river in the distance. It probably would've been nice for her if she wasn't thinking about being forced into a marriage with me. I looked back and noticed Rachel glaring at me.

"Can I speak to you for a second?" I asked Rachel, unable to cover up the clear discomfort in my voice.

"Speak," Rachel responded harshly.

"In private?" I asked, looking over at Josh for a second.

Rachel rolled her eyes and stood up before she followed me into the office. She closed the door behind her and then crossed her arms. For someone so small, she really knew how to fill up the room. In that moment, I felt small in her presence. I think it was because I knew how brutal she could be. Nicole and Rachel were both cut from the same cloth, but while Nicole's words would sting sometimes, Rachel's would cut through you like a knife.

"So, are we going to just stare at each other?" Rachel sighed.

"I need your help," I finally said, clearing my throat.

"Get in line."

"I need you to convince Nicole to say yes to this deal. It'll keep all of us safe."

Rachel gave me an incredulous look before she let her head fall back and laughed. I looked around the room uncomfortably. This wasn't funny.

"I'm being serious," I said.

"I know! That's why I'm dying. You want *me* to convince my sister to marry *you*? Does she look like some mob chick who is going to be down for your fuckery?" she asked me, taking a few steps in my direction, as if she were trying to challenge me.

"It's only until this whole board decision is over. Then, she can never speak to me again, if that's what she wants," I said, and I hated how sad I sounded when I said the last part.

Rachel looked up at the ceiling and then back down at me. She was still finding humor in all of this.

"Why are you so obsessed with my sister?"

"I never said I was."

"You didn't have to. You look at her like you would a well in the desert."

I was pretty sure she hit the nail on the head with that one. I was almost certain I did look at Nicole Smith like there was no other female on the planet, but I wasn't going to grant Rachel the satisfaction. My inability to get over her sister after two years was starting to get embarrassing for me.

"If you're really in love with her, aren't you worried about this messing things up forever?"

"Yeah, I am, but if it will keep her safe… I guess it's just what will have to happen," I said.

It was not rocket science that we were incredibly too young to get married. It had been two years since we had seen each other, and then we were suddenly thrown into this sea of constant secrets. I knew that I wouldn't find anyone that made me feel like she did, but I knew she would find someone else. I mean, it's Nicole. It was so effortless to fall in love with her. I knew I couldn't be the only one who thought that, and it was only a matter of time. When this was over, we would get divorced, and I would make sure she had as much money as she needed to be comfortable.

"Okay, this is getting a little too sad for me," Rachel sighed.

"Will you do it?" I asked.

"Yeah, I guess," Rachel said.

Chapter 7

I laid down on the loveseat that was sitting in the office. It was quiet enough for me to tend to my headache, but close enough for me to hear if anything was happening. It was on the edge of what I needed and what I had to do — just like everything else I had to do in my life. There were very few times I actually allowed myself to get what I fully needed. Unfortunately, my responsibilities heavily pushed my needs into the *want* category. I thought of the day I realized my needs were never going to be *needs* again.

***

Nicole's eyes looked at me as if she was pleading with me to bring the dead man on the floor back to life. They were searching for answers. They wanted me to make it go away and to tell her that it all wasn't true, but it was, and I couldn't.

I could hear my heart beating, and my lungs were clawing my body for air. All I wanted to do was lay down for a moment — just a moment so I could figure out what I had just seen. I couldn't. My mother was in the house, and I was pretty sure she was listening to everything that was happening. If she could stab Reggie a few times, her late husband's brother, then I had no idea what would happen to Nicole. She already didn't like her. I knew that, but I also knew that if something ever happened to her, I would cease to go on. She was my heart, and the world has tried to find a way to live without one of those, but failed.

"Nicole! Focus! You need to focus. We don't have time! Please," I pleaded as I grabbed onto her arms and shook her to listen to me, to stay with me. I was losing her to logic, but we couldn't work with that in my world — the world that I unintentionally brought her into.

"Noah, you're scaring me," she said with tears running down her face.

"Sorry. I just need you to listen to me. I need you to promise me you will tell the cops you… uh… went to ride your bike and got ice cream," I said, forcing myself to sound chill and sure when all I wanted to do was crawl into a ball and cry into the void.

"Noah—"

"Please, Nikki, if you never do anything for me ever again, please promise me you will do this. You have to get out of here and not come back, but I will come see you when I can. I need you to be safe," I said softly.

"I— I will try," she said, looking at me with wide, fearful eyes — full of disappointment, like I had told her all the tooth fairies and Santa Clauses of the world did not exist.

"I love you," I said, and, in that moment, I had never meant it more. She meant what she said. She was really going to try to do this unspeakable thing for me, something that I wasn't sure *I* would do for me.

Nicole blinked her tears back and nodded. She walked toward the door, trying not to look at the terrible sight in our presence. She looked over her shoulder at me before she opened the door and left. I stared at the door for a while, as if it would help take me out of my reality if I stared long enough. Then I heard my mother's heels click across the floor. I turned around and she was standing on the other end of the foyer, Reggie's body on the floor between us. I swallowed and looked her in the eyes. They were ablaze and it made my stomach turn.

"Well, look what you've done. This has become an even bigger mess because of the thing you insist on calling your *girlfriend*," she said coldly.

"Me? I didn't do this, and neither did she. You did this," I said, pointing to what was between us.

"Semantics. What I know for sure is we can't have someone walking around who knows what went on," she said.

"Well she knows. It's too late."

My mother shrugged nonchalantly and walked around the body as if it were a piece of trash on the ground. She tossed her hair over her shoulder and looked at me as if I was the lowest thing on her list of being worth her time. I was still trying to find enough oxygen in the air.

"It'll be sad, but she had a good run," she said.

"What do you mean?"

"Well, we're going to have to get rid of her."

My knees almost gave out and a chill ran through my body. No.

"No! You can't do that," I said, horrified, but not surprised about the fact she wanted to get rid of the only person I loved.

"Noah, I'm sorry, but your family and your people come first. She is a threat to us now," she said.

"She said she won't tell. I believe her. Unlike you, she actually loves me."

"I do love you! Don't you see everything I give you? You have everything, and yet you insist on disobeying me," she shrilled.

"Mother, Nicole has immunity, and if you break that, I will make sure you lose the only thing you love, your empire," I said, turning my back to her to hide the tears threatening to leave my eyes.

"She makes one wrong move, and I will see to it that her last few moments in this world are full of suffering," she said.

"You'll have to kill me first," I said through gritted teeth.

***

I opened my eyes to Nicole standing over me. Her lips were pursed, her arms crossed tightly over her chest. I sat up quickly and rubbed my eyes. I looked at the clock, and it was a little before two in the afternoon. *I must have drifted into sleep*, I concluded. My eyes scanned her, she was in her coat and boots again.

"I am not marrying you. I refuse to have you drag me into more misery. I'd rather die," she said.

"Where are you going?" I asked, ignoring the huge blow to my ego.

"Home. We need to get home by tonight. My mom is not going to buy us not being home like this during the holidays," Nicole said.

"You can't," I said to her as I looked over at Greg, who was watching with an exasperated expression by the door. I was sure he had gotten an earful during my nap.

"I am," she said before walking out and rushing past Greg.

"You could literally die," I said as I followed her out into the foyer.

Everyone had on their coats except Josh and Greg. I paused and put my arms up with a questioning look.

"You guys can't leave. What?" I asked.

"Dude, it's the holidays," Rachel said.

I rolled my eyes at Rachel before I looked over at Greg. He was next to me now. How could he let this happen? We had to hide out here to stay safe, and they wanted to just leave.

"Why are you letting this happen?" I sighed.

"The Table does not meet, and will not make any decisions, until well after the holidays." Greg shrugged.

"Are you coming?" Eliza asked.

My shoulders fell. I had nowhere to go. I was going to be alone for the rest of my birthday and Christmas. I shook my head slowly.

"Do you want to crash with me? I'm going home, and I'm sure my Dad's pissed, but he will still take you in," Eliza said.

"Or you could stay here," Josh offered with a small voice, "I've never had an exciting Christmas."

I looked over at Greg again, who nodded. I rolled my eyes. I knew if I didn't say yes, he would tell me I was wrong eventually and make me feel like shit. He thought I always should make the right choices, and, if I didn't, he made me feel like utter trash.

"Yeah, I guess I could stay here. Long Island is definitely not an option for me." I shrugged.

"Cool. Then let's get on the road. I want to at least be in the city by the time it gets dark," Rachel said.

"I'm driving anyway," Nicole said.

"No, you're not. It's my car, I am driving. Especially after how you spoke to me," Rachel retorted.

"I'm not fighting with you over this again," Nicole said with a raised eyebrow before glaring at me.

"Where are you going, Jason?" I asked.

"I'm getting dropped off at the train station. My family is already wondering where I am," he said, and I was waiting for him to make a jab at the fact that mine wasn't. He didn't. Instead, Jason and Josh gave each other a silent embrace. Jason promised he would come back to see Josh in the next few days.

I walked over to Rachel, who was looking at me with pity while everyone else started to head out toward the SUV. I reached for my wallet and handed her some cash.

"What's this for?" she asked.

"Cash for gas and whatever else you'll need on the way back," I said.

"Thanks, Crawford. Look, I'm going to speak to Nicole. She'll come around," Rachel said warily.

"Yeah… I wish… I don't know. Thanks, Rachel," I sighed.

"That's a whole mood. Happy birthday and merry Christmas." She gave me a sympathetic smile before walking through the door.

I stood in the doorway as I watched the car drive down the dirt road and disappear into the trees. I frowned before I turned around and looked at Greg and Josh, both looking at me expectantly.

"What?" I asked.

There was silence for a moment. Josh and Greg looked at each other warily before looking at me. I had so many questions about how they knew each other. Why would Greg keep something like this from me? He worked for me, yes, but I also considered him to be a friend.

"Are you guys just not going to explain why you insist on looking at me like that?" I asked.

Josh bit the inside of his cheek with an unsure expression on his face before he asked, "Are you going to be ok?"

That was a great question. I had no answer for it at that moment, but I'm sure I looked like shit and like the answer was no. My mother was going to try to exile me from The Table, and probably try her best to kill the woman I loved because that would break me. That's what she wanted. I also was running on only a few hours of broken sleep.

"I don't know," I answered.

"It'll work out. It always does," Greg said, stuffing his hands in his pockets. He sure did not look like he believed the crap that was coming out of his own mouth. I shrugged off his sad attempt at trying to make me feel better. He knew there was a slim chance Nicole was going to agree to this deal.

I walked past the two, about to make my way up the stairs when Josh cleared his throat. I turned around and looked at him. He looked very uncomfortable.

"Would you like to go for a walk or something before the sun goes down? There's a cool trail five minutes away. You get a nice view of the river. I go there to think… and maybe that's what you need," Josh said.

I wanted to say no, but the dude looked so eager, and Greg was giving me that look that meant "do the right thing Noah."

"Yeah, just give me twenty minutes. I need to have a word with Greg," I said, nodding for Greg to follow me upstairs.

I walked up to my room, and Greg followed me. He closed the door behind us and looked down with his hands in his pockets. If uncomfortable had a picture in the dictionary, it would be Greg in that moment. I stared at him until he finally spoke.

"Okay, so you're probably wondering what's going on," he finally said.

"Damn right. So you were going to look at me in the eyes and not tell me I have a brother?" I asked, my arms stretched out in frustration.

"Well, I was trying to protect him too. If you knew, then Tracey could find out and… she doesn't know," he trailed off.

"She doesn't know she has an adopted son?"

Greg shook his head slowly. There was more that he wasn't telling me. I could tell from his expression. He grabbed an envelope from the inner pocket in his suit jacket and handed it to me. It was in good condition, but still looked a little aged. It had my full name on it, Noah Carter Crawford. I opened it and almost dropped it when I realized it was from my dad. The last time I had gotten a letter from him was right after he had died. I read it.

To my beloved son Noah,

If you are reading this right now, you are probably extremely confused and possibly angry with me. If you aren't, then that might change by the end of this letter.

There were many reasons I kept your older brother, Joshua Crawford, from you. Like many decisions in my life, I'm not sure if this was the right one, and, if it wasn't, I'm unequivocally sorry. Joshua is not your stepbrother, but your biological half-brother. His mother, Erica Perez, now Erica Westbrook, and I had met when we were both in college. We were serious, and I was in love with her, but your grandfather did not support our relationship. Instead, he wanted me to

*marry your mother. That had been the plan for years. I tried to fight
for our relationship, but in the end, I chose your mother.*

*I did love your mother. She was the first girl I had ever fallen in love
with, but there was a fire I felt when I was with Erica. I knew this,
and I stayed away. That was until a business conference held in
Hoboken one weekend, some years after graduation. I bumped into
Erica, who was the manager of the hotel the event was being held at.*

*She told me she was pregnant a couple of months later. I told her it
was her decision in the end, but I would help her take care of our
child. That was when she told me she also had been married for a
year to Derek Westbrook. We finally came to the decision that it was
best to not tell him the truth of her pregnancy. I made sure to send
money to Erica, and would visit Joshua whenever Derek was not
present.*

*This went well for two years until your mother realized I had been
sending money to an account with Erica's name on it. Your mother
had been jaded by the nature of our business and a taxing pregnancy
with you. She threatened that if I did not put an end to whatever I
was up to, that she would deal with it herself or worse: have The
Table fix it. I knew she knew it was for a child, and I could not
fathom Joshua ever being hurt. I went on to deliver the cash myself
for the next year or so. I wanted Joshua to get everything he needed
and more.*

Your mother eventually caught on to this, as well, and had a watcher from The Table waiting for me outside Erica's house. I asked Erica if she was willing to meet me in another location, but she had refused. Derek already had his suspicions. I felt as if I had no option but to take matters into my own hands. I took Joshua away and raised him as if his family had died. I'm not proud of it, but I wanted to protect my son. I kept him in Soteria. I even brought you to play with him a few times when you were very young.

Unfortunately, I had to write this in a letter. I would've preferred speaking to you about this man to man. If you are reading this letter, then I was right, and I wouldn't make it to see that moment. There are many letters, and, as you reach different points in your life, I will make sure your assistant from The Table supplies you with them. Know that I love you and your brother very much. More than you will ever know. Make sure to take care of him. He's very special, like you.

Love,
Dad

I put down the letter on the foot of my bed and paced as I processed the information I had just read. Greg was silent and let me go through it. He was always good with knowing when to step in and when not to. I guess he knew I had to find out this way. I finally looked up at him.

"How long have you known?" I asked.

"About three years now. I was appointed as your assistant months before you knew, and I was given the tasks of taking care of your estate. This house is yours, so I came up here and sorted through the letters that were locked in the safe. They were never sealed… I'm sorry," he said.

"For what?"

"Because… you get a lot of things piled on you and you never get to distribute that weight to anybody else. I try to help, but it will never be enough. There are so many layers," Greg sighed.

I shook my head in frustration. I threw myself on the foot of my bed and closed my eyes for a moment before springing up again. Greg looked startled.

"I'm supposed to go on that walk with Josh. He's probably waiting by now," I said.

"You seem like you haven't gotten much rest."

"What's new?"

I threw on my coat and walked past him to make my way downstairs. Like I expected, Josh was sitting in the living room with his coat already on. He gave a small smile when he saw me and I tried my best to smile back.

My eyes couldn't help but scan his face to see if I saw Dad. Josh started to speak, and he laughed with a huge smile, and that's when I saw it. I heard myself choke. I willed my eyes not to get shiny, but I already felt them. I hated myself. I cleared my throat. I wasn't sure why seeing Dad in someone else made me emotional. I mean, I saw him in me every time I looked in the mirror. I looked just like him. I guess it was the idea that I finally had something to share with someone. I never was able to have the bond with a sibling that other people did. Seeing Nicole and Rachel's bond was so nice, and, while I was glad two beautifully different people were still so connected, I was sad that I never had that for myself. I felt the same things with other friends when I was in school. They would never be truly lonely when they were connected in the soul that way. For the first time, I felt that I would know how they feel.

"Earth to Noah… are you ok, man?" Josh asked, taking a few steps toward me.

"Yeah… let's go for that walk," I said softly, because I was sure if I spoke louder, I would sound like I wanted to cry. We couldn't have that.

Chapter 8

We walked along a winding trail lined with frost-crusted trees. The gravel crunched under our boots as we walked in another bout of silence. Josh had insisted that the view of the Beaver Kill river was amazing at the top of the hill we were going up. He said he went there to think sometimes and it looked like I had a lot to think about. My brother, you had no idea.

"I'm pretty sure we've met before," Josh said, looking over his shoulder back at me.

"Yeah? How so?" I asked, warming my hands in my pockets, safe from the cold air.

"Your dad used to bring you here when we were younger to play. It stopped after a while, but I think I remember it. I don't get to see a lot of people, so I remember who I do see," he said.

I took a moment to think about it. I used to come to this house with Dad up until I was in the first or second grade. I remembered playing with some kids, but I thought they were all the children of the help. Josh finally looked at me again, and then I saw the memory.

***

"Daddy, he said you were his daddy and I told him that he's lying," I said, hiding behind Dad.

"You shouldn't push people, Noah. You know better than that," Dad said, pulling me from behind him to look at me. He knelt down to my level and looked at me with his emerald eyes. I felt tears collecting at the corner of my eyes. I never wanted to disappoint him, and it made me immediately regret doing it.

"Sorry," I choked.

"Hey, little man, don't cry," he said, ruffling my hair.

"You're mad at me."

"No, I just want you to be better for next time."

"So I can be like you when I grow up?"

"So you can be *better* than me, Noah."

"But you're the best."

"Debatable."

"What does that mean?"

"Nothing. Go hug Joshy and tell him that you're sorry. We have to head home," Dad said, patting my cheek.

I turned around to see Joshy with his arms crossed in the doorway. His lips were in a perfect frown. I walked up to him slowly and wrapped my arms around him. I rested my head on his shoulder before the words "I'm sorry" left my lips. He finally hugged me back and rested his head on mine. I could feel his plush curls being pressed into my forehead.

"It's ok. I forgive you," he said.

"You do?" I asked.

"Yeah, you're my friend." He gave a smirk.

Joshy went up to Dad and hugged him too. Dad whispered something in his ear and he nodded. I remembered thinking that Dad was so great that I would want him to be my dad, too, if he wasn't. I was happy Joshy had him, too.

***

"I think I remember that. I pushed you the last time I saw you." I snorted.

"Yup! Ha, I'm still waiting to take revenge." He chuckled.

Something told me that he had no idea about the news that I had just discovered. Something also told me that it would be up to me to tell him. Like everything else, it was my responsibility.

We got to the top of the hill and looked out at the unrestricted view of the river, glistening in the little bit of sun left in the sky. It was peaceful. We both watched in silence for a while. I took a deep breath of the fresh, crisp air. Josh took a seat on a large tree stump. He moved over so I would have space, too.

"Told you this place was cool," Josh said triumphantly.

"That it is. You just went out one day and found it?" I asked.

"Yeah, well, I'm always here so I went out and tried to find cool things nearby." He shrugged.

"You're always here? You don't leave?"

"Yeah mostly. Caesar takes me to the doctor and stuff… I go to the supermarket sometimes, too, but that's pretty much it. Your dad had said it was dangerous."

"Wait, what did *our* dad tell you?"

"He said the same people who hurt my family were going to hurt me if I wasn't safe. So, I stay here." He shrugged.

I listened as I looked at the river. The letter mentioned how The Table could've hurt him. The thought of people hurting a child made my stomach turn. *Man, I have to change this thing*, I thought. I wanted to be The Head of The Table and change it.

"So, you and Nicole…" he began, breaking my train of thought. I knew he had been looking at her. I didn't blame him at all. Nicole was stunning, but that was not helping.

"What about us?" I asked.

"You guys have history," he said as a statement, not a question. I guess it was pretty obvious.

"Yeah, we dated a couple years back."

"And you still are into her."

"Yeah."

"Yeah, she's gorgeous. I get it."

"She's off limits," I said, finally looking at him.

"Relax… *little bro*. I wouldn't do that. I just liked her energy. She reminded me of myself in some ways… I knew the moment I saw you look at her. Plus, she looks at you like she loves you back," he said.

That was news to me. Nicole Smith's goal these days, besides being perfect in her Nicole way, was to rival me in any way she could. I was not on her list of favorite people.

"I don't know about that." I chuckled.

"It's kind of soon to get married, but I think she'll say yes. Rachel will speak to her," he said.

"That's true. Rachel is great. She knows how to get to her sister," I said.

"She seems cool… in a fiery way." Josh chuckled.

"Yeah, for sure. I appreciate her though." I smiled as I thought about how her words occasionally cut through me like swords.

"Then there's Eliza… She likes you, but is mad that she does," Josh said.

"How do you know that?" I asked, because that was pretty accurate. Did I have a psychic sibling?

Josh rubbed his stubbled chin for a moment as he looked down at his boots.

"She is frustrated that you look at Nicole the way you do. Whenever you look at Nicole like you're going to… do whatever you plan to… she looks really upset. You will never look at her like that, but she still likes you, and she hates it," Josh said.

"We had a thing for a short period of time. It just didn't work out because—"

"'Cause you're in love with Nicole," he finished for me. Those weren't going to be my exact words, but close enough. Okay, so maybe he was just super intuitive. This couldn't all be obvious.

We sat in silence again for a while and watched the sun descend behind the mountains. And just like that, the day was over. It was sad when such beautiful things, like the stunning view of the sunset, came to an end. It was a reminder that nothing lasts forever, and like my situation, I hoped it would reign true. It was going to get much darker soon. I decided it was time to make our way back and Josh agreed. When we got to the bottom of the hill, Greg was standing by the door with his long wool coat on.

"I wanted to see you two before I headed back downstate. Tomorrow is Christmas Eve, and I should be home for that. Be good. I'll be back in a couple days," Greg said, tapping his briefcase on the side of his leg.

"What if I don't feel like being good?" I challenged him out of pure boredom.

"Save that for when Nicole comes back," Greg retorted. Josh started laughing behind me. I shot him a look, but it didn't work.

"Very funny," I deadpanned, walking past Greg to the doorway of the house.

"I know," Greg said, before walking to his car. Soon enough, he was gone.

Chapter 9

I woke up to the sound of giggling coming from the hallway. I reached for my phone and oriented myself. Okay, it was the day after Christmas, and it was just after noon. I slept for almost fourteen hours. I guess my body needed to catch up on the lack of sleep I had been getting with finals season and the dumpster fire of events that occurred that past weekend.

I checked my notifications. There were a lot.

Eliza Craig: Update—my dad is disgusted, but there might be hope? Told you ol' Danny is getting soft. I'll keep you posted.

I guess that wasn't bad news, but Daniel Craig also had to answer to my mother. He used to be equal partners with my father, but he took a lesser role in the past few years. There was no explanation as to why, but that meant Tracey had more power. He might be able to help, but Tracey's decisions were final in the end.

Rachel Smith: No, I did not ask my sister to reconsider this bs on CHRISTMAS DAY. Give me some time.

Alex Ramos: Hey man! Long time no speak. Merry Christmas. Call me when you get a chance. I'll be on the island for the next few weeks.

Alex was my best friend from high school. With the turn of events, I became really distant and an all-around bad friend. Alex never cared. It was like he understood without us ever speaking about it. He visited me in rehab and stopped by when he could, even though I was no longer in the neighborhood. I texted him back to let him know I would meet up with him soon.

Mom: I'm calling you at 1pm so get up and pick up. Also, I hope you had a Merry Christmas. I didn't, not that you care.

If that was not a toxic text, I didn't know what was. I groaned in protest, but I clicked the time on my phone so it would set a reminder.

Greg Nelson: I hope you had fun with your brother yesterday and relaxed. If you didn't, make sure you do, because you don't get nearly as much time off that a guy your age should. There will be plenty of time to think about everything in the coming days. The Table is not taking any action for a couple weeks. Enjoy it. I don't say this as your employee, I say this as your friend.

I couldn't help but let a small smile crawl up my lips. Greg was a good guy and he cared. I texted back to thank him and wished him and his family happy holidays.

I heard giggling in the hallway again, and I finally sat up. It was a woman's voice, but I was confused since Caesar and the rest of the help weren't coming back from holiday leave until tomorrow. I opened my bedroom door and walked out into the hallway. There was no one there. The sound of the laughing led me to Josh's room. His door was ajar.

I peaked in and saw his huge gaming setup. There was a desk with two large laptop screens in front of him. Above, on the wall, was a huge flat-screen TV that was no less than sixty inches. On it was a split-screen display. One side had a girl who looked like she was watching from a webcam, and the other side looked like a new racing game I wanted to play but never had time for.

The girl had a headset over her long brown hair and looked over at the screen triumphantly. Josh groaned and tossed his controller onto the desk. He spun around and stopped when he saw me. He pulled his headset down to his neck and tousled his curls with his fingers.

"Hey sleepyhead," he said.

"Hey. Sorry. I heard laughing," I said, nodding at the screen.

"Oh, yeah, that's Nina. Say hey, Nina," Josh said over his shoulder nonchalantly to the attractive female on the screen.

"Hey," she said with a smile.

"Hey, Nina. Noah." I waved.

"Yeah, Nina and I just game together… Anyway, gotta go Nina. My *little bro* needs attention." Josh smirked.

"Catch you later," she said before signing off.

I raised an eyebrow at him and chuckled. He returned the look with a very confused one.

"So… Nina," I said, wagging my eyebrows.

"What about her?" he asked with a confused look that made me roll my eyes.

"You two are a thing?" I asked.

"No… We were at one point, but not anymore. She just wasn't the one," he sighed.

"You met?"

"Yeah, a couple years back. We were doing long distance, but I realized I just wasn't in love with her."

"Wow. Well, I just wanted to see what was up. I heard laughing," I said.

"A foreign sound?" Josh questioned, and it made me snort.

"No. I figured your laugh wouldn't sound like a female's," I deadpanned.

I made eggs as Josh told me about some game he was coding. I had no idea what the hell he was talking about, but I assumed he didn't have a lot of people to speak to. It was the least I could do. I pushed the eggs around in the pan and nodded along.

"Right now, I'm working on getting the motion graphics to operate smoother," he went on.

"That's cool… you should show it to me sometime," I said, looking over my shoulder.

"Yeah, for sure," he said happily.

I threw my eggs on a plate and brought it over to the kitchen island. I started eating, but when I glanced up, Josh was watching me with a concerned look on his face.

"I asked if you wanted eggs and you said no," I said.

"No. I don't want your *seasonless* eggs." Josh chuckled.

"I'm in a rush. My mother is calling in like ten minutes," I said, my mouth half full.

"You just seem stressed a lot. I mean… I just met you, but I feel it seems like this is your life. It's like life forgets to cut you a break."

"Life pretty much decided I don't get breaks."

"Things will work out. Nicole will probably say yes. Then that's cool you get to be married to *her*. Even if it's just for a little while. Greg will help you. The longest you'll have to endure this phone call is ten minutes," Josh said with ease.

I stared at my brother as I thought about what he had just said. It was true, but at the same time, it wasn't. I didn't know how to explain, so I nodded and finished my eggs instead. I wished I could look at things that way — in such a positive way, but I couldn't. I knew what things really were, and that's why I was on edge. Josh had a much simpler outlook because he didn't know, and it was probably better that way. I wanted that for him. Life was never particularly sweet to me, but it had been a lot better before I knew what I did now.

"My surgery went well. You forgot to ask me how I was doing after Elizabeth got convinced by you and your heathens to shoot me. I almost died," Tracey said over the phone.

I rolled my eyes so hard, I was surprised it didn't make a sound. I knew I could be dramatic at times, but she was painfully worse. Josh had stayed around for moral support, and I could tell he was nothing less than frightened by how crazy she sounded. He shouldn't have even been listening to what was going on, but he had already heard the events that had happened the past few days. Talking to him about everything was yet another thing on my list of "things Noah has to take care of because his world requires him to take care of everything."

"No one convinced Eliza to do that. She did that because you were planning to do something unspeakable to Nicole and Jason, mother," I answered dryly.

"I would only do what seemed fit for our people," she said, gasping as if what I said was so absurd.

"Why are we having this conversation?" I asked, tired of this absolute useless waste of time.

She was silent for a long moment. Josh looked up from his laptop with a raised eyebrow.

"I want to make a proposal," she said.

"A proposal?"

"Yes. A settlement of sorts. We can make this all go away," Tracey said.

"I'm listening."

"You give up your potential position as Head for a hundred million. You won't have to go through the hearing, and we'll forgive Eliza's actions," she said.

My eyes narrowed. There was definitely a catch. For as long as I could remember, there was always a catch when it came to making deals with my mother.

"I won't have to be involved in The Table at all?" I asked. Not having all these responsibilities sounded nice. I always wanted a break.

"Not at all. I won't ever ask you to do another thing," she said.

"And what about Jason and Nicole?"

"What about them?" she asked, clearly annoyed.

"Will they not be killed, mother," I said, exasperated.

"We can work something out with Mr. Westbrook."

"And Nicole will have immunity?" I asked.

"Well, honey, she won't. If you leave, then your requests as part of the board are voided," she said.

"No deal," I said.

"Be reasonable, Noah. You'll be free from this. You don't want this. I can make it go away. You want her more than freedom?"

I knew my mother hated Nicole, but this was an all-time low for her. She was really trying to get rid of her.

"Why do you insist on getting rid of her? What has she done? She literally saved us. What the hell is it?" I asked.

There was silence again. I looked up at Josh, who was frozen. His expression said it all. It was a mixture of fear, disappointment, and disgust. I knew it. I often felt those things too.

"I'm not having this conversation with you, Noah. *You're just like your father.* If you want to choose *her* over me, yet again, then I will see you at the first hearing in January," she said before hanging up.

Chapter 10

Josh made me a sandwich and sat it on the coffee table next to the couch, where I laid with my face buried in it. I grunted into a cushion to say thank you when my phone rang again. It was still on the kitchen island. I didn't care. The last thing I wanted to hear was someone telling me to do something or to tell me bad news because no other type of news existed here. I was tired — physically, mentally, and emotionally. Josh had asked if I wanted to talk, but I didn't even know how to put into words what I was feeling. I hadn't done it in a while, and it was like my brain had forgotten how. So, I just laid there and took deep breaths so I wouldn't explode, so I wouldn't drown in the mess that continued to flood in.

"It's a call from Nicole," Josh said from the kitchen.

I sat up so fast that my head hurt. Josh shook his head at me before handing me the phone. I cleared my throat and answered before the phone stopped ringing.

"Nikki," I said, failing at not trying to sound too eager.

"Noah, we need to talk," she said.

"Yes, okay," I said, returning to the couch to sit down.

"So, I see that you decided to get my sister in on your plans. She spoke to me for hours this morning," Nicole sighed.

"I only want to ensure that you're safe. I don't want to ruin your life."

"Again," she added and it stung a little, even though I knew it was true.

"Again. I don't want to ruin your life again," I said.

"Meet me down here tomorrow. We need to discuss this whole thing. I'll give you my decision then," she said.

"Okay, sure. I can do that," I said, not sure if I could, but I would find a way for her.

I called Greg and had him get a renter's car delivered to the house. It was a dumb amount of money, but I paid it. I offered to bring Josh with me. There was so much I wanted to speak to him about. He told me he wanted to stay here. That he would get in the way. I told him that he wouldn't, but he insisted he stay. I promised to come back in the next few days. Caesar and the rest of the help would be back in the morning, anyway, and he was used to having them around. I worried about him, but I had to deal with things back at home first. I couldn't stay up here forever.

The next morning, I left at sunrise and made my way back downstate. I thought about going to the house, but my mother would be there, and I knew I didn't need added aggravation. I went to my apartment in Queens instead. I had gotten it right after I graduated high school. I wanted a place to go when mother was too much and I needed a break. The only reason I decided to dorm was because I figured some human interaction would be good. I hated it, but at least I tried it. My ex-therapists would have been so proud.

I walked into the apartment and checked the security pad for alerts. It was super sensitive and any tampering would've given me at least one flag. There were none. It was still morning, and I had told Nicole I would meet her for lunch. I had loads of time. I got into my shower, shaved, and found something clean to wear. I laid back on my bed and closed my eyes for a moment just for the phone to ring. I groaned and tapped the phone without looking.

"Yes," I answered.

"Happy holidays, asshole," Alex's voice sounded from the other end of the line.

"Hey," I said groggily.

"You're still sleeping?" he asked with a chuckle, surprised.

"It's only ten something in the morning," I said.

"No, it's almost noon," he said.

"It's what?" I yelled as I sat up and looked at the time projected by my clock on the wall in front of me.

"Are you okay?" Alex asked, no longer amused.

"I fell asleep," I said.

"Clearly… I was going to ask if we could meet up at Joe's later?" Alex asked from my phone that was now on speakerphone.

"Um, yeah sure. It would have to be after six," I said, grabbing a pair of black boots to go with my grey sweater and black jeans.

"That works for me. I'll see you at 6:30," Alex said.

Just then, my phone started to beep from someone being on the other line. I cursed underneath my breath and ran over to the phone on my bed to see who it was. I was hoping it wasn't Nicole being super punctual like she normally was. I exhaled loudly when I saw Greg's name across the screen.

"I'll see you later, Al," I said quickly before switching to the other line.

I switched the line to Greg. I could hear the sound of him quickly typing on a keyboard — probably the one in his office. I slid on my wool trench coat.

"Just calling to tell you that someone came to pick up your rental since you have your own car there," he said, not waiting for me to say hello.

"Greg, what would I do without you," I said dryly, but really did mean it. He knew.

"Probably crash and burn into oblivion. Anyway, give me the updates," he said.

"I'm going to run many lights because I'm going to be late to meet up with Nikki… Nicole," I said, grabbing my keys.

"Thanks for clearing that up. I wouldn't have known who you were talking about. You have so many obsessions with people, I can't keep up," he said as he typed away.

I rolled my eyes as I waited for the elevator. I was not obsessed with Nicole. That made me seem like a creep.

"Why do you insist on making me sound like a creep?" I walked into the elevator. The shaft had a view of the outside and allowed me to stay on the phone.

"I am just messing with you. Tell me how it goes," he said.

"Tell you as my assistant and lawyer?" I asked.

"And as your friend, Crawford. Are you doing ok?"

That was a great question, and the answer was that I had no idea. I was content with the fact that Nicole and I were even going to discuss anything of this. I wouldn't have blamed her if she wasn't going to entertain this at all. She didn't want this. No one sane would want this, but she was doing it for me. *No, you idiot, she didn't do this for you, she's doing it so she doesn't fucking die.* I digress. Other than that, I was dissatisfied with pretty much everything else. My mother was trying to throw me out of something that was destined to be mine, and the only reason I didn't let her was because I didn't want the people I knew to suffer. I wanted to scream at the top of my lungs, but that wouldn't do anything, so I just let the pressure build.

"I'm as close enough to decent as I've been in the past few days," I finally answered as I drove out of the garage and into the dull vibrance of the winter's day.

"That's something. I know it's easier said than done, but one step at a time," Greg said.

"I appreciate you."

"Alright, you're not paying me to get sappy with you during my lunch break." He snorted.

"You're right. Start drafting details for the arrangement with Nicole if today goes well," I said.

"You got it. Don't strike out," he said, hanging up.

I drove up to the Smith residence with my heart beating a mile a minute. I put my car into park and took a few deep breaths before shooting Nicole a text.

Noah Crawford: I'm here.

I knew that she was expecting me, but I was freaking out just the same way I would if I was showing up unannounced — which I knew was high on Nicole's list of things that annoyed her to no end. The more I thought about it, the more I thought of the possibility that I had climbed my way pretty high on that list.

Nicole Smith: You're late.

Crap.

Noah Crawford: Sorry

Nicole Smith: I started walking toward Joe's. I'm walking through the park by the lake if you'd like to join me for the trip. Needed some air.

I found her walking along the lake. Her white coat made her stand out against the brown and grey of the dormant earth around her. The wind danced with the curls that hung from under an orange hat. The sight was beautiful, just like the girl who bore it, and I almost didn't want to interrupt her.

"Hi," she said without turning around to see it was me.

"How do you know it's me?" I chuckled, a little startled.

"I felt it," she said softly before she looked over her shoulder, looking at me as I caught up to her.

We walked in silence for a while. The only sound was cars driving in the distance and the sound of our shoes on the concrete. It's funny how time and experience could change so much between two people. Here, next to me, was a girl that I used to have endless things to say to. We would get in trouble for breaking curfew because all we wanted to do was speak to each other, and now I was struggling to find words to start a conversation. I could feel my heart beating in my chest.

"How was your Christmas?" I finally asked, only after practicing it in my head a few times.

"It was nice… I love my family and love spending time with them. I just wasn't in the holiday mood. How was yours?"

"It was okay. Josh is cool… and my brother," I said.

She tilted her head, then looked over at me with a confused look.

"Yeah, I thought we established he was your step-brother," she said.

"He's my blood brother," I said.

"Woah. I knew you two looked similar. How did you find that out?" she asked.

"My father left me a letter before he passed."

"That's a lot. How do you feel about it?"

"I mean, it's nice to have a brother. I was always jealous of what you and Rachel have… It's just a lot to process, and I don't really have time to do that right now."

"Right. Sorry."

"No, it's ok. Thanks for asking."

We made it out of the park and waited to cross the street to the diner. There were couples hand-in-hand window shopping and looking at the Christmas decorations covering almost everything in sight. The air was full of pure happiness, and, for some reason, it made things awkward. It was like we stuck out because of our pure misery.

The light changed and we walked in silence to Joe's Diner, an old fifties style restaurant that had the best burgers and milkshakes. We were immediately met with Elvis' voice floating through the air. Back in high school, I would've been elated to meet up here with friends, but now, I was dreading sitting down. It meant that we would have to speak about things — things that were the opposite of great. Even if she was going to say yes, it was going to be painfully awkward, because she didn't really want this. And even knowing that, I still wanted it to happen, which I undoubtedly hated myself for.

We sat down in a booth by a window and looked at our menus in silence. It was because we didn't want to look at each other. We had been here together, and separately, countless amounts of times and knew what was on the menu already. I wasn't even sure if I wanted to eat with how nervous I was, but I ordered anyway when the waitress came over and asked what we wanted. When she took our menus and left, Nicole and I looked at each other reluctantly with the realization that there was nothing left to do but speak about the elephant in the room.

I struggled to find the words to begin and Nicole realized shortly after, when she decided to begin. She clasped her hands together and put them in front of her on the table before deciding that she wanted them on her lap instead. She was nervous, too, and I selfishly found comfort in that.

"So, I have put some more thought into this whole... *deal* to fix things," she began, looking around to make sure no one was listening.

I nodded and made some disgusting noise that thankfully only I could hear because it made me feel nauseated with myself.

"What does me saying yes include?" she asked.

"Well, I don't have all the answers to that, but I'm sure we can adjust some things with Greg. You would most likely be there during board meetings and a few events that happen from time to time until the decision is made. Essentially, you want to please the people on the board. If you get on their good side, and show that you have their interests in mind, then they will vote in your favor. It's very much like politics. That's mainly up to me, though. You would have to be by my side. I haven't done this before, so I think it's best Greg explain this. The main reason I'm agreeing to even allowing this to be an option is so you can be safe," I said low enough so only she could hear.

She nodded and looked around as she thought about what I had just told her.

"I meant more like logistics. Do we really have to act married? Will we be watched constantly?" she asked softly.

"Often. I would say in public, yes. There might be some skepticism. The house upstate is wired to block any eavesdropping of any kind, but, outside of that, I would say we should."

"So, I would have to tell my parents we're together," she said.

"Uh… maybe you can say we're dating. I don't want your dad to kill me," I said, because I knew if he had found out Nicole eloped with the guy he probably didn't trust much, my ass would get kicked. I had enough people who wanted to do that. I didn't need to add to the list.

"Okay… So we just go to the courts and get married, right?"

"Something like that, I guess."

She nodded slowly again as she played with her fingers uncomfortably.

"Alright, I'll do it, but I have conditions," she finally said.

"Like what?"

"First off, I'm not going to sleep with you. I want to get briefed on what's happening. I will not just do things because you say so. I'm your equal in this... I want to be treated like one. Also, this is all over the moment you get to be the king of your little castle again. I don't want any part of this," she said.

"I'm okay with that. Greg will work out the small details in the contract," I agreed.

"Noah, I'm talking about you. I want you to do those things. You're going to respect me, and not because the contract says you do. If you *love me* like you claim, you're not going to just use me and treat me like I'm just a means to an end."

I was about to respond when the waitress came back with our food. Nicole's face immediately went from an ice-cold expression to a warm acknowledgement when she looked up to thank the waitress. It was so effortless for her, and it made me wonder how often she had to do that, hide how she felt for others. My chest hurt at the thought. I nodded kindly to the waitress before she left.

"I do love you, and I don't treat you as if you're a means to an end," I said. I thought about what Eliza had said to her. It had gotten to her head.

"You have. These past few months, you tried to control what I said and did without much explanation because it suited you. I don't like it. And no, you don't love me. You think you do," she said, pointing a french fry in my direction.

"So you're telling me how I feel?" I asked, crossing my arms.

"Fine, Noah, why do *you think* you actually love me?" she asked, challenging me with raised eyebrows.

I was not expecting to be asked that. The air got stuck in my throat and I thought I might choke. I knew I loved Nicole and that she made me feel things that no one else would ever make me feel. I never wanted her to not be around, but I didn't know how to put why I was feeling that into words. I ended up looking at her, unable to say anything, and that pissed me off. I was so damaged that I couldn't fully express how I felt anymore. My annoyed glare was interrupted when Nicole's face changed from challenging to mortified. She looked past me and started to sink in her seat. I turned around and saw Michelle

Solomon standing there looking at us with an irritated expression on her face. Great.

Chapter 11

Michelle walked over to us and put her hands over her hips when she got to our table. If looks could kill, Michelle Solomon's look would've, without a doubt, made it in the books for the most lethal. She would've put Tracey to shame.

"Hey girlfriend… Crawford," she added my name like it was something gross.

"Hi, Michelle. Long time no see," I said.

"Not long enough," she said, nudging Nicole so she would slide in deeper to the booth.

"Um, what are you doing here?" Nicole asked uncomfortably.

"I live in this town, babes," Michelle said sweetly, but with an edge that made Nicole give a small sigh.

"I know, but I thought you were away with your family," Nicole said.

"I came back earlier today. My parents start working tomorrow," Michelle said.

She looked back and forth between Nicole and myself while she nibbled on fries from Nicole's plate. Nicole looked as if she was praying for God to make it all go away.

"So, this is really a thing, isn't it?" Michelle asked.

"What do you mean?" I asked.

"You two dating again. I saw the flowers last week," she said.

I was confused for a moment, before I remembered the huge bouquet of flowers I had delivered to her house. It was to make her smile during all of the madness. I hadn't really considered anyone else seeing it. I gave an apologetic look to Nicole before what I said next.

"Yeah, you caught us. We just wanted to keep things quiet in the beginning," I said with a fake chuckle.

Michelle looked over at Nicole to verify what I had just said. Nicole was giving me a death glare with a forced smile. She nodded when she looked over at her friend. I was going to get an earful later.

"Sorry girl, I was just waiting until we were ready to tell you," Nicole said.

"Does anybody else know?" Michelle asked.

"No, just you," Nicole said with a look that told me that she had just found out herself.

Michelle smiled at the confirmation that her superficial best friend privileges were still intact. I took a bite of my burger and stared outside. It was starting to get dark and what I saw was partially obstructed by my own reflection. I focused on my reflection and realized how tired I looked. It wasn't only in a physical way. Yes, I needed sleep, but what I was feeling was a mental fatigue, and my expression showed it all. I felt like my emotional bank had run dry and I was being dragged through what life was throwing at me.

I was so zoned out as I looked out the window that I didn't realize that someone else was looking at me. I zoned back in to see my friend Alexander Ramos standing in the window with his arms crossed and a raised eyebrow. He was still smiling, but that didn't mean anything since it was like the kid didn't know what a frown was.

He finally walked in and Michelle got out of the way so Nicole could embrace him. They were holding each other and laughing at something Alex said while Michelle gave me a death glare. I raised my eyebrow at her.

"What?" I asked.

"Hurt her, and I will make sure your life is miserable," Michelle said before walking over to the others.

"Too late. It already is," I grumbled.

I stood up and smirked at my friend's expression that was as bright as the sun. His dimples dove deeper into his tan skin when he opened his arms. I rolled my eyes as I walked into them.

"Look who it is, The Don," Alex said, tapping my back and ruffling my hair with his other hand.

"What's going on, Al," I said with a snort.

"I was walking back from returning a gift and then I was like *look at this shithead eating without me*," Alex said looking at Nicole and Michelle with his "get a load of this guy" look.

"Join us, then," Michelle said, as if she was invited in the first place.

"Hell yeah," Alex said, grabbing a menu from another table and sliding in with Michelle. I slid in next to Nicole.

I grabbed my milkshake and took a long sip while Michelle and Alex did the mindless flirting thing they always did. Alex was definitely the worst when it came to that. He flirted with everyone, and I mean every living, breathing human. I watched as his attention moved to Nicole, who smiled at him fondly. They were always only strictly platonic, but I knew if she ever gave him the green light, and we weren't friends, he would forget what breaks were. The Smith girls had that effect on everyone. Rachel's beauty was a kind that was slow burning. The more you looked at her, the more you couldn't look away. But Nicole Smith's was one that hit you all at once like a disease, and no one was immune. I hadn't found a cure for it, and it was clear my best friend hadn't either by the way he was laughing at what she said.

"I miss seeing you around all the time," he said with a smile.

"Aw, Ramos, that's really sweet," she said, gushing at his charm.

I rolled my eyes and took another sip of the milkshake. I looked up at Nicole, who gave me a frown.

"That's mine." She chuckled looking at the almost empty glass. I hadn't realized.

"Sorry, you can take mine," I said, handing her my hardly touched glass.

"So… you two are back at it again," Alex said, which made us both freeze.

"Apparently," Nicole said nervously as she looked down at her plate.

The meet-up with Nicole was clearly over. There was no way we would be able to discuss anything of substance with our best friends around. After Alex and Michelle ate, we all walked in the direction of Nicole and Michelle's houses. Nicole and Michelle led the way as they spoke amongst themselves in hushed voices while Alex and I trailed behind.

"I'm happy for you, man. She's good for you," Alex said softly, a moment after Nicole looked over her shoulder at us.

"Oh… thanks," I said awkwardly.

"When did this happen?" he asked.

"When did *what* happen?"

"You getting in there with Smith. You never mentioned it."

"Err… about a month or so." I struggled to find an answer.

"Well, you should hold onto her this time. You dating her was the happiest I'd seen you ever, and yeah, I know, you have to find your happiness in yourself and not other people. That's true, but maybe she's part of you and you can't be happy if part of you is missing," Alex said, tapping my back.

I frowned as I thought about what he said. It could've been true, but it didn't really matter if the other person was not a fan of you.

"Art school has made you soft." I chuckled.

"Maybe. Don't tell anybody." He laughed.

We reached Nicole's house, where we all spoke for a little longer — making promises about hanging out before the next semester started. I was about to stand next to Alex and Michelle at the bottom of the stairs to the entrance to her house when I realized I was supposed to do the boyfriend thing and walk Nicole to the door. I walked with my fake girlfriend and soon-to-be, *even better*, fake wife up the stairs. She gave me an annoyed smirk when we got to the door.

"Bye," she said with a snort.

"See ya," I said before turning around.

"Oh c'mon, Crawford. Kiss her! Don't let us interrupt you from time with your girl," Alex said, and I gave him a death glare as Michelle hit his arm.

"Turn around and give them privacy," Michelle said, dragging him around.

I turned around to see Nicole giving me a *don't you dare* look in the dim light of the little lamp by her door. Despite the fierce look, I wanted nothing more than to kiss her goodnight. I sighed and spun her around in my arms so my back was to our two very annoying friends several feet away from us. I held her face and brought my forehead to hers. She looked at me with frightened wide eyes. I wasn't going to kiss her until she wanted me to — even if that time never came. I wasn't that type of guy.

"I will tell Greg and he will meet with us to draft a contract tomorrow," I said in a whisper, rubbing one of her tight hair coils between my fingers.

"Where?" she asked, closing her eyes.

"I'll let you know," I said.

"Okay… Good night," she said softly.

"Night, Nikki," I said.

I stared at Nicole for a moment — her browns to my greens — before I let her go. She stared back at me before I turned around and walked down the stairs. Alex walked Michelle home since my car was there. I sat in the cold car for a while, thinking. So this was really going to happen.

Chapter 12

We met at the CCT building. It was still the holiday season, so no one from the board would be there. I took Nicole downstairs to the meeting room. She scrunched her nose at the dark room with the long oval table.

"What?" I asked.

"You guys call it The Table 'cause of this room?" she asked with an expression that showed just how unimpressed she was with the idea.

"No, it's called that for the Knights at King Arthur's Table. The members all met to keep order in the kingdom," I said.

She gave another confused look as her eyes ran along the length of the table in front of us. I rolled my eyes, now amused because I already knew what she was going to say. Why was I in so deep with such a nerd?

"It's not a circle," she said, looking up at me with a smirk when she saw my expression matched hers.

"There are too many people. There are twenty-one board members, if you include The Head, and the room isn't big enough for a big circular table. It's round enough," I said, pulling out a seat for her to sit.

"Don't lie. You've thought about it, too," she said, hitting my arm with the back of her hand at my judging chuckle.

"Maybe," I said as Greg walked in wearing a navy-blue suit and a smile.

He was silent, as if he was trying to assess the room's energy before he spoke. That was Greg: never missing a detail ever.

"Good afternoon, lovebirds," Greg said with a satisfied smile like what he had said was really that funny.

"Ew," Nicole said, straightening in her large chair and crossing her arms.

He gave her a little smile before he sat down and opened his briefcase, taking out his laptop and various papers. Nicole and I watched in silence while he typed a couple things on his keyboard. He finally looked up at Nicole.

"Nicole, I was told that you have some conditions. I will add them to the contract now," Greg said.

Nicole nodded and grabbed a folder from her bag. My eyebrows raised in surprise, and Greg smiled in appreciation. She was always on top of her shit. I shouldn't have been surprised.

"Any decisions that Noah has to make that will alter my livelihood must be run by me first. He is not allowed to just tell me what to do," she said after glancing down at her typed up list.

"Any objections?" he asked, looking over at me with amusement in his eyes.

"No," I said.

He typed for a moment before he nodded for her to continue. She continued to read the list. She wanted to be viewed as my equal during the time being with no ridiculous rules that made it seem otherwise. I agreed. The list was pretty reasonable, I realized as she read it off, and I continued to agree.

"Anything else?" Greg asked.

"Last thing is Mr. Noah Crawford will not try to sleep with me or make any other physical advances," she said.

Greg's eyes widened for a moment before he looked over at the beautiful woman sitting in front of him and then looked at me with the utmost sympathy. I sighed inwardly.

"Well, we also want to make this look as believable as possible. An occasional kiss or holding of the hand should occur in front of the board members," Greg said with an uncomfortable smile before I could say anything.

Nicole looked over at me with a tired glance. Happy was the furthest thing from what she was. She looked down at her list again and nodded.

"Not unless I say you can," she said, looking up at Greg.

"Whatever, fine," I grumbled, just wanting to get out of there.

Greg typed on his laptop dutifully while side-eyeing me occasionally. I knew he thought this was funny, my small miseries. Never the big ones. It was the minor inconveniences that caught me off guard or made me stumble on my words that entertained him. He finally looked up at both of us.

"So, just some housekeeping… Nicole, this is still an actual marriage, legally, so I will need you to sign a prenup. Noah and I have a settlement of five million dollars, but if this is not satisfactory for you, we can discuss it further," he said.

Nicole's eyes widened, and she looked over at me. She shook her head. Even now, she didn't care about my money. It was never about that with her. The fact that she thought she would do this for free made me feel worse about putting her through this in the first place, but I wasn't surprised.

***

Nicole dropped her book bag on the ground and started to look through my record collection on the shelf. When she got to the row of collector's pieces, she looked in awe.

"How did you get your hands on this?" she asked, holding my favorite record of them all. It was an original copy of the *Rumors* album signed by Stevie Nicks herself.

"I got it at an auction that I went to with my dad a few years back," I said.

"Did it cost a lot?" she asked, running her finger over the signature.

"Yeah... like twenty-five grand," I said.

"That's a lot," she said, giving it a thoughtful look.

I hated speaking about money. Once people knew you had it, there was never any going back. It was either they treated you nicely so they could benefit from it somehow in the future, or they assumed you thought you were better than them and they hated you over it. I couldn't care less about it. It was just there. I didn't even make it myself. There was no reason for me to be overly proud about it.

I sighed inwardly as I watched Nicole run her fingers over the album again before sliding the record out and putting it on the player. She was going to ask more and find out my dad had been one of the country's most wealthy men. I liked how things were going with us, and I really didn't want them to change. Actually, that's false. I did, *very much*, want them to change, but in a way that made us an item. I just didn't want it to be because of my money.

She started bobbing her head to "Dreams" by Fleetwood Mac as it played through my speakers. She didn't ask any other questions about money. I was shocked.

"That's it?" I asked.

"Oh sorry, did you want to talk about the auction more?" she asked, turning down the volume.

"No, I just thought you would ask more about it," I admitted.

"Like what?"

"The money part or what my family does, I guess."

"Hmm, well, I know your dad was a really rich guy, so that makes you a rich kid, but I don't really care about that stuff. *Not that I don't care about your family*. Please feel free to talk about them if you want, but I know you don't like to. I just think… If the world started caring more about who people are instead of what they have, we would be in a better state. I don't know if that makes sense," she said, tapping her chin.

I felt my lips curl into a smile, and I nodded. My shoulders, that I didn't realize were tense, relaxed, and I leaned further back into my chair. She gave me a small smile before looking down at the list of songs on the back of the album. Her lips mouthed the lyrics that came from the speakers as she swayed to the music. Her hair was curly and pulled into a bun on the top of her head. Her blue sweater revealed the tops of her perfect shoulders. She was a whole vision, one that I was unable to stop looking at.

"What?" she asked, breaking me out of my train of thought.

"Huh?" I asked, being pulled out of the staring contest I was taking part in on my own.

"You're just staring at me, smiling." She giggled.

"Sorry, you just look nice."

"Thanks, you look nice too." She chuckled.

"Nikki… Nicole," I started.

"Mhm?" she asked.

"Can I take you to dinner sometime?"

***

"That's a lot, Noah. When you said money, I thought you would pay next year's tuition or something," she said.

"Five million, it states, to ensure the continuous comfort of Ms. Nicole Smith," Greg read.

"It's really no big deal, seriously, Nikki. Take it and use it to go to school or travel or whatever makes you happy," I said softly.

"But—" she began to argue.

"I will not settle for anything less," I said.

She sighed and looked back at Greg with a nod. He handed her the document and told her where to sign. I signed afterward. He moved on to other things and I zoned in and out, signing when I needed to and agreeing to what I needed to agree to.

"We can go to the courts as early as tomorrow and get this done," Greg finally said, putting the signed documents away. He looked at me for an answer.

"That's okay with me." I shrugged.

"Yeah, I guess," she answered shakily, and Greg nodded at her with a sympathetic smile.

Greg tossed me a little blue box. I opened it to look at a light-catching diamond ring. I had told him I had no clue on the first thing of picking an engagement ring. He tried to give me tips. Greg wasn't married, but he said he had gone with friends to help pick out rings before. He was the details guy after all. When I expressed my lack of desire to do it, he said he would take care of it. I awkwardly looked at her, not sure if I was supposed to kneel.

"Don't," she said, putting her hand out to stop me.

I handed her the box and she looked at the ring. She slowly took it out the box and slid it on her finger. It was a perfect fit.

"How'd you know my ring size?" she asked, looking between myself and Greg.

"I have my ways," Greg said.

"Rachel?" she asked.

"Maybe," he said with a small smile.

It was settled. We were going to get married in the morning. Nicole hardly said anything for the rest of the meeting. I would've paid crazy money to know what she was thinking at that moment, but I knew it probably had something to do with how insane the whole thing was. We were getting married to save our lives and the ones of those we cared about.

I went for a drive later that afternoon and decided to stop by Eliza's. I drove through the opening of the huge iron gates that surrounded her house and parked next to her car. It was the only one there, so I knew she was home alone. Eliza opened the door and stepped back to let me in. I closed it behind me.

"So, when's the wedding?" she asked as she crossed her arms and stood in the middle of her foyer.

"Tomorrow," I said.

Eliza nodded slowly before walking to the living room and sitting on the couch. She started swiping on her phone quietly. I followed her into the room and took a seat across from her. Her eyes were shiny and I sighed. She was upset.

"I'm sorry, Eliza," I said softly.

"You're not. This would've happened eventually," she said dryly.

"We are only doing this to fix things," I said.

She gave a bitter laugh and threw her phone on the couch so hard that it bounced.

"You are *in love* with her. You would find some way to make this happen. If it wasn't going to be now, it was going to be a few years down the line. Your precious Nikki," she said.

"Eliza," I breathed.

"Don't *Eliza* me. What's done is done," she said, taking a sip of wine from the glass that was sitting on her coffee table.

"I didn't know that any of this would happen. I didn't even know I would see her again," I said.

***

I felt the touch of feathery fingertips run down my chest, tickling me out of my deep sleep. I swatted at them gently and tried to fall back asleep. Then I felt lips giving me light kisses from my temples to my cheek to my chest and lower. I let out a tired laugh.

"Please, I'm tired. Nikki, you wouldn't let me sleep last night," I said, and the kisses suddenly stopped.

That's when I realized what I had said. I hadn't been with Nicole last night. I was with Eliza. I slowly opened my eyes to see her looking at me with a horrified look on her face. My eyes widened, and I tried to figure out a way to backtrack what I had just said. There wasn't. I braced myself for a punch to the face, the family jewels, or anything that would hurt a lot, but instead, she just stared.

"Eliza, I'm—" I began, having no idea how I could ever end it successfully.

"I'm so stupid," she said through her teeth before she reached to grab her shirt on the foot of the bed.

"No, Eliza, I didn't mean it," I said, sitting up.

"Don't lie to me, Noah. Just leave," she said, getting up and gathering the clothes on the floor.

Her dark red hair hid her face, but when she finally did look at me, my stomach dropped. Tears wet her cheeks, and it alarmed me because it was the first time I had seen her cry. The first time she ever let herself seem defeated in front of me.

"It was a mistake," I said.

"Correct. Last night was a mistake. Now, get out," she said as she threw my clothes at me.

I quickly pulled on my clothes before I walked over to her and tried to do something to fix this. She pulled my hands from her face.

"Eliza, please talk to me," I pleaded.

"About what? About how before we started going out, I asked you about this and you lied?" she asked.

"I didn't know," I breathed.

"Leave," she said again.

"Can't we talk about this?" I asked.

"You still love her, don't you?"

I wanted to tell her no. I wanted to say that seeing Nicole at school a few days ago didn't mean anything to me. That I didn't care, but that was a lie, and I couldn't lie to her at that moment. Not when she looked like she was going to die because of what I said. I just exhaled sharply. She shook her head in recognition before giving me the hardest slap to my face in my life. I almost fell over.

"Get out, Noah. I can't see your face right now."

***

"Your heart knew where it was, even if your head didn't," she said, taking another long swig of wine.

"Perhaps," I said, hanging my head because I couldn't argue with the statement.

"So what are you here for? Are you going to get in my pants and call me Nikki again one last time? Better get on with it then," she slurred.

I stood up and took the wine glass out of her hand. I picked up the bottle nearby, it was empty. I sighed and looked back at her. She looked down ashamed. I put the bottle and glass down and sat down next to her. I hugged her because that was the only thing I could do. She buried her face in my chest and sobbed.

Chapter 13

I woke up to the sound of my alarm and reached over to stop it on my phone. I groaned, which turned into a yelp when I saw Greg standing a few feet away, looking at me with an unamused look.

"You should be up already," he said.

"It's only 8:45 and the ceremony is at eleven. I live ten minutes away from the courthouse. Let me sleep a few more minutes," I grumbled.

"Why are you so grumpy?" he asked, handing me a mug of coffee.

"I got home late," I said, grabbing the mug.

"Why?"

"I was at Eliza's."

"Last hurrah before your wedding day?" he asked with judgement in his voice.

"No. I didn't. I went to tell her today was happening. She hates me for it," I said.

"She's hurt," Greg said.

"I know, and it's something I can't fix," I sighed.

"It's only been a few months. Give it time."

"I don't think time will fix it," I said.

"What life has taught me in the past twenty-nine years on this planet is that you can't force yourself in or out of love with anyone. Sometimes the heart is stronger than the mind, and the more the mind pulls away, the more severe the loss in the game of tug of war. You can't force yourself to be out of love with Nicole," he said.

"I'm not trying to do that anymore. I just want Eliza to stop hurting because of it."

"She'll fall in love again, and you will be there for her when it happens, as a friend. You guys were really great friends before you decided to date," he said.

I stood in the men's bathroom of the courthouse. I looked at the guy staring back at me in the mirror. I had imagined my wedding day many times, and it wasn't anything like this. Same girl, but everything else — different. The idea of a large wedding was never a turn-off for me. Celebrating something so important seemed to be the only way to go. Nicole Smith was definitely someone to celebrate being married to, yet we were doing the smallest ceremony possible.

Greg walked into the bathroom and looked at me with a smile. I gave him an exasperated look in the mirror before I looked at him straight on. He walked up to me, straightened my suit, and looked up at me like a proud parent. I rolled my eyes.

"You ready?" he asked, tapping my cheek.

"Farthest thing from it, but let's do it anyway," I said.

"You got yourself a stunning wife out there and I have the wedding bands. Sounds ready to me," he said.

"How long until the ceremony?" I asked.

"Fifteen minutes… You look just like your dad right now... I'll see you out there," he said before leaving me alone once again.

I looked back at myself in the mirror. I did look like Dad. It was so apparent that I couldn't dispute it. I reached into my pocket and took out a picture of us. It was from the family portraits we had gotten done when I was seven or eight. The photographer had told us to make a serious face and Dad had done it effortlessly. I, on the other hand, was smirking, and, because I was young and cute no matter what I did, we kept it. Dad always kept it in his wallet, but I saved it once he died. I brought it with me on special occasions. I wasn't sure if a fake wedding counted as one of those, but since it was with Nicole, I brought it just in case. I had brought the picture with every other milestone that had to do with her. When I had asked her to be my girlfriend, the homecoming dance, and even when I told her that I was moving. I brought it along to anything important, good or bad. Was this good, or bad?

I looked at Dad in his suit, staring intently at the camera with his green eyes. I looked up and saw almost the same thing in the mirror. Really, the only difference was our hair. I got my midnight black hair from my mother. Dad's was more brown.

"Help me figure this one out, Pops," I said softly.

I walked out into the large hall of the courthouse. I started to walk in the direction of the spot where I knew everyone was when I saw Eliza and froze. I had told her she didn't have to come if she didn't want to and figured she would take me up on the offer. She kept walking toward me, then threw her gauzy scarf over my eyes.

"Eliza, please, I'm almost a married man." I snorted.

"Noah, please, not everyone wants to jump your bones," she retorted as she tied the scarf to my head.

"Why am I blindfolded right now?"

"Because your sister-in-law requested that I prevent you from seeing the bride."

"What if you mess up my hair?"

"You don't give a shit about your hair… You have enough mousse in it, though. The scarf won't do anything," she said, guiding me down the hallway.

We walked slowly in silence for a while. I heard people quietly walking by. I still felt bad about the night before. For someone who had been crying so much the night before, she looked so put together. She wore a grey dress with long heels that made her almost my height. Her dark red hair cascaded down one side of her head. She looked as if she was ready to take on the world. Emphasis on *looked*. I couldn't see her anymore.

"Are you okay?" I asked.

"The world is disappointing, but since that's the norm, I guess we can say I'm okay," she said.

"I feel that." I snorted.

"Are you ready for the first day of the rest of your life?" she asked.

"Isn't that like the speech for the end of high school or whatever it is?" I asked.

"Who cares? Are you?" she asked.

"Eliza, you know this isn't really a wedding, right?" I asked in a low tone.

"You sure about that?" she asked. *What did that mean?* Of course I knew.

I could tell we got to the group because I heard everyone's voices. Rachel's excited voice, and Nicole's soothing one. Greg's amused voice… and one that sounded so familiar, but I couldn't pinpoint it.

"Who's here?" I asked Eliza.

"Everyone. Your bride, Rachel, Greg, Jason, and Josh," she said.

"Someone call me?" Josh asked, and his voice got closer.

"How'd you get here? Can I *please* take this shit off my eyes?" I asked louder for everyone to hear me as Eliza led me a few steps forward.

"No! You can't see the bride until the ceremony," Rachel said.

"I told her all of this was not necessary," Nicole added.

"Can't Nikki see me?" I asked.

"No, my back is to yours," Nicole responded, knocking the back of my arm.

"Why does she get to not be blindfolded?" I asked.

"I spent all morning doing her makeup. We can't ruin my art," Rachel said.

I sighed and heard Nicole giggle. It made a smile show up on my face like a reflex.

"You alright?" I asked.

"I guess. This is a lot of fuss for a fake wedding," she said softly.

"Sure is," I agreed.

"You know there's supposedly a reception later," Nicole said.

"There's a *what*? Rachel? Greg? Who did it," I said loudly, and I heard Greg laugh.

"We're ready," I heard a woman say, and everyone shuffled before the sound of doors opening echoed in the hallway. I felt my heart start to beat quickly in my chest.

"Okay, you guys can see each other now," Rachel said as someone spun me around and pulled the scarf off my eyes.

I opened my eyes to see Nicole spinning around to look at me. It was one of those visions you wish you could play on loop forever. She wore a light blue dress. It was her favorite shade, periwinkle. I didn't know many shades of blue, but I knew that one.

***

"What's your favorite flower?" I asked, holding Nicole's hand as I walked her home from school.

"Hmm… periwinkle hydrangeas," she said, looking up at the sky as she thought.

"What's periwinkle?"

"It's a type of blue. It's my favorite color, and on hydrangeas, it's the most beautiful. Why do you ask?"

"Well, you're my girlfriend now. I have to get you flowers sometimes."

"You don't *have* to get me flowers."

I gave her a playful look and snorted as if what she had just said was absurd. She shook her head and gave me a smile.

"I just don't want you to feel like you have to spend money on me," she said softly.

"I know I don't have to, but I want to. At least sometimes. It'll make you smile," I said, putting my hand over our already clasped ones.

"How do you know it'll make me smile?" she asked.

"Flowers always make women smile. My mom hardly smiles, and she even smiles at flowers." I chuckled.

I was right. Nicole got flowers. No matter how rough the day, or if we had gotten into an argument, she always smiled at a bouquet of periwinkle hydrangeas.

***

The dress fit in all the right places and had a low neckline. It seemed to effortlessly form to her body until it decided to flow at the bottom. It just grazed the ground with her heels on. The bouquet in her hand were hydrangeas, of course, an arrangement of periwinkle and white. Her eyes had a touch of glitter that sparkled whenever she moved her head, but you could only tell if you paid attention. Her full lips were glossy with a touch of red. Her hair was straight with some large curls at the end. I tried to take in as many details, as quickly as possible, before it was obvious I was staring.

"Don't look at me like that," she said, using her bouquet to lightly push my mouth closed. She looked down, embarrassed. I wondered if she had seen herself. How could I not marvel at the sight of her? I hadn't realized my jaw had fallen. I saw Rachel taking pictures on her phone at the corner of my eye. I probably looked completely dumbfounded in the pictures, but I didn't care. It was the truth. I was.

"I thought wedding dresses were white." I chuckled softly, and I wanted to kick myself. Why was that the first thing I said to her?

"I thought I'd save that for my actual wedding day," she said softly so only I could hear.

"You look really beautiful, Nicole," I said, matching her tone.

"So do you," she said with a small smile before looking away again.

"Alright, you two. Save it for the wedding night. Are you ready?" Rachel asked.

We both looked at her with a look that was probably full of bewilderment. We were not ready for any of it, but saying yes was a lie, and there was no use in saying no. It was going to happen anyway. Everyone walked inside the courtroom and found a seat up front. Greg walked in behind us to be the witness and handed us the rings.

As we slowly walked up to the judge, Nicole grabbed my hand and we both squeezed at the same time. My nerves were all over the place.

"You ok?" I whispered.

"No, you?" she asked.

"I don't know, honestly. Just think of it as two friends putting on a show," I said to her right before we got close enough for the judge to hear.

The judge spoke and we listened when we needed to, repeated when we needed to. We stared at each other intently, silently begging each other to stay calm. Greg handed each of us the rings, and we shakily slid them on each other's fingers. It was just a thin silver band, but it held so much meaning. We spoke some more when we needed to, and then we were at the most important part.

"By the authority vested in me by the state of New York, I now pronounce you husband and wife. You may kiss the bride," the judge said.

I leaned in and put my hand softly on her face to tilt it up toward me. She gave a slightly amused and scared look as if to say "do you realize how insane this is?" and my eyes scanned her face for a second. It was like I wanted to look at her one last time before everything was about to change, forever. Her eyes searched mine for a second, too, before she closed them. I closed mine and brought our lips together.

There were several things I realized during that kiss. The first was that I had forgotten why I loved kissing Nicole Smith so much. Her lips were soft, pillowy, and warm. This was what I had been missing the past two years. I hadn't realized how much I missed the feeling. The second was that this kiss was way longer than a peck, and while it probably didn't phase the judge, I'm sure everyone else in that room was aware of it too. The third thing, which was the most scary, was that Nicole was kissing me back, and this kiss was not just friendly.

Chapter 14

I glared at my new sister-in-law and my assistant when we walked through my apartment elevator doors. My apartment had been turned into a little reception hall. The dining table had a three tier cake and large bouquet of periwinkle hydrangeas. There were two people from a catering company setting up large platters of food in my kitchen.

"Why," the words came out of the mouths of Nicole and myself at the same time.

"Because, life is about to suck soon. You might as well have a party before that happens," Rachel sighed as if our confusion was strange.

"She's right. Let's just eat. I'm hungry," Josh said, walking past us and to the platters.

Nicole looked up at me apologetically for her sister and sighed before she let go of my hand, that I didn't even realize she was holding, and walked farther into the apartment. I immediately felt the cold absence and how much I wanted her hand back. *You are supposed to admire her from afar, idiot,* I scolded myself.

We ate and spoke about random topics. We spoke mainly about college, the upcoming semester, and made fun of Greg for being old when he really barely looked older than me. Later, the conversation shifted to summer and what we wanted to do for the warm months. It was almost as if everything that was yet to be sorted out never existed. It was better that way. It made the time more enjoyable. We cut the cake, and the conversation broke off into smaller groups. Greg went to answer messages on his phone. Rachel and Eliza moved to the couches. Josh and Nicole sat at a corner of the table while they spoke passionately about their favorite books. I was left with, obviously, my favorite person in the world, Jason Westbrook. Not only was he the reason why life had been particularly more miserable the past few months, but he also was my wife's ex.

We ate in silence until I excused myself to the bathroom. I did what I had to do and took my tie off. I sighed in relief as I unbuttoned the first couple buttons on my shirt. I rolled up my sleeves and opened the door to see Jason standing there with an intense look in his eyes.

"Jason," I said, waiting to hear why he was waiting for me.

"We need to talk," he said.

"Okay, go ahead."

He took a step closer to me and pointed a finger hard into my chest. I looked down at it for a second before looking back at him. He thought I was going to cower at this? *Oh please.*

"Nicole is not just any girl. Don't hurt her, or I will make your life a living hell," he said in almost a growl.

"Oh, Jason, did you not realize that you made the lives of myself and Nicole more miserable than it has been in years? This all happened because of you," I said, taking a step forward to tower over him.

"I didn't mean to hurt her," he said.

"Me neither," I said.

"Oh my God. Will you two just stop?" Rachel's voice interrupted us, and I looked up to see her with Eliza and Nicole at her sides, and Josh lingering in the back. Great, a party to see me kick Westbrook's ass.

Jason walked away and made his way down the hall back to the main area of the apartment. I looked over at Rachel, who had a travel bag for a suit or probably a dress in her arms. Eliza had a duffle bag on her shoulder.

"What's this stuff for?" I asked.

"We have to get your wife out of her dress," Rachel said.

"Stop calling me that." Nicole laughed.

"Well, you are his wife, for now," Rachel said cheekily, making her sister's eyes roll up to the ceiling.

"So, both of you need to help her?" I snorted, deciding not to comment on the wife-remarks.

"There are like forty buttons in the back. I need help," Nicole said, turning around to show the little buttons in the back of her dress.

"I can help you." I flashed my eyebrows.

"No," Nicole said, pushing me out the way to get into the bathroom.

"You tried." Eliza snorted before following the sisters into the bathroom and closing the door behind her.

Jason left soon after, explaining that he had to get back before it was too late. Greg was at my dining table, typing on his laptop with his headphones in while the caterers cleaned up. I sat next to Josh on the couch.

"How does it feel?" Josh asked as I sipped my glass of champagne.

"What, the champagne? I offered you some and you said it was gross," I said.

"Alcohol tastes like medicine. I don't get how you can drink that stuff and enjoy it," he said with a frown.

"Not all alcoholic drinks taste like that."

"The stuff I've seen you drink does. You had cognac for Christmas, and now you're drinking the bubbly tonic of death."

"It helps calm you," I said with a chuckle.

"I guess I don't have much to not be calm about." He shrugged.

"I envy you, brother. Anyway, how does *what* feel?" I asked after finishing my glass.

"Being married."

"I don't know. It's fine, I guess. It's not real," I said.

"It sure did look real when it happened… the kiss, I mean," he said.

It sure felt that way, but I didn't say that. There was no sense in even dwelling on it. It would all be over in a couple months.

Just then, Nicole, Rachel, and Eliza all emerged from the bathroom. Nicole was in a white long sleeve shirt and jeans. Some of her makeup was off. She no longer sparkled when she moved. It didn't matter. I could still stare at her for hours. I was still looking at her when her eyes met mine. She gave me an expression that I couldn't read before turning to smile at Rachel, who had handed her a long brown coat. *Wait, what was that? What did that mean?*

"I guess we're all set," Nicole said after she had pulled on her coat.

"How are you getting home?" Greg asked, standing up from the dining table.

"Rachel's driving, which is why your champagne isn't finished." Nicole nodded toward the bottle on the coffee table.

"I do not drink *that* much," Rachel retorted as they walked toward the elevator.

Nicole gave us a pointed look with a smirk over her shoulder before she walked toward the elevator. Greg and Josh chuckled. I, on the other hand, was concerned about other matters. I didn't want her to leave. I wanted to be alone with her. I wanted her to bring up the kiss because I knew she eventually would.

"You're leaving already? It's only six," I said.

Nicole's boot heels clicked on the floor as she swung around to look at me. She wouldn't look straight into my eyes. She glanced at me, then looked at Greg instead.

"We have a meeting tomorrow morning. I should get some sleep," she said shyly.

"What meeting?" I asked, looking at Greg.

"To brief.. Mrs. Smith-Crawford on what to expect at your first event together and an upcoming board meeting," he replied.

"Smith-Crawford?" I asked, liking the sound of it.

"I like my Smith. Plus, I want a distinction between your mother and myself," she
started to explain.

"Plus, you'd both be N. Crawford which is *so cute*, but probably not in Greg's law world," Eliza added dryly.

"I like the Smith-Crawford… and what event?" I asked, finally breaking my attention to look at Greg.

"The Spinelli New Years' Gala," Greg said.

"I told you I was going to skip that," I sighed.

"It's best if you make an appearance and start playing nice before the board meeting next week," Greg said.

"I thought it was longer than that," I said.

"Your mother moved it up," Eliza said.

"And I need to be prepared to help make *you* look good so *I* don't die." Nicole gave me a sarcastic smile before walking over to the open elevator doors.

I immediately felt like weights were placed on my shoulders. Social events were not my strong suit. Most people didn't notice, and I couldn't understand why. I never put much effort in trying to hide it. Greg said it was my "pretty boy charm" that blinded them from the fact I was a complete jerk. I was not a jerk. Attractive? Yes, but not a jerk. I did not feel the need to play nice with people I didn't care about. I used to be good at it, but after almost losing my mind because of the Reggie incident, I no longer saw the point of it all. There were some things that no longer mattered. In that way, I wondered if Tracey had taken some of my spark away.

Nicole and I made eye contact for a second before the elevator doors closed. Even though I would see her the next day, I didn't want to see her go.

The plan was to get some time alone until Greg pretty much told me that Josh would be staying with me for the night. I did not have a problem with Josh at all. I just wanted to recharge my social battery, as Nicole had called it. I sat in my pajama pants on the foot of my bed. I swiped through my texts, but stopped when I saw one from someone I cared enough to respond to.

Alex Ramos: Throwing a party next weekend. Come through. Bring your girlfriend.

Noah Crawford: Maybe

A few minutes passed before I got a response.

Alex Ramos: Show the world that pretty face before you wrinkle like a raisin or some shit.

Noah Crawford: We're 19.

Alex Ramos: No, I'm 18. That means you're one year closer to death and you have to party.

Noah Crawford: If I say I will try my best, will you leave me alone?

Alex Ramos: Yeah asshole, that's good enough for now. Night.

Josh appeared in my doorway with damp hair in one of my t-shirts and pajama pants. He took a few long strides to the futon across the room.

"Texting your woman?" he asked.

"No." I snorted before plugging my phone in on my nightstand.

"Is your favorite color black?" he asked.

"I guess," I said, looking around at the black and grey interior of my room.

"Why?" he asked.

"It's simple and goes with everything. My mom always liked the colors black and grey, I guess I just got used to it," I said.

He nodded and looked around for a while, probably taking everything in. It was another moment where I saw Dad in him and it made me smile. I guess it was like what people saw when they looked at me.

"This is probably a really bad time, but I've learned that I'm not good at timing anyways. So, Dad wrote me a letter and I want you to read it. You don't have to read it now, but I want to give it to you for when you are ready," I said, handing him the letter I had folded on my nightstand.

"I can just read it now." He shrugged with no hesitation. It had been so long since I approached something without hesitation. Everything these days seemed to hold so much weight.

He opened it and read. I didn't know what to do, so I just watched as his eyebrows furrowed over the piece of paper. His lips mouthed the words and stopped at one point. He glanced up at me for a moment before he kept reading. When he was done, he slowly handed me back the letter. He stood a few feet away from me and just stared.

"What are you thinking?" I finally asked.

"Bro, what am I *not* thinking," he said.

"That's fair."

"I usually work through things fine. For the most part, nothing really confuses me. But this is a lot," he sighed, as he sat next to me.

"Yeah, I get that." I nodded.

"Do you miss him?" he asked, and I immediately knew who he was talking about.

"Everyday," I said.

"Me too. You look just like him. When I think about Dad when I was younger, the image is pretty much you now."

"Today, I was looking at a picture of him and I saw it."

"Is your life always like this? Just full of things to do, fix, and find out?" he asked.

"Pretty much." I chuckled.

It was silent for a while. We were both letting our truths sink in. Then, I asked the question that had been looming in my mind over the past few days.

"Do you want to see her?" I asked.

"Who?" he asked.

"Your mom."

"I don't know, but let's tackle one issue at a time. You have to survive this hearing," he said.

"Oh, yeah," I said.

"Otherwise, I'm going to have to deal with Rachel on my own. That sounds like a new version of hell," he said, and we both laughed.

Chapter 15

Nicole was always the best student. She was so organized and on top of her game that I used to find it intimidating when we were in school together. Everything was always color-coded and filed neatly away in a binder or the little organizer she had in her locker. I had remembered this, so I wasn't sure why I was surprised by how seriously she took Greg's briefing. He gave a smile that seemed as if he felt so validated that she highlighted the things he had emphasized. He had told her she would have to be social and well-liked during the board meetings, and, while I knew she was not interested in that, she didn't complain. She just nodded and continued to listen.

"That should be it. Do you have any more questions?" he asked.

"No, I don't think so. I'll make sure to call you if I do, Greg," she said smoothly.

"And what are your talking points for tomorrow?" he tested.

"Dr. Jen Spinelli went to NYU. We'll talk about the school and how I am doing in the program. Brian Spinelli is in the music industry, and I will congratulate his new deal with The Recording Company. I like music, so I can wing that. Daniel Craig will be there. He probably will not be open to discussing much with me, which makes sense, so I will go for mentioning football. He likes the Patriots. Do not bring up Eliza. Senator George Kaplan will be there. Congratulate him on his win and say I'm looking forward to the talk he is giving at NYU in a couple months," she said, only glancing down at her notes a few times.

"You'll be great. Keep this one in check, too," Greg said, tilting his head in my direction.

"I don't need to be kept in check. I'll be fine," I sighed.

Greg gave Nicole an exasperated look, and she chuckled while she put her papers away in a crisp folder. Then, she put her pens and highlighters away in a little bag that went in her larger bag. I wondered if the outward order soothed any of the chaos that must've been going on within. I knew she had to be stressed, even if she didn't show it.

We got up to leave. Greg had a meeting with all the other assistants of The Table soon. These meetings happened much more often and helped the board members have more time to take care of their actual businesses.

"Good luck at your meeting, Greg," Nicole said as she walked toward the door to exit the board room.

"Thanks, Ms. Smith-Crawford," he said.

"Please, Nicole is fine. You're literally helping save my life over here." She chuckled.

"Okay, Nicole. Oh, one thing before you leave," he said, and I could see a blush threatening to become very apparent on his pale cheeks.

"What's that?" she asked.

"Wear something more form-fitting tomorrow night," he said.

I laughed, and Nicole gave him an incredulous look.

"I can't say I object, but why?" I asked.

"An eighteen and nineteen year old are getting married. Someone is going to assume a pregnancy is the reason. Let's refute that assumption for the next few public appearances," Greg said uncomfortably.

"I see. Thank you, Greg. Is that all?" Nicole asked.

"Yes," he said.

I followed Nicole upstairs to the glass doors that led outside. She did not seem to have anything to say to me. When she got some feet from the building, she took off her rings and put them in her bag.

"Hey, Nikki, do you have a minute?" I asked.

"Yeah, I guess," she said as she turned around to look at me.

"I was wondering if we could talk."

"We are talking, Noah." She shrugged.

"I mean, about everything, over lunch," I said.

"I don't have time for that right now. I have to find a dress that won't look like I'm trying to hide our potential supposed baby, start reading for this winter class I decided to take before I was forced to play house with you, and I have to get my nails done today, so I can focus on this party tomorrow," she said, grabbing her car keys from her bag.

"Oh, I see, that's a lot."

"Yup."

"Well, when can you fit me in?" I asked.

"Don't you think I am fitting you into my life with all of this?" she asked before she opened her car door and got in.

I got back to my apartment to see a crisp, three-piece tuxedo hanging up with a thin plastic bag over it to keep any dust off. The apartment smelled extra fresh, like it had just been cleaned. I walked into the guest room to see Josh looking at the letter again as he laid on his bed. He looked tired, like he had not gotten a lot of sleep. I knocked on the already open door, and he tilted his chin as a greeting.

"How was the meeting?" he asked after I sat.

"Good. It was mainly for Nicole." I shrugged.

"You're back early. Did you guys get to speak?" he asked, looking down at his digital watch.

"No, not yet," I sighed.

"Some ladies named Becky and Millie came here to clean up and drop off your tux. They looked startled to see me, but I mean, who would've thought Noah Crawford would have a black guy walking around his apartment saying he's his brother? I'd probably be startled, too." Josh snorted.

"They're nice." I chuckled as I put my feet up on the little couch.

"They are. Also, does Nicole get help now with all of this stuff that she has to do, too?"

I sat up and looked at him. He gave me a confused look. Josh had a pretty calm demeanor, but he probably seemed ten times more alive than I did in that sense. I hadn't shown that much excitement in probably years.

"You're a genius," I said.

The security pad near my front door dinged at six-thirty, and I pressed the intercom icon on the screen to answer. It was security telling me that the car had arrived. It had picked up Nicole first, then swung by to get me before we were to head to Gotham Hall in the city. I rode the elevator down to the first floor and said hello to the security guard before I walked over to a large black SUV. The driver opened the door for me, and I slid into the seat next to Nicole. Her hair was up, and she was wearing a strapless, dark red, form-fitting dress with a black shawl to cover her shoulders. I stared and knew I was, in fact, going to die.

"Hey," she said softly, as if she didn't know how she looked.

"Hi, uh, you look amazing," I said.

"Thanks. I like your tux." She gave a small smile before looking back down at her phone again.

"Thank you… How was your ride here?"

"It was okay. You didn't have to send me a ride. I could've driven here or something," she said.

"I just thought I could help make it a little easier," I said, and she nodded, looking out the window again.

We rode in silence for a while as we inched along in the holiday traffic. She finally looked up from her phone when we had gotten too deep into the Midtown Tunnel to get a signal. She sighed. I knew she was using it as a way to not speak to me, but now she didn't have it as a security blanket.

"How was the reading for the class?" I asked.

"Boring. It's a philosophy class," she sighed.

"That's my minor," I said.

"Oh, I'm sorry. I just," she began, then she stopped when she saw my smile.

"I'm just messing with you, Smith… Smith-Crawford," I said, and I hated how tender my voice sounded when I had said her name.

"It's all so strange, isn't it?" she asked softly after a long moment of silence.

"Yeah, I didn't see myself getting married before I even finished my teens."

"Me neither... I always wanted to fall in love, the kind of love where it's so deep that it hurts, and then get married once. Kind of like my parents. I guess sometimes life just doesn't work out the way you want it to."

I felt like shit. I wanted to punch myself in the face, and this marriage thing wasn't even completely my fault.

"I wish it could have been different, for your sake," I said, putting my hand over hers on the leather seat between us.

We drove up to Gotham Hall and security ushered us into the building past all the paparazzi taking pictures outside. I had been here multiple times for events, but it was Nicole's first time. She tried to conceal her expressions as she marveled at the high ceilings. When we got to the main event room, many heads turned our way, and I felt her hand reach for mine. I gave her hand a squeeze. I was used to being looked at. I was the next Head of the CCT Network, but the looks were even more intense now that I had a woman by my side.

I looked over at Nicole, and she took a deep breath before she plastered a smile on her face. I soon saw the Spinellis walking over to us. Jen and Brian Spinelli, two board members, smiled at us warmly while their son, Gerard, observed Nicole with his eyes going up and down her body. He was a couple of years older than us, and he had a reputation of being a complete asshole that followed him.

"Noah, I'm so glad you could make it," Jen said with a smile as she leaned in and kissed both of my cheeks.

"I'm glad I… we could make it as well," I said.

"You have to introduce us to your stunning date," she said, giving Nicole an adoring smile.

"This is my wife, Nicole," I said, and I wondered how saying something could make me so happy and sad at the same time.

"Wife? I didn't know you had gotten married and *so young*. Well, I would hold on to her, too, if I were you. How do you do, dear? Dr. Jennifer Spinelli, but please, call me Jen," she said, wrapping Nicole in a warm embrace. I could see Gerard's expression become grim when he heard the word *wife*. I smiled to myself at the small victory.

"Hi, Jen. It's so nice to finally meet you. Noah has told me such great things, and I told him we had to attend," Nicole said in a soft and welcoming voice. Jen beamed at her and then me.

"Oh, how darling! Come, come, let's get you a drink. We have to chat," she said, whisking her away.

Nicole gave me a wide-eyed smile before she was gone in the crowd.

"So, Noah, how have you been doing?" Brian Spinelli asked me with curious eyes. I knew he had heard things from the board meeting. He probably was confused, and had a much harder time hiding it than his wife did. Ditto, apparently.

"I've been doing well. I recently finished my first semester at NYU," I said, trying to think of what Nicole would do. I wish I had listened to more details about Brian from the meeting.

"Oh, that's just fine. What are you studying?" he asked.

"Psychology. It's really interesting to see how the mind works. Congratulations on your deal with The Recording Academy," I said.

"Thank you! Yes, my company will take part in planning the Grammys next year," he said proudly.

"That's exciting." I smiled, and I really did mean that. It was pretty cool.

"So, how has married life been treating you? She's beautiful, son."

"I have to say I don't mind it. We're newlyweds, so I'm still learning new things all the time," I said.

"That never changes. I've known Jen for twenty-seven years and have been married for twenty. I learn new things about her everyday," he said with admiration in his eyes.

"I hope Nicole and I can be so lucky," I said and I wished it, but knew it wouldn't happen.

"Just remember, son. You are a team, and teams don't give up," he said.

I finally found Nicole in the crowd. She was speaking not only to Jen, but to two other middle-aged women. They giggled and looked at her with wide, adoring eyes. I inched my way to the group, and she looped her arm into mine. I was in awe of how well she was playing this off.

"Hi, I was just telling everyone about things at NYU. Noah's studying psychology. It's all really fascinating," she said adoringly, making the women gush over the way she hung on my arm. I smiled at her.

"Nicole is going into the medical field. I can't wait to see what she accomplishes," I said.

"Aw, what a lovely couple," Jen gushed, putting her hand on her cheek and holding a champagne glass with the other.

"It was nice meeting you, ladies," Nicole said before I walked away, pulling her along with me.

"That was fantastic," I said, and I wanted to kiss her at that moment, but I didn't.

"Thanks. Let's find our seat and get ready to eat," she said.

We sat at a round table with a huge arrangement in the middle. There were flowers of all sorts gathered together, and it looked just as beautiful as it was chaotic. We were eating the first course of our meal when Gerard came over to sit with us. He gave Nicole a charming smile.

"Mind if I join you?" he asked.

"Not at all. I'm Nicole," she said, offering her hand to shake his, but instead, he kissed her knuckles. I felt my neck get hot. *Chill out, Noah.* You can't kick his ass when you want his parents to like you.

"Gerard Spinelli," he said as I got pissed off that he didn't even address me.

"Nice to meet you." Nicole smiled politely.

"The pleasure is all mine," he said as his eyes lingered down to her cleavage and stayed there for too long.

"How are you doing, Gerard?" I nodded.

"Noah, good and yourself?" he asked in a clipped manner.

I nodded before I went back to eating. His eyes went right back to Nicole as he flashed a huge smile that contrasted with his olive skin.

"I thought Noah would be a bachelor for a little bit longer. How long have you known each other?" Gerard asked Nicole, and I knew he was here to get answers.

"About six years now. Are you dating, Gerard?" Nicole asked.

"Interesting. Well, I always thought I would leave marriage to my later years. What made you decide to get married so young? You're eighteen, right?" Gerard asked.

I saw Nicole's smile falter just a little. There was something that was very invasive and uncomfortable about the conversation. Of course he would think that. Gerard was known for his antics with multiple girls a night, partying at his family's residences around the world.

"Sometimes you just know. No need to waste time, right," I said, stretching my arm to the back of Nicole's chair and letting my fingers dance on the smooth skin of her shoulder. Gerard looked at her intently to see how she would react.

Nicole leaned in to sip soup from her spoon and acted as if it were normal. Gerard seemed to get bored after that.

"Well, Crawford, you're a lucky man. Hold onto her. Nice meeting you, Nicole," he said before getting back up and disappearing behind the sea of tables.

I felt Nicole's hand slowly go behind my neck, which made me shudder before she pinched a small bit of my skin really hard. I almost yelped, but I held it in my throat.

"What was that for?" I asked.

"Stop touching me," she said, hardly moving her lips before I realized that my fingers were still stroking her shoulder.

"Sorry," I said with a smirk that made her scowl deepen.

The main event area turned into a dance floor. I asked my wife if she wanted to dance, and she shared that she would rather read more Aristotle, but still let me drag her out to the dance floor. The music was upbeat and fun. We didn't really look at each other, but were still in pretty good sync with each other and the music. The Spinellis came over, Brian asked if he could dance with Nicole, and Jen didn't really ask me. She threw my arms around her.

"How are you enjoying yourself, Noah?" Jen asked, loud enough for me to hear her over the music.

"It's a wonderful party, Jen. Thank you for having us," I said with a small smile.

"Nicole is just a delight. I'm so happy you brought her." She smiled with a smile that was so warm, mine grew bigger.

I looked over to Nicole, who was saying something that made Brian laugh. He dipped her and they laughed, this time together. They seemed to be doing fine.

"She's fine, Noah. Listen, I wanted to ask you about the decision that was made last week," she said, and I felt my stomach drop. I wasn't expecting sweet Jen Spinelli to bring this up during a holiday party.

"Yes, about that. It's all just a huge misunderstanding," I said.

"Brian and I figured. We decided to vote, but I wanted to find out more. You and Nicole seem just splendid with nothing out of sorts," she said.

"Thank you, Jen. I appreciate it."

"I think you would make a wonderful head to the organization. You know, Brian and I will be opening up an after school music program for disabled children. It would be great if CCT would consider endorsing us to get the word out there. We are looking to expand nationally in the next few years," she said. There it was. No matter how nice the person was, they still wanted something. At least, that's how it was in this world. It was for a good cause though, and it would probably get my vote for her.

"That sounds like such a great cause to get behind. Please let me know how we can help," I said with a smile.

We danced for the next song and then we switched partners again. My nerves eased a little when Nicole walked back to me. She looked calm and unbothered. She went to the ladies' room, and I went over to grab another drink. I sipped slowly and watched as everyone moved on the dance floor in the dim lights.

"Noah Crawford, you would've sworn it was Carter in the flesh. How are you, son?" Senator Kaplan said, walking up to me with the typical politician's smile. The kind where there's always a catch. His silver hair reflected off the lights of the room.

"Senator Kaplan. How are you?" I asked, reaching out to shake his hand.

"I can't complain. Your mother tells me that you're going to my alma mater. How was your first semester?" he asked, giving my hand a firm shake.

I tried to remember what Nicole had mentioned. He was planning on speaking at our school soon. I reminded myself to add yet another reason I had to thank her on my list.

"Great. I can't see myself going anywhere else. I hear you will be giving a talk at the school soon," I said.

He laughed, like finance was funny, and spoke about it for way too long. I smiled and nodded along. I knew Dad would've loved it if I had decided to study business, but there was nothing more boring to me.

"I want to help businesses, and I think a public endorsement from those who have pull would help all of us in the end," he said.

"I see. I will definitely look into the matter. It sounds rewarding," I said, completely unsure of what he had just said.

"Looking forward to discussing it further, son. Also, congratulations. Your new wife and I had a great conversation about the stock market earlier tonight," he said.

"Thank you," I said.

It took a while for us to find each other again. Everyone had decided to cram into the main room as the last few minutes of the year were upon us. I felt someone tug on my sleeve and turned around to Nicole, who had a thoughtful look on her face.

"Another year is almost upon us," I said.

"Yup," she said uneasily as she looked at the countdown projected on the wall behind the live band.

"You alright?" I asked softly, taking a step toward her so she could hear me over the noise.

"Yeah, I guess," she said, pulling her scarf over her shoulders.

The crowd started to countdown from thirty. I chuckled as everyone started yelling out the numbers. There was no reason to start before ten, but here they were.

"You're not going to countdown?" Nicole asked.

"I start at ten. I'm never that excited about anything," I said.

She nodded thoughtfully until her eyes widened a little as she looked behind me. I turned around slowly to see Daniel Craig staring at us intently. His wife, Margaret, was speaking to him with a beaming smile, but instead, in these last few seconds of the year, he looked at us.

"Your first New Years' as a married couple! Cheers," Jen said cheerfully, clearly feeling the effect of the wine and spirits of the night.

Ten. Nine. I smiled at Jen and Brian Spinelli and turned to lift my glass to Daniel Craig. He did the same gesture back.

Eight. Seven. I realized that I wasn't smiling, which felt normal to me, but did not fit the scene of what was happening. Couples held each other as they screamed the numbers louder and louder. Everyone raised a glass. We were the only ones who stood out, and not in the good way.

Six. Five. Four. I plastered a smile on my face and pulled Nicole into me. She smiled at Jen, after she gave me a *don't you dare* glance. In my head, I begged her to not hate me for what I was about to do.

Three. Two. Everything around us became a blur. I could still feel eyes on us, and I knew I couldn't back out now. I guess it was time to give our audience the show they weren't sure whether they would get or not.

One. I leaned in and kissed her. It was like everything around us had faded into the farthest of backgrounds. When I pulled away, Nicole just stared. I had seen her facial expressions a bunch of times, but this was one I couldn't read.

"I need a drink," she sighed before she quickly ran off.

There are certain things a man does not want to hear when he makes a move. *That was terrible. Yuck. I am repulsed. I'm going to run away and get drunk to forget that just happened.* I know, it wasn't supposed to be a real move, but after it was over, it felt like one. To me, at least. I was screwed.

Chapter 16

I felt the knots my nerves were tied in loosen just a little bit the moment we got in the car. Emphasis on *just a little bit*. Next to me, a very inebriated Nicole leaned on the door on the other side of the row.

"How much did you drink?" I asked.

"Two glasses of wine, but a lot of champagne, ha ha." She laughed. Dear God. I could not let her go home like this.

"Nicole, you don't usually do this. Do you?" I asked, assuming that I knew, but so much time had passed since I could assume anything of value with her.

"Um… I don't remember. I guess it's working," she hummed.

I sighed and pressed the button to lower the partition. The traffic was pretty slow, and the driver turned his head a little to acknowledge me.

"Bring us to my building, please," I said before putting the division between us and the front row back up. Didn't want to share her not so shining moment with everyone. This was probably my fault somehow anyway.

"I'm going home," she slurred.

"I will drive you home when you are sobered up and your parents won't want to kill me," I said.

"*My* parents don't kill people. Only *your* mom."

"...That's very fair. What do you want to forget? The kiss?"

"Yeah, because none of this is real. You're not for me. You're for Eliza."

"What?" I asked, sitting up, alert.

"She's the one with red hair." She giggled.

"I know who she is, but I told you, we are no longer together," I said.

"Her dad said she's going to be your wife," she said sleepily.

When we got to the apartment building, Nicole was not only still quite drunk, but now she was tired. It was faster to just carry her, so I did. She tried to protest, but I ignored her as we walked through the glass doors. The security guards looked at me with a smile, but I scowled in response. This was not the fun situation they probably thought it was.

The elevator doors to my apartment opened. I stood Nicole on her feet, and she swayed a little. I helped take off her shoes and sat her down on the couch. I went to get her a bottle of water.

"Hey guys," Josh said, looking curiously at Nicole from the hallway as she slowly walked to the bathroom.

"Hi, Josh," Nicole slurred a little.

Josh glanced at me with a questioning look. I sighed.

"She's drunk," I said, handing him the bottle of water.

"I see," he said before opening the bottle as he walked over to her.

I knelt in front of the fridge as I looked for the loaf of bread when I heard Josh gasp loudly. I stood up quickly and saw Nicole puking on his bare feet. Poor guy. I handed him a roll of paper towels before taking Nicole into the bathroom.

"Sorry," she finally said after throwing up some more into the toilet bowl.

"It's okay," I said softly, holding her hair back.

"No, it's embarrassing," she sighed in her normal tone. She was starting to sober up.

"I've been there, Nikki. You don't have to be embarrassed around me," I said.

She didn't answer, but instead, sat down and looked away. I didn't want to bother her, but my curiosity got the best of me. I had to know what Daniel had said to her.

"What did Daniel say to you?" I asked.

She was silent before she turned to me with a distant look in her eyes. I wasn't sure why, but I immediately felt a chill spread across my skin. It was one of those things where you knew that the answer was not one that you wanted to hear.

"You were supposed to marry Eliza. You were going to go through with it, too. Apparently, I ruined whatever your agreement was. That's why everyone hates me, Noah, right? I *messed up* whatever was supposed to happen to keep the money close. I was your way to escape. Was this your plan all along? Lie and tell me that you love me so I would somehow agree to this?" she asked, choking on her words, two little streams of tears ran down her face.

"Nikki, stop, that's not true. I didn't plan any of this," I said, shifting toward her on the floor.

"Noah, did you know that this would happen?" she asked as she backed up to the closed, fogged-glass door.

"No. I knew there would be trouble, but I had no idea what would happen. I definitely did not think this would happen. I love you, but I would never want this for us," I said.

"Stop saying that. I'm not going to let you break my heart again. You don't love me, and there is no us. But, here I am caught up with some lies and pretty eyes," she said before she stumbled out of the bathroom.

I woke up the next morning wrapped in the embrace of my blanket. I sat up and saw I was still in my shirt and slacks. I saw my suit jacket thrown on my little couch across the room. The clock on my nightstand read ten-thirty in the morning. I had slept for several hours, but it felt like I had hardly gotten any sleep at all.

I threw on some sweats and walked to the kitchen. Josh was at the stove flipping pancakes, and Nicole drowsily sipped on some tea. When he saw me, Josh gave me a smirk.

"Morning, brother," he said before looking over his shoulder at Nicole. She glanced up and gave me a nod before she looked back down at the mug.

"Morning. What are you doing?" I asked.

"Cooking. Want some pancakes? I made a bunch," Josh said, gesturing at the stack of pancakes sitting in front of Nicole.

She grabbed a fork and put one on the plate in front of her. I sat down next to her and grabbed two from the stack.

"Are you ok?" I asked her.

"I feel like death," she grumbled.

"That's what happens when you guys drink poison for fun," Josh chimed in from across the kitchen.

"Joshua," Nicole said.

"Yes?" he asked.

"Don't test me today," she said.

"Okay, okay," he said, cowering with his hands up.

"You have a hangover," I said, feeling her forehead just to confirm that she wasn't sick. She wasn't. She, in fact, felt a little cold. That explained my hoodie that was swallowing up her little frame.

"I'm aware," she sighed.

"You should eat. It'll help," I said.

I heard the faint ping of the elevator. Who was coming up, and why did security not notify me? I stood up and started to walk to the elevator when it opened to reveal Rachel. She was in sweats and a flowy t-shirt. Her hair was in a high bun and she wore sunglasses that covered half her face. She scowled at me and went straight for her sister.

"Aw, your first hangover. New year, new you," she said, patting Nicole's head lovingly.

"I regret calling you already," Nicole deadpanned.

"Eat. You'll feel better," Rachel said before grabbing the plain pancake that was on my plate. My eyes cut to Josh, who was laughing at the sight.

"Help yourself, I guess," Josh said dryly, despite the fact he was entertained by it.

"Thanks, *Joshy*," she said sarcastically.

I wanted to dwell on what was behind that exchange, but I had bigger fish to fry, like salvaging my fake marriage. After last night, I knew there were eyes on us.

"If I eat a little, can we go?" Nicole asked.

"Can we speak first?" I asked.

"Oh God. Make it quick, Crawford. I have shit to do. Not all of us have a month off from school like you guys," Rachel said.

"One more year, Rach," I said.

"Just because you're married to my sister does not make it okay for you to call me my nickname. Let's go, Josh," Rachel said, dragging Josh from washing the pan.

"I thought I was Joshy. *Ouch*." We listened to his voice as they disappeared down the hallway.

Nicole shook her head before looking back down to her half-eaten plate.

"I wanted to explain myself," I said.

"You don't have to explain anything to me, Noah. In a couple months, this will be over, and you can do whatever you want," she said.

"I do," I said.

***

"We think it would be nice if you two got to know each other. You're almost eighteen. You should be out there sowing your wild oats," my mother said as we walked up the steps to The Metropolitan Museum of Art.

"I'm going to pretend that you, my mother, the supposed biggest *role model* in my life, did not just say that," I said as I smiled at people who acknowledged us as we walked by.

"I'm just saying that you deserve to be happy again," she said. She was right about that, but I wasn't sure if I would be just as happy with anybody else. It was too late anyway.

We walked through the crowd until we found Daniel Craig, who was standing with two redheads at his sides. One was his wife, Margaret, and the other was a younger girl with hair that was slightly darker than her mother's. She stared at me, as if she was assessing whether I was worth her time. I remembered who she was. It was Eliza. I hadn't seen her since we were about twelve. She had gone to boarding school, and after that, she was barely around. We used to sit in her yard's treehouse and shoot snails at the neighbors with a slingshot. It *definitely* did not look like she was doing that anymore.

"Noah," she said.

"Elizabeth," I replied.

"I still go by Eliza," she said.

"The last time we spoke, we shot a snail right into your neighbor's lemonade," I said.

"There have only been a few highlights in life since then." She smirked.

"Why don't you two go get a drink?" Margaret said, and Eliza looped her arm into mine while we walked to the waiter that poured champagne into a tower of glasses.

"Did you get the memo? You're supposed to whisk me off my feet tonight," she said as we slowly walked through the crowd.

"Were you provided with the very important detail that I am not really looking for anything right now?" I asked.

"Yeah, your heart is all broken because of your ex. That'll pass," she said.

"Eliza, you're telling me you're down with this whole thing our parents have planned?" I asked as the man handed us glasses of champagne.

"Why not? You're good-looking. It's not like I would barf myself to sleep every night. Plus, I'm bored. I like a project," she said.

"While I am so glad I surpassed your ever so high standards, I'm just not ready," I said.

"I can help with that. We can make this shit show of a life bearable for each other. Maybe we can change a few things, too. I'm not a fan of some of these policies," she said.

"So, that's it. You don't believe in love? You want to be in a purely transactional relationship?"

"Look, our parents are always on our cases. If we try it and it works out, they'll leave us alone, and we'll get to clean up some of the messes they've made the way we want to do it. Also, I'm convinced I can get you to fall in love with me anyway," Eliza said.

I didn't answer immediately. It wasn't that I did not think Eliza Craig was attractive. I did. She was objectively beautiful — hot even. Her black dress fit her perfectly, and she was tall like a model. She had big blue eyes and lips that were hard not to pay attention to. I knew we would get along most of the time, and that she was even right about getting our parents off our backs. There was only one problem, a ginormous one. I was still in love with someone else, and I wondered if you fell so tragically hard for someone that if your heart decided that you would never fall for someone like that again, could you change its mind? I decided to find out.

"Alright, you're on," I said.

***

"So it didn't work?" Nicole asked.

"No. She's beautiful, we're friends, and I love her in that way, but not in the sense of a monogamous relationship." I shrugged.

"Why didn't you tell me?"

"I don't know. I guess I never thought there was a need to," I said.

"So she still has feelings for you, and everyone else wants you two to get married," Nicole said.

"But I don't want that. I do love you, but I'd never use you as an out. I knew things would get complicated if my mom found out Jason was digging into things, but I never thought it would be like this," I said.

"Noah?"

"Yeah?"

"Why?"

"Why what?"

"Why do you love me?"

If there was going to be something that I was sure about, so sure that I felt it in my bones, it was that I was in love with her. Was the sky blue? Did the sun rise in the east? Were violets blue? Did I love Nicole Smith? Yes, undoubtedly. I had always had good comebacks and been smooth with words. That was my thing. It always helped me with girls and getting out of trouble in school. Once again, it was like I physically couldn't get myself to tell her. The only person I wanted my words to work for and I couldn't use them. It was like my brain went blank and I had gone mute. After a moment, she sighed.

"I really miss when you only said things you meant. I miss that... Rachel, let's go," she called, and the conversation was over.

Chapter 17

It was the morning of our first board meeting of the new year. Greg had been working double time. He had driven Josh back home and had been meeting with or conference calling with Nicole day in and out to make sure she was ready. We met some blocks away from the office building so Nicole could get in the SUV I was being driven in. Greg said we should cover as many details as possible. We traveled together because we were married. We would hold hands as we walked in to show unity. I would turn and smile at her occasionally to show I was in awe of my new wife. I wasn't completely sure what Greg had briefed her on, but I prayed as we walked down that hall she was ready. It felt like bringing a gentle butterfly into a war zone.

Nicole wore pumps with a deep gold dress, its sleeves reached right over her elbows. Her hair was straight again. She looked stunning, like a breath of fresh air against the cast of grey that I knew would fill the room. She kept a small smile on her face and walked as if she was in possession of confidence for the both of us. When we walked in, everyone looked. Jen and Brian nodded politely. The senator assessed us without much expression. The people that I didn't care enough to know all whispered amongst themselves. Daniel turned to my mother, who looked like she was going to explode.

"Mr. Noah Crawford and his wife, Mrs. Nicole Smith-Crawford" was announced by a man standing by the door.

I guided Nicole to the seat all the way to the left, and I sat next to her, taking the second seat. It was switched, but I wanted everyone to see her importance. It was a silent statement. Greg sat at the seat on my right. My mother glared as Nicole opened her pad-folio and grabbed a pen.

"Well, we have a lot to discuss today. I suppose we should begin with congratulating my son on his *recent marriage*," mother said. Everyone gave a vocal acknowledgment, and I nodded to the rest of the group.

"Thank you," Nicole said kindly.

"Wish we could have attended the ceremony," Daniel said.

"It was very small. We couldn't wait," Nicole said, looking over to me.

"Well, I guess we can discuss the matter later. Hopefully you can wait for that," my mother said. I squeezed Nicole's knee for reassurance. Tracey was pretty vile. I was used to it, but it had been years for Nicole.

The first thing that was discussed was the incident. There was a recount of what had happened, which, of course, was told in a manner that made my mother look like the victim. I tried my best to block most of it out.

"I'm still recovering physically and mentally," Tracey added after Daniel read the recount.

Then, there was silence. I looked around and saw looks of sympathy and shock. *Great*, I thought, things were not going to look good for us.

"If I may add something?" Nicole asked, raising her hand. There was an audible gasp by a few of the board members. *What was she doing?* I sat up to stop her, but Greg put a hand on my arm to stop me. She slid a typed paper out of her portfolio.

"No," Tracey said bitterly.

"According to your charter, any board member is allowed to make a statement. I'm a board member through marriage," Nicole said.

"She's correct... Please stand to give your statement… Mrs. Smith-Crawford," Daniel said in a bored tone.

Nicole gave a small smile before she stood and walked to the front of the room. My heart was beating so fast. What she was about to do would make or break us. She had to have known that, but she looked so relaxed.

"I wanted to give an account of what happened the night of the incident, but I thought it would be in good judgement to review how this all began. A major reason The Table has not been dismantled is me. When Reginald Crawford was killed over two years ago, it was me who threw investigators off their course by mentioning that there was no way Noah could have been there that day. To this day, they have been unable to find Reginald. When Jason Westbrook started to investigate the matter, I worked with Noah to stop him from getting any leads. When Jason decided to go to Williamsburg, it had been after I pleaded with him not to. It was, therefore, out of my hands. When I was almost poisoned and my phone was temporarily blocked in my apartment that night, it had come as a major surprise, as I had shown nothing short of loyalty to The Table. When I was called in and asked by Ms. Crawford to sign my immunity away to save Jason Westbrook's life, I found myself even more surprised and confused," Nicole stated. Everyone listened intently.

"What about your visit to this building a couple weeks ago when you went to look in our files? Was that being loyal, Smith?" Tracey asked.

"*Smith-Crawford*, and I appreciate you reminding me of that very important point, Ms. Crawford. You see, I planned to get the information Jason would eventually receive and tamper with it to push him in the wrong direction. My word would not be enough. He needed information presented to him with just a piece missing, a piece so small that he would not realize it was missing. That piece would save us all. Does that clarify my intentions?" Nicole asked as she looked over to Tracey.

My mother did not answer. She looked at my wife with narrowed eyes. Nicole just smiled at her kindly before acknowledging the room again. I knew Tracey's blood was boiling, and I used all the strength in me to hold my smile in.

"What happened next that night was in violation of the charter. My husband, a primary member of this society, was injured by employees of Ms. Crawford. The safety of everyone in the room was in danger until Ms. Elizabeth Craig arrived to put a stop to all of it. According to the charter, if a primary member of the board is injured by a lower member or employee, it shall be stopped by whatever means necessary. So, to conclude, I think there are a few points we should all keep in mind. The first being, Ms. Tracey Crawford knowingly violated the charter. Not only did she have her own son hurt, but she ordered me to sign away my immunity, despite all I had done. The second, Elizabeth Craig's actions were in order, due to her duty to the charter. Third, if you would look at my charming husband sitting here with you today. He is fully aware and versed in this charter and was there to save his future wife. That sounds like a man who is alert and fully capable to be the next Head of The Table," Nicole said.

It was one of those mic drop moments, and, if we were not in a serious meeting, I would've clapped as she walked over to her seat. Instead, I stood and held the chair still for her to sit. I could hear the sound of the members whispering amongst themselves. The room was stirred. I was sitting back in my seat when Nicole slipped me a paper that was typed. I thought it had been a summary of what she had shared a moment before, and I would've happily kept it, but it wasn't. It was titled "Noah's Talking Points," and I looked up at her in confusion.

"What's this for?" I asked her quietly. I had no intention of speaking. I had no idea how this was going to go. I looked over at Greg, who was quickly reading the paper over my shoulder. He looked confused, too.

"Noah, would *you* like to add anything?" Daniel asked, loud enough for the room to hear, with a challenging look. He knew I hated to speak in front of the board. If I said no, I would look weak. If I seemed unprepared, I would look like an idiot.

"Yes. Thank you, Daniel," I said, smoothing my suit as I stood up and walked to the front of the room.

I looked down at the paper in my hand. What was on it was nothing short of brilliant. I glanced at Nicole, who kept her composure and did not show any expression.

"First, I would like to thank my wife, Nicole, for her detailed and eye-opening statement. As you all know, marriage is taken very seriously within our organization, and the charter states families are immune to any harm that may come due to the actions of this organization. I had granted Nicole immunity when I had turned sixteen. I knew I intended to marry her then, but it was not time. To keep her safe, I guaranteed immunity to her. While who I marry is up to me, there were many instances in which my mother expressed her intention to stop this union from happening. I had seen my mother toy with the rules of the charter in the death of my uncle, and I refused to see it happen with my wife. I did receive help after the incident of my uncle, Reginald, but the purpose was to get some distance from my mother, who had not followed the rules. With this knowledge, I needed time to prepare for what atmosphere of chaos she had created. I was only sixteen and under the age the charter calls for any activities the law might deem as unlawful, but I had no choice but to endure it. I leave you with a question. Is Tracey Crawford someone you want to be in charge of the precious balance this society holds with her inability to follow the rules of our sacred charter?" I asked.

The room erupted with chatter. I refused to look at my mother, but I could feel her glare burning through my skin. I sat down and looked at Nicole, who squeezed my hand. Then I looked at Greg, who gave us both a pleased look.

"I don't know how you did that, but you single-handedly saved his ass," he whispered.

It was decided that the board would make a decision in a week. Greg told us that Tracey would delay the vote, but it was only a matter of time before the live vote would have to take place. Jen Spinelli walked over and spoke to Nicole with a smile. Nicole returned the smile and seemed to be thanking her. I looked around the room. My mother spoke angrily to the Bow Tie and Waxed Mustache. I really should've learned their names, but they were the most uninteresting-looking old white guys you could imagine.

"That was something," Greg said softly to me.

"Didn't you help with that?" I asked.

"No. I told her that your mother might try to spin the story in her direction, but we would call for a recess to come up with a strategy. She said she would prepare for all the scenarios I gave her, but I did not expect that. She should consider law," Greg said, looking over at her.

"I told you she was a genius," I said proudly.

"Yeah, but that was brilliant. Lunch is on me," he said.

"Actually, Gregory, I would like to celebrate my son's new marriage with a lunch with him and his *charming* wife," my mother's voice startled us.

"Not today," I said.

"Yes, today," she said.

"Where?" I sighed.

"Al Forno. See you there at two," she said with a devious smile before she walked away.

I hadn't been to Al Forno in seven years. I vowed I would never step foot in the restaurant again. The only two people who knew why were my mother and myself.

***

"Why are we getting fancy food, Dad?" I asked as we sat in the dimly lit restaurant with mahogany wood walls.

"I wanted to have a special day with you, son," he said, which made sirens go off in my head.

Dad never called me son unless something serious was happening. He had called me son when he told me Grandpa died. He called me son during the talk. "Son" was reserved for the most sad, or the most awkward, occasions. So when Dad had me stay home and took me out to Al Forno, our favorite restaurant, *and* called me son, I knew something bad was happening.

"What's wrong?" I asked.

He sighed and took a few more bites of food before he looked at me with a look that would haunt me for the rest of my life. It was a mixture of regret, sympathy, and fear. I felt my stomach drop, and I was no longer hungry.

"You know that I won't be here forever, right?" he asked.

"Why are you saying that?" I asked. I knew what he said had been true. No one would be here forever. I had lost grandparents, but they had been much older. My dad was young and had looked the same the whole time I had known him. He wasn't even forty yet. He ate healthily, and he would go to the gym with Eliza's dad all the time. Carter Crawford wasn't going anywhere anytime soon. He wasn't supposed to.

"Life is short, and if anything were to happen to me, I'd like to know we had moments like these, us sneaking a day away together to eat our favorite food," he said.

"Yeah, but why are we doing this now?" I asked, confused.

"Because I love you, son," he said, ruffling my hair, and, for a moment, I thought I saw a tear in his eye.

I was sitting in social studies when I found out. The principal walked into the room with a grim look on his face and told me to bring my stuff. I was annoyed. I had just missed school the day before, and I wanted to stay, but I listened anyway. When we made it to the office, my mother was there. I gave her a confused look. She never was the one to pick me up before she had to. It seemed like she didn't want me around more than what was required by the law.

"What are you doing here, Mom?" I asked.

"I'm so sorry, sweetie. Your father had a heart attack. He's gone," she said, tears running down her face.

Nothing would ever be the same again.

****

Chapter 18

I shook all throughout the car ride. I tried to stop myself, but I couldn't. I hated her for this. She was going to try to get me at my most vulnerable. I had no choice but to tell Nicole, who was holding my hands to comfort me.

"Breathe, Noah, breathe. This will all be over in a couple hours," she said softly.

"Yeah, I'm sorry. I'm being weird," I said, completely embarrassed that she was seeing me this way. I always kept it together for her, and she had never seen me like this. *All you need to do is chill out*, I told myself.

For years, I had to hold it together. The last time my mother had seen me reveal my emotions was when Dad died. Since then, it was my usual poker face, and I suppose my poker face turned into a poker soul, if you will.

"No, you're not," she said.

"I am," I said, my voice trembling.

I was. There was no reason why I shouldn't have been able to walk into that restaurant. Dad died seven years ago, and I knew it wasn't Al Forno that killed him. He liked it there. I should have wanted to go there because it was our place, but I physically couldn't. The very thought screwed up every fiber in my body.

"Noah, he told you something that every kid fears the day before it happened. I think it would be strange for you to not have a reaction. I don't even know what I'd do if something like that happened to my parents," she said, leaning on my shoulder.

"I miss him. A lot," I said, and I wasn't sure why I felt the need to vent to her.

"I know. I'm sorry… He would be so proud of you."

"I'm not sure about that." I snorted.

"Well, I am. In a world that is full of darkness, you choose to be light. Everyday, you choose to do the right thing. That's all a parent could ask for," she said as she wiped a tear rolling down my cheek.

Nicole held my hand as we followed the waiter to the table my mother was already sitting at. Tracey gave us a forced smile as we sat down. I willed myself to not look around, to just pretend like it had been any other restaurant. Nicole still held my hand tight underneath the table. I knew she was only doing it to keep me calm, but I still appreciated it.

"Finally," Tracey said, not hiding her annoyance.

No one spoke at the table for the next few minutes. Nicole watched me from behind her menu. I probably looked like the definition of shit. The waiter came to us, and we ordered before we frowned at the fact that our protective shields were now gone.

"So, how long?" Tracey finally broke the silence and startled both of us.

"How long what?" Nicole asked.

"How long have you been legally digging your claws into my son?" she asked harshly.

"We have been married for a little over a week," Nicole said evenly.

"I thought you did not want my son. You said so yourself," Tracey challenged.

"I… I don't recall," Nicole answered.

"I see. So you either are pregnant, or my son insists on ruining his life to keep you safe," my mother said.

She knew I was not strong here. She wanted me to be unable to protect Nicole. I couldn't let that happen. Nicole deserved so much more than that.

"Why are we here, Mother?" I asked.

Tracey's face turned into a cold expression that I was sure scared us both. She leaned in to our side of the table.

Here. We. Go.

"I wanted to congratulate you on your win, but this is yet a battle, and you're not ready for the war you just started," she said, looking at Nicole.

The room felt cold all of a sudden, and I worried about what she meant. She smiled at both of our grim expressions until Nicole gave her a proud smirk.

"If your version of winning is emotionally damaging your son and hurting other people as a means for power, then I think I'm the true winner here. I know you never liked me Tracey. I don't like you either. That's something we can agree on. I guess it's best to start there because I'm not going anywhere," Nicole said, holding her gaze on her mother-in-law as she drank a glass of freshly poured water.

My mother raised an eyebrow and looked at me as if to say "would you get a load of this." I smiled inwardly at Nicole's words. She was not the same shy and timid girl that she had been when we were in high school.

***

It had to have been one of the worst ideas that I ever had the audacity to think would work in my favor. I was going to puke before we made it to the Smith's residence.

"Why on Earth did I agree to this," my mother groaned as we walked in the cool air of the fall evening.

She carried a store bought cake in the box as she dragged her body to our location. I rolled my eyes. *My mother was not racist*, I told myself. She was just *painfully ignorant*.

"We should've done this at our house. Have you eaten there before? What do they even cook?" she asked huffily as if we were talking about aliens from another planet and not an esteemed family in the neighborhood.

The Smiths were the definition of a perfect family. Two doctors who had two beautiful daughters. Mr. and Mrs. Smith were so kind. Mr. Smith even helped teach me how to drive.

"Yes Mother, I've eaten there countless times, actually. They cook a bunch of things. All food — if that's what you're going to ask me next. Why are you acting as if this won't be a normal dinner?" I asked, looking over at her.

My mother didn't answer. She gave me an incredulous look before sighing loudly. We had reached the house, and I rang the doorbell. Soon, a smiling Malcolm Smith answered the door. His wife, Jasmine, came rushing up behind him to greet us. Her smile lit up the atmosphere, just like her daughters'.

"Hi, I'm Malcolm, Nicole's father. It's so nice to finally meet you, Tracey," Malcolm said, shaking her hand before pulling me in for a hand shake and back pat.

"I'm Jasmine, her mother. It's nice to meet you. Let me take that from you," Jasmine said, giving both of us a warm hug before taking the box from her.

"Hi, it's a pleasure… What a beautiful home you have," my mother said as if she were in shock.

"Oh, thanks! I try to redecorate from time to time when work allows." Jasmine smiled with a proud shrug.

"What do you do?" my mother asked.

"I'm a doctor," Jasmine answered.

"Of what?" my mother asked, confused.

"I'm a pediatrician," Jasmine's voice carried from the kitchen as she hurried to put the box down.

"Let me take your coat, Tracey. What do you do?" Malcolm asked as my mom shrugged out of her coat.

"Business matters. I help run my late husband's company now… CCT. How about you, Malcolm?" my mother asked.

"Oh, that's right. Noah mentioned that. You must be so busy. I'm a plastic surgeon, but as you know, you make the time for your family," he said as he hung her coat in the closet.

My mother gave me a thoughtful look. I had told her this already. I guess she had to hear it from the source. Nicole and Rachel came down the stairs.

"Hey guys. I'm glad you're here, Ms. Crawford," Nicole said kindly. I gave her a quick kiss on the cheek.

"Nice to meet you, Ms. Crawford. I'm Rachel, Nicole's sister." Rachel shook my mother's hand.

"Pleasure, I'm sure," my mother said.

"Hey, you," Rachel said challengingly.

"Hey." I smiled.

"Well, let's eat," Malcolm said, catching his daughter locking fingers with me. He chuckled before he turned toward the kitchen. We followed, tickled that we'd been caught.

At the dinner table, I sat next to my mother and across from Nicole and Rachel. Jasmine and Malcolm sat at the two heads of the table. Jasmine had cooked like it was a holiday. There was mac and cheese, roasted chicken, potato salad, vegetables, fresh rolls, and a bunch of other things.

"You cooked this all yourself, Jasmine?" Tracey asked, and I caught Rachel giving her a look.

"Yes, I love cooking when I get the time to." Jasmine beamed.

"I do as well," my mother lied in response. The house would be up in flames.

"I'm so glad that you finally got to join us this evening. We've been trying to get Noah to bring you around," Malcolm said.

My mother had refused to come the three other times the Smiths had told me to bring her to dinner. She made me make up an excuse for her each time, and I had told her I wouldn't make one for her this time. She flushed and looked around shyly.

"I had told Nicole to bring you all over to the house. She told me that you would be busy," she said, and I almost audibly groaned.

Nicole looked up at her confused.

Oh. My. God.

"Oh Nicole, we would've found the time," Jasmine said.

"I'm sorry about that, Tracey. We hope you weren't insulted," Malcolm said, frowning at Nicole.

"Yeah, sorry about that," Nicole said softly.

Rachel gave me a look that told me to fix what just happened, and I shrugged helplessly. She rolled her eyes and glared at my mother until she noticed.

***

We were silent on the way to Nicole's house. I was so tired from shaking that I drifted in and out of sleep. When I was awake, I looked out the window and watched the houses pass by in the darkness of a winter's early evening. The driver notified us that we were only a few minutes away, and I finally looked over at my wife. *Ha, my wife*. The beautiful woman, whose face was illuminated by her phone like she had a halo, was my wife, and I felt like the most inadequate joke that walked the earth. She had not only saved my ass once, but twice that day, and all I could do was stare at her.

"Nikki," I said softly so I wouldn't startle her.

"Yeah," she said, looking over to me.

"Thanks for today. You really had my back out there. That was phenomenal," I said.

"You're welcome… for what happened at the restaurant. The rest was for me, no offense," she said.

Ouch.

"None taken." I shrugged.

I would've liked to think that it was all for me, but her life was on the line. Mine wasn't. I couldn't fault her for not wanting to do this for me when I had put her here in the first place. I watched as she slipped her engagement and wedding rings in her purse. I wanted to punch myself for having an emotional reaction to that, too, but I did. I needed a nap, or maybe a drink. Both.

"What are your plans for the weekend?" *You idiot.* She does not want to exchange niceties with you.

"I have to catch up on my class. I have a huge paper due in a couple days, and then a midterm," she answered, sliding into her coat.

"That sounds like a lot," I said.

"It was really due today. I had to ask for an extension. There was just too much to do these past few days," she said as we came to a stop in front of her house.

"Oh, I'm sorry," I said.

"I'll be hibernating and probably injecting tea into my veins." She snorted and began to leave the car.

"I'll walk you to the door," I said, getting out.

"I'm perfectly capable of walking myself," she said as we walked up to the house.

"Completely, but I'm doing it anyway," I said, smiling at her incredulous look.

"Well, thank you for walking me those thirty or so steps. We're here," she said, turning to me when we got to the door.

"You're welcome. You never know what could happen in those thirty or so steps," I teased.

She chuckled while she reached in her bag for her keys. It was a small victory, but it felt like a big one to see her smile. The front door opened before she could put the key in and we both jumped. There stood Malcolm Smith in his scrubs, sliding his glasses onto his face. Oh boy.

"Noah… I thought I heard my daughter speaking to someone. How are you, son?" he asked.

"Hi, Mr. Smith. I'm doing alright," I said, but I was not doing alright because the last time I saw him, I was ruining his daughter's life. Great how things went full circle.

"I heard you're going to NYU, as well. How is it?" he asked.

"Great, I love it," I said.

"Well, Noah was just going. Bye, Noah," she said.

"Night guys," I said, backing up quickly.

I almost ran to the SUV before he could say anything else and hopped in. I could see in the mirror that the driver was amused. I rolled my eyes at him and sighed.

When I had gotten back to my apartment building, I nodded at security and they smiled back, but they looked confused. I didn't think much of it until I made it upstairs, and it felt like someone was just there. The lights weren't on, and, when I turned them on, nothing seemed out of place, but something didn't feel right. There was the feeling of energy you felt when someone else was just around and they hadn't completely left yet. I slowly walked deeper into the apartment. First, I walked around the living area, and then the kitchen. Nothing seemed out of place. I heard the ping of the elevator like someone was coming up. Only people who had a key or the code could come up. I walked into the kitchen and went to grab the largest butcher's knife, but … it was missing. I looked in the sink, but it wasn't there.

The next moment, I felt like I watched from outside of my body. The elevator opened to one of the security guards with a gun. I put my hands up with wide eyes. The guard shot his gun, and I felt a sharp pain on my shoulder, heard the clang of metal hitting the floor, and my vision blurred a little. I touched my shoulder, and my hand felt wet. I looked, my hand was red. It was blood. I turned around, and saw a middle-aged man dead on the floor. I looked back at the security guard, who was running toward me. He was yelling something, but I couldn't hear. He caught me before I fell.

Chapter 19

I woke up to Greg standing over me with a nurse by his side. He was holding me up as she was doing something to my shoulder. It looked like I was getting stitches. I had figured something like this would've hurt, but I couldn't feel the needle at all. I looked past Greg and saw the security guard speaking to some other security guards.

"What happened? Why can't I feel anything? When did you get here?" The questions groggily poured out of me at once as I started to wake up more.

"They called me, and I got here a little less than an hour ago. Someone snuck into your apartment and..." he trailed off with a frown, and all I could do was sigh, annoyed.

"Okay, great. Now what?" I asked.

"I need you to stay upstate. I'm doubling down on security, too," he said.

"The house has a top notch system. What are more security guards going to do? Clearly nothing... No offense guys," I said, putting a hand up to the security standing fifteen feet from us.

"None taken," one of them said.

Greg sighed before his eyes widened, and he grabbed his phone quickly from his back pocket. He tapped his screen a few times before he put the phone to his ear. Even muffled and tired, I knew her voice.

"Sorry, Nicole… Yes, I know you had a long day… No… Actually, it is a request," Greg said.

"I'm finished," the nurse said, giving me a small smile.

"Thanks," I said, breaking my attention from Greg to her.

"You were lucky," she said softly, which, in return, just emphasized how close to unlucky I probably was. I felt my stomach turn.

"Yes, upstate… tonight," Greg continued, and I could see by his expression he was uncomfortable with whatever she was telling him.

"What's happening?" I asked, slowly sitting up on my own to look at Greg properly. He was now standing across the living area. He had a heavy jacket thrown over a white button-down and grey pants.

"Okay, I understand… S-see you soon," he said before he hung up.

He looked over at me and frowned. She was upset. I could tell by the tone of her voice that I heard occasionally when some sound escaped the phone. I was fully aware how scary Nicole could be when she was mad. It was usually really angry at first, and then tears later. Sometimes it would be in reverse, or just one, but that was usually how things went down. Either way, it was scary to see women having the ability to just show so much of their emotions. Society failed to give me the luxury. Regardless, I hated whenever I revealed what I was truly feeling. I didn't want other people to know what was going on in my head.

"Security says the apartment is clear. I'm going to pack a bag for you. Any requests? Oh right, you have no fashion sense," he said.

"And you do? You just wear suits everyday," I said.

"My suit and tie combos are killer. You wear dark colors like you are constantly at a funeral, or mourning."

"I am. I'm not sure if you've been following along with what's been happening the past few years, but it's been shit." I opened up my arms for emphasis, and it hurt a lot. I yelped.

"Try not to kill yourself while I get your stuff," he said, but stopped as soon as he turned around.

"It's ok," I said before he could say anything.

"I didn't mean——" he began after he turned around.

"I know what you meant," I said, staring back at him.

He just stared at me with wide eyes full of sympathy. I shrugged and laid back down on the couch, closing my eyes. I was tired, and I didn't want him to look at me like that. I had too much to worry about. Someone wanted me dead, and it almost happened.

***

I hadn't slept in weeks. The investigation seemed over. I was safe. I was in our new neighborhood. Things were quiet now, and that was the problem. Quiet meant you were alone with your thoughts, and one's own thoughts, something you conjured up on the inside, could be scarier than any threat that came from the outside. Today, my thoughts were at their worst.

I stared at the gun on my bathroom counter. It was Dad's, and my mother had it locked up at our old house, but she hadn't gotten around to having his artillery closet set up yet. So, I had this. It would be fast, and there would be no turning back. I picked it up and looked at it. I wondered if Dad felt somewhat similar. If he was going to die, at least it would be fast.

"What are you doing?" Greg asked, walking into my bathroom. I hadn't heard his footsteps.

"Greg, not now," I said.

He took a step near me and grabbed the gun before I could react. I didn't look up at him. I couldn't.

"The drinking and now this? We have to do something, dude," he said calmly, but I could hear the emotions laced in his voice.

***

I wanted to drive myself upstate. I hated the idea of being stuck without a car in the middle of nowhere. Stuck. That's all I had been feeling lately. The older I got, the more stuck I felt. I was pretty sure that I had a lot more freedom when I was younger. It was like the older you got, the more freedom actually meant anything but actually being free. Maybe I never was, but maybe ignorance offered a bliss that I missed.

There was some type of attack going on that night. On the way up, Eliza texted me that she was okay. When I questioned why I would think she wasn't, she told me that someone followed her around at a party. When she tried to drive home, they almost made her swerve into a pole. She told me that it was suggested she go upstate until the matter was investigated.

When I got into the house, I found Jason sitting on the couch in the living room. His coat and shoes were still on, like he had just gotten there. He was hunched over with his elbows resting on his knees as he looked at the flames of the burning fireplace. He finally looked over at me, but he remained silent. He looked a little shaken, like something had just happened, and it probably had if he was here. Why else would you want to be in the middle of nowhere while on break?

"Something happened. What happened?" I asked.

"Someone cut my break line," he said, and his hands trembled ever so slightly, but I still noticed it.

"What? Wait, how did you get here?" I asked.

"I drove him. Looks like we're all targets," Nicole called as she walked downstairs in an all-white crop top, loose pants, and cardigan. She was the brightest thing in the dim house. It was fitting.

"My phone said there were a bunch of missed calls and texts from Nicole saying she needed help. I tried calling back, but she wouldn't answer, so I hopped in my car, but a few miles out, I realized I couldn't stop. I was thankfully able to stop in some bushes off the highway," Jason said.

"When he finally got through to me, I told him I never called him. I picked him up. I don't think it's a coincidence. Someone is trying to kill us... *again*," she said, hugging herself as she sat on the arm of the couch.

My mind was reeling as I tried to find something to say. It had to be the working of The Table, but I wondered what was happening. Would they really hurt me? Eliza? Nicole was my "wife" now. She was supposed to be untouchable, but would she have been next if Greg didn't get her out of there? I took off my coat and threw it on the couch chair. That's when Nicole gasped. She stood up as her eyes looked at my shoulder. I looked over and saw some blood.

"What's that," she said.

"I got stabbed," I said, probably much more casually than I should have. But really, how else do you say it? *Ah yeah! I was stabbed! Pretty wild, right?* First off, there was no reason to be dramatic about it. The statement carried enough drama on its own, and saying things like that was not really my style, at least, not in recent years.

"You what? I just saw you like four hours ago. Where?"

"My apartment. Someone broke in. I'm okay."

"What about security? You need to get the bandage changed. Josh, bring down a first-aid kit," she hollered, and it echoed in the house.

"That looks pretty bad... Did you go to the hospital?" Jason asked, breaking his silence.

"I can't. They would have to file a police report, and that will make things messy. Greg had someone take care of it," I said as Nicole tugged my shirt to the side to look at my shoulder.

"Just take your shirt off," she said, pushing me down on the chair.

"I like this game," I said, sliding my shirt over my head and flashing my eyebrows.

Jason scowled before he shook his head and stood up to leave. Nicole rolled her eyes at me before she diligently examined the bandage on my shoulder. She went into the kitchen to wash her hands before she pulled the bandage off and did not grimace once. She nodded like what she had seen made sense. I watched her intently as she inspected the fresh stitches on my arm. She looked at me in the eyes, and, for a moment, I thought she was going to kiss me. I really, *really* wanted her to in that moment, and maybe she would've, but then she looked above my head.

"Hey, I brought the first-aid kit. What's wrong?" Josh's voice called from behind my chair.

"Thanks. Your brother got hurt earlier tonight," she said uneasily, as if she had been caught doing something wrong.

Josh walked around, and his jaw dropped at the sight of my shoulder. He looked up at Nicole speechless and looked at me for answers.

"I was stabbed. Someone broke into the apartment," I sighed.

"Don't move," she said, sliding off her cardigan.

"Now I *really* like this game," I said.

"You're so annoying," she sighed as she took a few alcohol swabs out the kit and ripped them out of the packaging.

"That burns," I said through clenched teeth when she brought it to my wound.

"Sorry," she said softly before grabbing a roll of gauze from the kit.

I watched as she slowly wrapped my shoulder in gauze. She was kneeling over me on the couch. I let my eyes roam before I caught Josh smirk and slowly walk away to leave us alone. She didn't notice.

"Thanks for this, Nikki," I said, much softer than I wanted to.

"I'd be a pretty bad future doctor if I just let your injury get infected," she said with a smile as she cut the gauze.

She used two clips to keep everything in place. She looked me in the eyes again, and I pulled her into my lap. I put my hand on her cheek, and she lowered her face closer to mine. Then, it was like she realized something, and she was out of my grasp within seconds. She stood up and started to pack the kit.

"We shouldn't," she said.

"I was only going to kiss you," I said.

"That's the problem. We shouldn't be doing that *either*," she sighed.

"Why?" I asked.

"This isn't real. This will all be over in a few weeks, and I can't get caught up in something that doesn't exist," she said.

"Nicole," I breathed, "my feelings will remain whether a paper says they are or aren't."

"I wish I could believe that," she said softly.

I stood up and walked over to her before the front door opened. Eliza walked in seconds later with a bored look on her face. She scanned the room for a moment and sighed before she started walking past the entrance of the living room and toward the stairs.

"Don't let me stop you," she said in her bored tone.

"There's nothing to stop," Nicole said, looking up at me.

Chapter 20

I opened my eyes to the sun insistent on having me start my day at that very moment. I stretched in X formation and reached for my phone on the nightstand. There was a text from Alex.

Alex Ramos: Hey I stopped by your apartment and the security almost killed me. What's going on?

Noah Crawford: There was a security breach last night. They're on high alert. Sorry about that. You okay?

Alex Ramos: I'm alright. I was just checking if you were still coming this weekend

Noah Crawford: Saturday night?

Alex Ramos: Yeah. My place at 8.

Noah Crawford: Okay. I'll try my best.

Alex Ramos: You owe me AND you need to live a little.

Oh friend, I don't know if I will be living much longer if I go to this party. Something told me that whoever was after us already knew about this party and was hoping we would be there. I knew I would have to not show up, but I frowned at the thought. I really did owe him. We hadn't hung out in months.

My train of thought was broken when I heard a knock on the bedroom door. I sat up and grunted as an answer before the door opened. Eliza walked in, dressed in her matching black sweats. She sat on the chair near the window and looked at me as if she was waiting for me to say something.

"What?" I asked.

"You're just laying around while the rest of us are trying to figure out what the hell happened last night," she said, tapping away on her phone.

"Excuse me for getting sleep, something my body needs to sustain itself," I deadpanned.

"Speaking of sleeping… you and Nicole?"

"Not that it's any of your business, but no. Where is she?"

"It sure looked like something was about to go down in the living room last night. She's somewhere probably being followed around by Westbrook, who keeps trying to apologize about everything," Eliza sighed.

"Yeah, well, it's a little late for that," I said, standing up and walking to the bathroom.

"I *almost* feel bad for him. I mean, it's like he actually thinks she would give him another chance after this," she called from behind the closed door.

I didn't answer. I continued to stand by the toilet and think about what she had just said. Nicole and Jason were dating up until a couple weeks ago. Would she consider taking him back? No. She wouldn't do that to me, right? I mean, to herself. This had nothing to do with me at all.

"They do look cute together, though. Hmm, why does she get all the good-looking ones?" Eliza sighed.

"Please stop," I said, opening the door after I washed my hands.

She sauntered over and looked at me in the bathroom mirror as I brushed my teeth. I narrowed my eyes at her and she smiled.

"You're jealous," she said.

"Of who? Jason does not stand a chance with Nicole. I don't care anyway. Besides, she's married to me right now," I said after I spit out the toothpaste.

"For now. I hate to admit it, but she's pretty perfect. She's not going to want to be in a fake marriage for any longer than she needs to be. She'll probably want to find some tall, dark, and handsome doctor or *lawyer*." She shrugged as she played with her hair in the mirror.

I just stared back at her as I continued to brush. She smiled because she could tell the thought bothered me. Eliza didn't like to hurt people. Instead, she liked to know what caused people to tick. Half the time she didn't use it, but she liked when others knew she had the upper hand. She knew the idea of Nicole being with someone else bothered me, especially if that someone else was Jason.

"I don't care what she does after this," I said after washing my mouth out.

"Do I look like I was born yesterday, Crawford? You're not worried that she'll be gone after all of this is over?"

"I really am not hung up over this like you think I am." I shrugged and winced, reminding me that my shoulder was hurt. I could use some new bandages and wondered if Nicole would help me wrap it again.

"Hmm, looks like you're going to need to get fixed up. Wonder who you'll ask." She chuckled before walking away.

I walked into the living room to see Nicole and Josh staring intently at a paused TV screen, as you do. It looked like it was on some celebrity gossip channel. Nicole finally looked up at me with questioning eyes. I raised my eyebrow at her because I never took her as being obsessed with celebrities to the point of staring at them like this.

"Noah, do you know that guy?" she asked, pointing to the TV screen.

I sat next to her on the arm of the couch and studied the large screen in front of us. The screen was zoomed in, and there was a fuzzy image of a young man in a dark atmosphere. His face was too shadowed, but it was his eyes that stopped me from saying no. They were too familiar, like I had seen them recently.

"Yeah, but I don't know how," I said.

"That's what I was saying… I feel like I've just seen him… Why do I feel like I've spoken to this random guy?" She chuckled, beside herself.

The three of us stared at the screen for a moment, and the feeling that this was just beyond my grasp gnawed at me. My eyes moved from the man on the screen to Nicole, who was now standing up and looking at me.

"Could it be one of your drivers or security guards?" she asked.

"What would they be doing there with celebrities? They work for me," I said.

"This was a story about some secret meeting that took place with some of New York's socialites," she said.

"Rumor has it that your mom and Eliza's dad made a quick appearance," Josh added.

There was no way that my mother and Daniel would let themselves get caught in a meeting by the paparazzi. It was messy, and the only reason they would be messy would be so I could see it. Something registered on Nicole's face that made me guess that she might've been coming to the same conclusion. I continued to look at the picture, and that's when it hit me. That was the guy who tried to kill me in my apartment. And the reason why the guy who stabbed me looked so familiar to Nicole was because he worked security in my apartment building. *Holy shit.*

Caesar appeared at the entrance to the living room. Nicole jumped when she noticed him and grabbed onto my bicep as a response. If my security personnel couldn't be trusted, then who could? Were all my employees in on whatever this was?

"Mr. Noah, it's good to see you're awake. Would you like me to tell the cook to prepare brunch? It's a little late for breakfast." Caesar smiled.

"No thanks, Caesar. Josh is going to cook breakfast for us," Nicole said, patting my brother's arm.

"What now?" Josh asked.

"I owe you a favor. Just do this for me," she whispered.

He rolled his eyes at her before standing up. She flashed him a disarming smile before he made his way to the kitchen. Caesar stared at the paused TV screen for a moment, and Nicole quickly took it off.

"Well, let me know if I can be of any service," Caesar grumbled before he slipped away.

Nicole grabbed my hand and pulled me upstairs. I had a dream like this once, minus the possibility of my life being on the line. The maids looked at us with raised eyebrows as she pulled me down the hall. She locked the door of her bedroom and looked around the room nervously. I gave her a confused look.

"This is an inside job. I don't know who is in on it or not, but we're not safe here," she yelled in a harsh whisper.

"I don't even know what to do next," I answered honestly.

She sighed before she grabbed her phone from her back pocket and tapped a few times on the screen. She started pacing as the phone rang on speakerphone. The call finally was picked up, and Nicole jumped when she heard the noise.

"Rachel— Rachel, I need your help. This is a disaster," she said.

"What am I, FEMA?" Rachel snorted from the other end of the line.

"How can I tell if a room is bugged?" Nicole asked, ignoring the remark.

"Well, step number one, definitely don't have a conversation about this if you're talking about the room *you're in.* You need to go to the bathroom and run water. Stand in a shower," she said.

"Why would I do that?" Nicole asked.

"It will mask your voices. I'm going to send you an app. It will scan the room for frequencies. I'll talk to Josh, too," Rachel said.

"Why?" Nicole asked.

"He knows tech stuff, and I don't have time to teach you," she sighed.

"Okay. Good luck at the competition. You'll be great," Nicole's voice hummed, even in a stressful moment like this.

"Thanks. Love you. Call you in an hour, Coco. Don't make our lives worse, Crawford," Rachel said before she hung up.

"No promises." I snorted.

Josh's fingers feverishly typed on his keyboard as a bunch of letters and numbers showed up on the large screen on his wall. Nicole tiredly watched as she leaned on my shoulder. It was Jason and Eliza's turn to check the other half of the house for any frequencies. So far, there wasn't anything found.

"How much longer? We've been doing this for an hour," Nicole said.

"We?" Josh scoffed while looking over his shoulder at her.

"Semantics," she shot back, finally standing up and leaving my arm cold in her
absence. She started to pace around the room while she tapped on her phone. Her
shoulders eased before she noticed me looking at her.

"Good news?" I asked.

"I aced my paper," she breathed.

"Shit, I forgot you had to do that. When did you get it done?" I asked.

"Last night after you striked out, we got that paper done. Can't have anything ruining that nice GPA. Not even her husband," Jason said, walking in with a smug look on his face.

"Thanks again for staying up with me," Nicole said, not catching his jab at me.

"Of course, Smith. I owe you one... or several," Jason said, sliding his hands into his pocket with a small smile.

"It's Smith-Crawford now," Eliza said as she stood by the doorway of Josh's room.

"It doesn't matter." Nicole shrugged.

"Well, it's your name, is it not?" I blurted out.

"We are not really married. I would never actually marry you. I've been put through enough," she said harshly. My chest hurt, but I didn't say anything. She looked at me for a moment like she knew, but didn't say anything either. It had already been said anyway.

"Definitely a very different beat from last night when he was trying to break your headboard… Guess you remembered it was your heart you should be worrying about. Right?" Eliza taunted her.

"Speaking from experience, right, Eliza? Anyway, did you guys find anything?" Nicole shot back with a sigh.

Eliza slowly turned to me, and I decided that showing no emotion was the best way out of this. Nicole was just giving it right back to her. It wasn't her usual mode of operation, but she was tired. We all were.

"No, except now I know for sure that the staff hates us for snooping around," Jason sighed.

"Maybe Nicole is just paranoid and there isn't anything in the house," Eliza said.

"Nicole, hand me your phone," Josh said at the perfect time because I was not in the mood to see them argue.

"Why?" Nicole swung around to look at him.

"What's your number?" Josh asked as she handed it to him reluctantly.

"Not you too. You can't want her, too," Eliza said with a face as if she had tasted the most vile thing ever concocted.

"I'm not even going to acknowledge that. I'm getting somewhere. Just give me your number, and I'll explain in a sec," he said.

She raised an eyebrow at him before she recited her number. He typed it quickly in his laptop, and then his shoulders tensed. He started typing again after a long pause. The mood of the room turned tense as all of us watched my brother type away.

"So, there's some good news, and there's some bad news," he said after he slowly turned around.

"What's the good news?" I asked.

"The good news is that I was able to turn off the feed that they have of what's going on in the house," Josh said, rubbing the stubble on his chin.

"What's the bad news, then?" Nicole asked.

"The bad news is that I'm not sure how to permanently dismantle it. It's this weird system that is triggered every time a phone rejoins the wifi that's in this house. And, even when I turn off the wifi and turn it back on, it still turns on the feed. I've never seen anything like that before." Josh scratched his head.

"What feed? Where is it going?" Jason asked.

"It's feeding information from your phones. Recordings, texts, locations... all of it is going somewhere. I don't know where, though. It's hard to follow. I'll keep trying, but I wouldn't be surprised if it was somewhere in the city," Josh said.

"So now what?" Eiza asked.

"No one leaves the property until I try to take it off," Josh said.

"Do you think the help knows about it?" I asked.

"I don't know. I would like to think Caesar has no clue and just hates us for not letting him do his job, but I don't know," Josh said, turning around before typing again.

Nicole's phone vibrated against Josh's desk. He picked it up and answered without hesitation and put it to his ear. Nicole raised an eyebrow and started to walk over to him to get her phone back, but Josh put his arm out without even looking.

"Who are you talking to on *my* phone?" Nicole asked.

"Yeah we did, but it's not in the house. It's on our phones," he said.

"It's probably Rachel," I said.

"I know that. I'm not stupid. I checked the network already," Josh continued.

"Joshua," Nicole warned.

Josh gave her a tired side glance before he put her phone on speaker. Nicole was about to grab her phone from him when Rachel spoke.

"Your stuff is being hacked into, and it's probably by someone you guys know," Rachel said.

"Who would that be?" I asked.

"I don't know. We need more time to figure it out," she answered.

"Who do we know that's on the inside besides Noah?" Nicole asked.

"The only person I can think of is Greg," Rachel said.

Everyone turned to me with questioning eyes. Greg would never do something like this. We could trust him. Right?

Chapter 21

Greg walked through the doors of the house at dusk. He looked a little frazzled, unlike his usual pristine look. Before he walked into the living room to join the rest of us, he assessed the foyer with worried eyes.

"Why did you text me and say that I had to get here immediately?" he asked.

We stared at him for a moment in silence. There was no good way to sum up what was going on. His eyes scanned each of us before they returned to mine. Then, they shifted to the cluster of cell phones that sat on the coffee table.

"What's going on?" he asked.

"Can we trust you, Greg?" Eliza asked accusingly.

"What?" Greg asked, putting down his briefcase.

"We are being watched through a weird feed, and not that many people would be able to orchestrate this," Josh said, looking up from his laptop.

Greg looked at me quizzically.

"Greg, please tell us that you're not part of this," I said after a moment.

"Watched how? Like how I keep tabs on you?" Greg asked, still confused.

"No, not like that. More like hacking our phones to listen to conversations and know our whereabouts before we're actually there," Nicole said.

"No. I don't even know how to do that," Greg said.

"Can I see your phone?" Josh asked.

"Have at it," Greg said, reaching into his pocket and handing his phone over to Josh.

He sat down and waited patiently as Josh plugged the phone into his laptop and started typing away. Greg seemed annoyed and yet still at ease. His fingers tapped silently on the arm of the chair.

"His phone is being tapped into, as well," Josh said.

Greg nodded curtly as Josh handed him back his phone. He excused himself and went into the office. I followed him and closed the glass door behind us. He didn't look at me, instead, he looked out the window at the navy sky.

"We just had to check," I said.

"I know," he said.

"So you're not mad?" I asked.

"I'm just tired."

"Of us?"

"No, I'm tired of this situation, but my job doesn't involve sharing my feelings. You have other things to worry about," he sighed.

"You listen to mine. You can talk to me, Greg," I said.

"Maybe another time when you're not in danger," he said.

I sat on the couch as *Good Will Hunting* played on the screen. It was Nicole's favorite movie, and she watched intently, but the small smile she usually had when she watched a good movie was absent. She looked uncomfortable. Jason, who was sitting on the other side of her, asked if she wanted more popcorn, but she said no. I looked over at Eliza. She was sitting on the other side of the room as she watched us with an intrigued grin. She caught me looking at her and raised an eyebrow. I pulled my phone from my pocket and texted her.

Noah Crawford: Stop looking at me.

Eliza Craig: You guys are just so funny to watch.

Noah Crawford: There's nothing funny about sitting on the couch.

Nicole stood up and walked out the living room. I heard her footsteps on the stairs, and, before I could go after her, Jason was walking out and up the stairs too. No. Over my dead body. I went upstairs after a moment to think about it, but not before I could hear Eliza laughing.

When I got upstairs, the hall was already clear. I walked down the hall toward her room, but was stopped by Josh, who called me from his room. I sighed. Now was not really a good time, but I turned to look at him through his open door.

"Yes?" I asked.

"I finally followed it to three addresses. It's being fed to three different locations," he said.

"Did you find a way to turn it off?" I asked, walking into the room.

"Yes. Rachel helped, but yes," he said, rubbing his eyes.

"That's great. So now what?" I asked.

"I'm texting you the addresses. Now it's time to find out why," he said.

"You didn't look them up?" I asked.

"*No*, I'm going to bed. You seem to have enough time to follow my brother and Nicole into rooms. You can look it up." He snorted as he judged me in his smooth voice.

"Fine," I sighed.

I stood at Nicole's door for at least five minutes before getting the courage to knock. There was a long pause before she told me to come in. Slowly opening the door, I found her sitting up against the plush headboard of her bed. She typed on her laptop and didn't look up at me. Her face was illuminated by its light as her eyes raced back and forth on the screen.

"Hey," I said.

"Hi," she said.

"I just… wanted to see—" I began.

"You wanted to see if Jason followed me to my room," she finished.

I didn't answer. That was the best option. She was completely right, but I couldn't let her know that. I had too much pride.

"He did, but he's gone now," she said.

"What did he say?" I asked.

She sighed and looked up at me reluctantly. She shook her head before she started typing again.

"Nothing important." She chuckled.

I took a few more steps into her room. Her suitcase rested on the bench at the bottom of her bed with a few pieces of clothing folded neatly on top of it, like she was only staying for the night. She didn't want to stay any longer than she needed to. I didn't blame her.

"What are you doing now? I figured you would want to watch your favorite movie downstairs," I said.

"I have things to do… Plus I prefer not to sit in between two of my exes. It's just strange," she said.

"Things like what?" I asked, ignoring the second part.

"Another paper for my class," she said.

"I can keep you company," I offered.

"You're just going to watch me work? Sounds like high school." She snorted.

"I only did that a few times. And no. I actually have a few things I need to look up," I said as I chuckled at the memories of me being happy to watch Nicole get her work done.

"Sure. Take a seat wherever." She shrugged.

I had a few options. There was right next to her, which would come off as too eager. There was a couch chair by the window. That was too far away. I sat at the foot of her bed. It was close enough, but not too close. I slowly sank onto the bed, and, again, she didn't look up from her laptop. She focused on her screen while my mind reeled. It didn't matter what was going on, I always wanted to be around her.

I finally looked down at my phone and started to look up the addresses that Josh had sent me. I stared at them and thought hard on whether they were familiar or not. Two of them were, but the other wasn't. The unusual address led me to an apartment on the upper east side of Manhattan. I couldn't think of anyone I knew that was based there. The other addresses were the CCT office and the Williamsburg warehouse — two places I really held *so* dear to my heart.

I looked at pictures of the apartment building, but nothing jumped out at me. I texted Greg.

Noah Crawford: Do you know if anyone we know lives at the address I sent you?

Greg Nelson: It looks familiar. I'll look into it and get back to you in a bit.

Noah Crawford: You're the best.

Greg Nelson: When I'm not being suspected of being a Brutus.

Noah Crawford: Are you going to be mad about this forever?

Greg Nelson: Only until you screw something else up.

Noah Crawford: I never believed it was you. You're like a brother to me.

Greg Nelson: Yeah, yeah. Go talk to your wife. I have work to do.

I looked up at Nicole, who was typing at what sounded like a thousand words a minute. She had her breakthrough face on, like she had just hit some spring of inspiration and the words were flowing out of her now. I hated how much I could stare at her without getting tired of it. She was like a piece of art that got better every moment you looked at it.

"Earth to Noah," she said, breaking my concentration.

"What?" I asked.

"Do you believe in destiny?" she asked.

Did I believe it was destiny that wanted us to be together? Hell yes.

"Maybe. What do you mean?" I asked.

"Like, do you believe that we were always meant to sit here together tonight, or was it by chance?" she asked. I wanted to say yes.

"I mean, I would love it if it was always destined for this moment to happen, but what if I had decided to leave right this moment?"

"What if that was predetermined as well?"

"I think the big things are predetermined, but maybe our roads of getting there are our own. I think free will is still a thing," I said.

"Big things like what?" she asked, closing her laptop halfway. Her expression was extra curious. She wanted me to say it. I know she did.

"Like this whole thing. Maybe we were always supposed to do this," I finally answered after a pause.

"You think we were always supposed to end up … married like this?" she asked, glancing at her phone before changing what she was going to say before.

"Maybe one way or another we were supposed to end up together." I shrugged.

There wasn't a line written in the sand between us, it was in concrete. And maybe this was the only thing that could drill through it.

"Don't say things like that," she said softly.

"Like what?" I asked.

"Like what you're saying. You say it while you look at me like that. Just don't," she said, looking away.

"Why can't I?" I asked softly right before my phone vibrated and startled both of us.

"Because it's dangerous," she sighed.

I sighed, too, and looked down at my phone. It was Greg, so I answered.

"Yes," I said.

"I don't know who lives in the apartment building, but I do know someone who has frequented there," Greg said.

"Who?" I asked, sitting up from being stretched on the bottom half of the bed.

"Alexander Ramos," he said.

"*Alex?* As in my friend Alex?" I asked, frozen with shock.

"Wait, Alex did it?" Nicole asked.

"No… He would never, but maybe he knows the person who did. Maybe the person is a girl," I said.

"You can't just ask him," she said.

"Yup… so now what?" I asked Greg.

"Nothing. You do nothing right now," he responded.

Chapter 22

I had almost forgotten that security was keeping an extra eye on the house until I tried to go for a walk the next morning and was met with five men who told me I couldn't. Something about there being some threat to my livelihood or some shit. I closed the door and decided to workout instead. I knew I had to be careful with my shoulder, but I needed something to do.

When I got downstairs, I found Nicole running on the treadmill. She barely acknowledged me, besides a small glance, as she continued to run. I got on my least favorite machine, the elliptical, and warmed up for a bit before I headed over to the leg machines. It was all in silence, and I couldn't get myself to put on my headphones because I found myself so desperate to have her say something to me. She didn't, though. Instead, when she finished running on the treadmill, she wiped her face with a towel and went over to pick up a few weights next to me. All without a word.

She looked at herself in the mirror as she did some bicep curls and squats. I found myself staring and finally turned on my headphones after a while. *Get a grip, Noah, she's not interested.* You might as well not even look and entertain this.

"Shouldn't you be paying attention to your workout instead of mine?" she finally asked as she passed me to put the weights back.

"Shouldn't you at least say good morning to your husband in the mornings?" I shot back after turning down my music.

"Maybe, if he was real, and I knew who he was." She snorted.

"Last time I checked, I was quite real. Feel free to check." I flashed my eyebrows, which made her roll her eyes so hard, I was surprised it didn't make a sound. In her defense, it was a lame attempt at flirting.

"I'll pass," she said after a long glance that said so much, but was unreadable at the same time. What was that?

"What was that look for?" I asked, and I could hear the curiosity in my voice.

"Nothing," she said before looking at the small letters on the inside of my bicep.

That afternoon, I looked through Alex's social media. Every single photo. Every single picture of an art gallery or "candid" photo of himself or his friends. I needed to find any clues that I could, but I was not successful. Greg was the type of weirdo to not have any social media accounts, so he was no help to me. I knew who I had to ask.

I searched the house until I found Eliza, who was in the hot tub in the back of the house. She raised an eyebrow when I slid the glass door open.

"Wow, you're looking for me? That's a change," she said.

"It's about social media," I said.

"Proceed," she said.

"How can I know if one of my friends knows someone at The Table?"

"Did you search through their friends list?" she scoffed.

"Yes, but I couldn't find anything. What else?"

"Well, I don't know. That's not something you can just ask someone," she said.

"I know that. That's why I wanted to find out this way," I sighed.

Just then, Nicole walked outside in a black bikini and quickly got into the steaming hot tub. I wasn't sure what my face said, but it must've been obvious I was checking her out when Eliza rolled her eyes at me.

"Hey guys," Nicole said.

"I'm leaving," Eliza sighed before she stood up and walked out.

Nicole snorted when she left and sank deeper into the water. I broke the silence.

"Can I get your opinion on something?" I asked.

"Maybe," she responded.

"How can I find out if someone knows someone else I know?"

"Social media," she answered.

"Besides that."

"Are they our age?"

"Yes."

"If they are going to the same events and speak to one another, maybe you will run into them eventually. Why are you asking me?" She hugged her legs to her chest.

The party. Maybe this person would be there. There weren't many people my age that would know about The Table, but this person could've been hired. I had learned that anything could be possible these days. I tried to keep an open mind and not let what I saw on the surface affect what I needed to find out.

"You're so brilliant, you know that," I said.

"Thank you?" she said more as a question than anything else.

"I'll talk to you about it later," I said before I rushed back inside to find Greg.

I found Greg in one of the spare rooms, texting on his phone with his tie off and feet up on the window seat.

For a moment, he looked normal and not super professional, like he usually did. He stiffened when he saw me peeking through the opening of the ajar door. I waved him off when he moved to straighten up. I wasn't sure who told Greg he had to be professional when I was around — I couldn't care less. As long as he helped me survive The Table, he could walk around in pajamas, and I probably wouldn't think twice about it.

"So, how long do I have to stay here? I have plans for this weekend," I said as I sat on the foot of the bed across from him.

"Plans?" he asked with a raised eyebrow.

"Yeah, I need to go to a party," I said.

"I never took you as stupid," he said.

"I think the person who has been watching us will be there," I said.

"You almost died a few days ago, and now you want to help them along later this week?"

"I'm very aware. I'll be careful."

"Since you don't care about my opinion, where do I come in?" Greg sighed, finally putting his phone down.

Nicole sat shotgun, and I sat in the back while Greg drove us back to civilization. The first hour of the ride was quiet, except for the occasional comment from Greg, who mentioned that Nicole and I should not be going to the party. Nicole, who really didn't want to go much, would agree, and I would say something to shut them up.

"You owe me, Crawford," she sighed.

"Greatly, I know, *Crawford*," I hummed.

She rolled her eyes and turned back around to look at the open road ahead of us. I could see Greg giving me a look in the rearview mirror. I raised an eyebrow to question it, but he just looked out the window again.

We dropped Nicole off down the block from her house since she had told her parents that she would be at her apartment for a few days. Greg and I watched in silence until she made it inside. We weren't even completely off the block when Greg spoke.

"Do you want her or not?" Greg scoffed.

"What the hell are you talking about, Greg?" I asked, looking back at him.

His eyebrows were drawn as he held the wheel with one hand and waved the other one around as he tried to find the words to say next. Greg hardly shifted from his usual mood of a disgruntled neutral, and, when he did, he was upset. The last time I saw him like this was when I punched Jason in the face. I still had yet to find remorse for that.

"I mean, I get it. You're Noah Crawford, you're cool, you don't bow for anyone, and you always have something smart to say, but you are literally killing things with Nicole," he said.

"I can't kill something that is already dead," I said.

"And, with that attitude, it will actually be dead," he said.

"What are you talking about?" I snorted.

"You both love each other, but you're also both so stubborn that it's going to be ruined," he sighed.

"She *does not* love me," I groaned.

"Who told you that?"

"Who told you that she does?"

"I have eyes. Sometimes I don't even want to be in the room with you guys cause the amount of energy in the room increases exponentially whenever you're together," Greg exclaimed.

"I told her I love her, and her response was that I, in fact, do not," I grumbled.

"Well..." His voice went really high.

"What?" I asked, looking up to the ceiling of the car.

"You don't really act like it. I know that you're obsessed with her and almost died of heartbreak when she was dating Jason, but she doesn't know that," Greg went on.

That was an exaggeration. I did not almost die of heartbreak. I almost died because she was going to waste her time with a guy like Jason Westbrook. You saw how he ruined everything, didn't you?

"I'm not even going to start that with you again," I said.

"All I'm saying is that if you acted a little more tender and romantic with her, you would, *at least*, make this a lot more enjoyable for the both of you. And hey, you never know, you might be able to make this work." He shrugged.

"Make this work as in staying married after the trials are over? I am nineteen," I yelled through the laughter that erupted from my lungs.

"My parents got married one drunken night on a college trip to Vegas when they were nineteen, and they have been married for forty years. I met my girlfriend when I was sixteen, and I'm probably going to marry her, " he said.

Greg hardly ever spoke about his personal life. He knew all of my personal details, even the reason why Eliza hated me, yet, he never shared anything about his life, and I never asked. I considered him a friend, even. I didn't have many, due to the nature of my life. He was the only person who knew everything about me and didn't hate me for it. I was paying him a shit ton of money, but even money couldn't hide the true bearings of your soul forever. Yeah, Gregory Nelson was a real one, but I had always assumed he would never want to share with me. Like maybe I wasn't allowed into that other part of his life. I respected it, and I wasn't even sure if that was the case. Maybe I was just scared to find out that the friendship was only one-sided all along.

"You never mentioned her before. That's really cool, man," I said.

"Well, you never asked. You probably don't want to hear about my rocky relationship with the woman who is usually peeved I'm not around as much as I should be," he said.

"You can ask for days off. I don't care," I said.

"You would literally burst into the flames, Noah. Have you not been paying attention to what's happened the past few years?" He laughed.

"Fair, but once this is over, I want you to take a vacation." I chuckled.

"This conversation isn't about me," he said.

"I don't know what you want me to do, Greg. No, I don't want this to end, but that makes me a selfish jerk," I sighed.

"Not wanting things to end with her doesn't make you a selfish jerk. Do what made you two fall in love with each other in the first place. You used to have me send her special flowers, and you would write her sweet letters and plan nice dates. She likes that stuff," Greg said.

"I think she needs more. What she knows about me now… what I've put her through, she deserves more than those things could ever bring her."

"So, you're not perfect."

"Let's not get carried away, Gregory," I deadpanned. I was the worst candidate for a suitor in history.

"Effort goes a long way," he said as we drove into the night.

Chapter 23

A security guard took the elevator up with me to my apartment and took a look around. The coast was clear. He showed me the new security system that had been installed, going on about all the features and nonsense that I apparently spent money on. Truthfully, the only thing I cared enough to take note of was how to turn it on and off. I did not want to hear alarms every time I got home.

When I was finally alone, I got in the shower and let the water warm my skin. It was always like time would race forward whenever I was in there. It never failed. It was after ten when I got out of the shower. I looked at my phone, and there were two missed calls. I sighed because being left alone was clearly way too much to ask for. When my phone unlocked, I realized one was from Alex, and the other was from Nicole. Before I could think about what to do next, Alex called me again.

"Hello," I said, putting my phone on speaker so I could dry off and get dressed.

"So you're coming tomorrow! Nice to see you deciding to be fun," Alex answered.

"Who told you?" I asked.

"Michelle found out from your girlfriend," he said.

"Well, yes, I'll be there. Who else is going?" I asked, pulling on a pair of pajama pants.

"Mostly people we know, and a few friends from college that could make it," he said.

Alex liked to use words like few when he spoke about parties, but that always meant a lot. He liked being around a lot of people. There could never be enough of them around in his eyes. I knew there would be at least thirty people there.

"What time again?" I asked, bringing the phone with me to the kitchen.

"Come anytime after seven," he said.

"Will do."

"So…" he began.

"Oh no," I groaned.

"Rumor has it that you and Nicole went away together for the past week," he said.

"How the hell did you come to that?" I asked.

"Michelle," he said.

"You've been speaking to Michelle quite a bit," I observed.

"She is my way of finding things out since you don't tell me anything anymore," he sighed.

"Or you're seeing her," I said.

"I'm not seeing anyone. Anyway, back to you and Smith's week long rendezvous. Where did you guys go?" he asked.

I threw some mac and cheese in the microwave as I thought about an answer. I didn't even think about what would happen if something like this came up.

"Michelle didn't tell you?" I asked.

"No, she said Nicole got off the phone in a rush," he said.

"We just spent some time upstate. Just chilled and relaxed," I said, unable to be creative at the moment.

"I'm sure you did a lot of *chilling*." He chuckled.

"I'm hanging up." I rolled my eyes.

"No shame! I would be doing the same thing if I were you. Later, man," he said.

"Bye." I chuckled.

The microwave dinged, and I took the cup of macaroni and cheese out. I grabbed a fork and sat by the kitchen island taking a bite. I tapped my phone a couple times and called Nicole back. She answered on the second ring.

"Hello," she answered in her cool phone voice.

"So we went on vacation… Sounds nice," I said.

"It was the easiest way for Michelle to not bother me if I went MIA for some days." She chuckled.

"If it comes up, we went upstate and just chilled. Alex asked," I said.

"How creative," she deadpanned.

"It's late, and I'm tired. I saw that you called. Is everything okay?" I asked.

"I was trying to figure out what to wear. You're really bad at this husband thing. I don't like events, and that's all you are bringing me to," she sighed.

"I'm still working out the kinks," I said dryly, making her laugh.

She didn't say anything else. Instead, I heard her shuffling around. I imagined her dancing around her room on the fluffy white carpet. I knew her room like the back of my hand. I had climbed the tree nestled by her window countless times when I had decided that seeing her during every possible daylight hour wasn't enough.

"What are you up to? Did you figure out what you're wearing?" I asked.

"Yeah, I did. Right now, I'm just looking outside," she said.

"Why?" I asked.

"Because I missed the little lake, and now, it's like it's new all over again," she said softly.

Nicole's house had a pretty nice view of the lake in the neighborhood. The memories of us watching the moonlight glisten on its surface started to rush back in, and just the slightest longing to go visit her came to mind. It used to give my chest that jumping feeling whenever I would go. Things were different now. She wouldn't let me in.

"Nikki?" I asked after a moment of silence.

"Yeah?" she asked.

"Do you hate me?" I asked.

"No, I don't. I just miss you," she said.

"I'm... right here," I said confused.

"I miss who you were with me before everything happened. It's just different," she said.

"Oh" was all that could leave my lips.

"And I know we're not sixteen anymore. I just miss us. I guess life just got complicated and changed us... I mean, I'm sure I changed, too," she sighed.

"You just get better overtime, like a fine wine," I said softly, and she gave a small laugh. One of the best sounds that would ever bless my ears.

I jumped out of the car and rang Nicole's doorbell. I expected her to open the door, but instead, it was her mom. She smiled brightly and pulled me in for a hug. It had been so long since someone had hugged me like that, that if I had let myself, I could've probably cried about it. I definitely wasn't getting that from my mother.

"Noah, you look great! How are things?" she asked with a voice that was just as warm as her embrace.

"I'm doing alright, Mrs. Smith. It's so great to see you," I said back with a smile.

"So, where are you two headed to tonight?" she asked as she backed up to let me in.

"A party," I said, walking in, unsure if she was cool with the idea. I mean, the last time she asked me that, we were underage, but every house had different rules, and the Smiths were strict.

"Well don't look so scared. I'm not going to tell you two no. I was just curious," she said with a smirk.

Just then, I heard footsteps, and, soon enough, Nicole appeared at the top of the stairs. She walked down in a short dress and boots that reached up passed her knees. She gave me a smile before she looked over her shoulder at Rachel, who was following behind her. I never minded Rachel being around, but the vibe definitely changed when she was. She was now older than Nicole and I were when we started dating, but I knew the night would be different with Nicole taking the time to make sure she was okay.

"Don't forget curfew," Jasmine Smith said to her youngest daughter.

"But I'm with Nicole, and she doesn't have a curfew," Rachel sighed.

"Yes, I could move it back to eleven if you'd like to push it." Her mother crossed her arms.

"Let's go before you screw yourself over." Nicole snorted.

"Have fun, guys," Mrs. Smith said.

We walked a few blocks to Alex's party. Rachel walked ahead of us while Nicole and I trailed behind. I didn't realize I had been looking at her for a while until she looked over at me with a raised eyebrow.

"What?" she asked lightly.

"Nothing… You just… You look nice," I said.

She didn't answer. Instead, she smiled and looked down at her feet as they clicked on the concrete. Rachel looked over her shoulder for a moment before she chuckled and shook her head.

"You okay over there, Rach?" I asked.

"Yeah, just looking forward to ditching you two lovebirds for drinks and fun," she said.

"We're here for business, not pleasure," I said.

"Oh, *right*," she said, unconvinced this would change any of her plans for the weekend.

"If something seems off, we leave. That means you too, Rachel," Nicole said.

"Here we go," Rachel said in a sing-song way, but I knew she was annoyed.

Rachel's shoulders rose and fell silently in what looked like a dramatic sigh. Those two are like night and day. I found a smile curling on my lips. I felt Nicole give me a pointed glance before she looked forward to walk up the stairs to Alex's porch. The sound of music pumped out of the house. We entered behind Rachel, who disappeared into the crowd when someone called her name.

"This is a lot of people," Nicole said into my ear.

"We'll find a good spot to people-watch," I leaned down and said near her ear.

I found our fingers locking as we made our way into the crowd. There were entirely too many people for the size of the house. Alex's house was big, but he didn't live in a stadium. I'm sure word got out about the party, as they do, but I was also sure this was another case of his eyes being too big for his stomach.

I grabbed a beer in a cooler, and Nicole grabbed a can of ginger-ale before we made our way to the top of the loft of the second floor to look down on all the guests. There were less people around, and it was easier to hear Nicole against all the noise. We finally spotted Alex, who waved with a drunken smile as he danced with a couple girls.

"Look who's here," a voice said behind us.

I turned around to see Michelle Solomon smiling with a red solo cup in her hands. She hugged Nicole, and they chatted for a moment before she raised her cup to greet me. I raised my beer in response. The two continued to whisper amongst themselves as they locked arms. I kept a lookout for anyone who I thought was familiar. The problem was, a lot of people were familiar. I went to high school with half of the crowd.

That's when I felt it. Someone was watching me. I looked back at Nicole, who was looking around, while chatting with Michelle. She didn't catch my disturbed glance. I looked around again around the area where Alex was when I saw him. Gerard Spinelli. I almost laughed when I saw him staring back at me.

I started to ask myself a series of questions. Why would Gerard be here? Me, probably. He went to some prep school in Manhattan and probably barely knew anyone here, if at all. Why would he want to be here? To probably trip me up. The guy was the epitome of annoying. Why would he want to do that? It was because of The Table… I knew that. It was the only thing holding us together. Then, I realized what it was. It was literally right there in front of my face. If I screwed this up, Gerard would be the one to get it. Tracey could only keep her seat for so long. Eventually, the Spinellis would be the ones in power.

I kept my face calm, despite my realization. What I wanted was for Gerard to not know that I knew what he knew. I looked over at Nicole, who was looking at me now with a questioning look. She excused herself from Michelle and walked over to me.

"What's going on," she said.

"Gerard… two o'clock," I said, leaning into her ear so Gerard couldn't read my lips.

She smiled at him after a moment and raised her soda can to him. He mirrored her movements with his bottle. That's when she stiffened. I did the same and wrapped my arm around her tighter.

"What's wrong?" I asked.

"I don't have my ring," she mumbled.

"Well, I don't either, but we couldn't wear it here," I said.

"So what do we tell Gerard?" she asked.

"I don't know… we don't say anything," I said.

"I think he's going to eventually ask," she said.

"He's definitely going to ask," a familiar voice said behind us.

We both jumped. When I turned around, my jaw dropped. How?

"What are you doing here?" Nicole asked.

The music was loud, even in Alex's bedroom. The floors vibrated, but at least I could hear Nikki, Eliza, and Jason without leaning in and yelling in their ears. While I wouldn't mind getting close to Nicole, whose hair smelled like coconut, herbs, and a bunch of other amazing stuff, I really was not interested in being any closer to Westbrook than I needed to be.

"Aw, what's wrong Nicole? Not happy to see us?" Eliza teased.

"I never said that. I just asked what you were doing here," Nicole sighed.

"And, while you're at it, how did you get here?" I asked.

"My brother convinced Caesar to drop us off at the nearest train station," Westbrook responded smugly.

I glared at the fool for a moment. He was our brother. I hated that we had to share anything at all, but it was true. He was trying to get a cheap reaction out of me, and it wasn't going to happen. Thankfully, Nicole had something to say.

"He's literally a brother to you both. Stop it. He's not a toy," she sighed.

That's my girl. Jason's shoulders sank a little at her scorn.

"So Josh is here? Where is he?" I asked a little worried. He probably was somewhere having culture shock over the utter chaos that was taking place on the other side of the door.

"Looking for Rachel. He figured out the loser listening was Gerry Spins," Eliza sighed.

"Yeah, he's here," I said.

"So why are we in here?" Jason asked.

"Because you're not supposed to be here," I said.

"What if I was invited?" Jason said.

"Oh my God, Jason, shut up please," Eliza whined, hiding her face in her hand.

"Alex is Noah's best friend. Why would he invite Noah's girlfriend's ex to his party?" Nicole asked.

"I didn't think of that… but… but, maybe I came here with Eliza," Jason said.

"I don't know Alex. Not really," Eliza said.

"Good enough." Jason shrugged decidingly.

There was a knock on the door before the knob rattled. Eliza unlocked it and opened it to reveal Josh with a disgruntled Rachel next to him. When the door shut behind them, Rachel turned to me with her hands on her hips.

"What did you fuck up now? It's only been an hour, and, all of a sudden, Captain Lame is here ruining my night," Rachel exclaimed.

"I did not ruin your night. Your friends like me. That girl Ashley thought I was cute." Josh smiled smugly.

"They're drunk," Rachel deadpanned.

"Wow." Josh feigned pain with a hand on his chest.

"What's the problem, Noah, Coco? Why are we all here? As much as I'd like to play *Breakfast Club* again, I have things to accomplish in the next few hours," Rachel said, looking at the both of us.

"Like what?" Josh asked.

"Like dance with attractive men and hook up with one who does not make me want to deck them in the face," Rachel said.

Josh pointed at Rachel as to say "would you get a load of this," and Nicole leaned into me as she sighed. I'm sure she didn't want to hear that, but she would be lying if she said she didn't know about it. It was Rachel. She was always known as the exciting one.

"Let the girl live. Why does she have to be here if Gerry is scouting out you and Nicole?" Eliza chuckled, looking over at me.

"What if this dude's dangerous and tries to hurt us? Look at what happened to Noah. He probably knows Rachel's her sister. I mean, they pretty much look alike," Josh said.

"Who are we talking about?" Rachel asked, sitting down on Alex's desk.

"Gerard Spinelli," I sighed.

"He's not dangerous. He's a spoiled rich kid who wants everything he sees," Eliza said.

"Sounds like someone else I know," Nicole added.

"Here we go again. You're just mad I screwed your boyfriend." Eliza crossed her arms.

Everyone paused at that with wide eyes and looked at Eliza and me. I rolled my eyes and looked down at my feet. Nicole detached from me and went to lean on a chest of drawers across the room. I glared at Eliza, who gave me a strained, apologetic smile.

"While I have *so* many questions, what are we going to do about this guy? He thinks Smith and Crawford are married, and if she walks out there without a ring on her finger, it'll probably be weird since there are a lot of people around," Jason said.

"So let's just leave," Nicole said, and I could tell she was not happy.

"Yeah, there's probably a back entrance or something," Josh said.

"Let's go. I'm tired," Eliza said.

"Coco, Mom's going to wonder why we're back home so quickly," Rachel said.

Before Nicole could say something, the door knob rattled again. Nicole unlocked the door and opened it.

"Who is i—" she stopped short when she opened the door to reveal Alex and Michelle on his arm.

"It's Alex, and why wasn't I invited to the party in my room," Alex said, raising an eyebrow at me.

"Alex and Michelle… I knew it! I thought I saw you two making out at the movies," Rachel said.

"Michelle, oh my gosh! Hey girl," Eliza said.

"Eliza? What are you doing here?" Michelle asked dramatically. She definitely had a few drinks.

"You two… know each other?" Nicole asked.

"Know her? She's my girl! We hang out with the same people." Michelle laughed.

Nicole looked at Rachel and mouthed the words *my girl*. Oh boy.

"Oh my God! You're Jason! I was rooting for you! What happened?" Michelle asked.

"I'm going to throw up," Nicole said.

"Alright, let's go guys. Alex… I have to jet. I'll call you tomorrow," I said, giving him a questioning look.

"Yeah, later man," Alex said, looking a little uncomfortable.

Josh led the way out, and we all followed before Alex closed the door behind us. When we got downstairs, we walked to the kitchen and walked out of the glass doors that led to the Ramos' backyard. The air was so cold that it even hit me, and it never usually bothered me much. I buttoned a few buttons to close my coat in. Nicole tied the sash of her coat, and I put an arm around her to warm her up. She didn't look up at me, but she didn't push me away either.

We made our way to the gate that bordered us from a walkway that led to the front of the house when we heard someone clear their throat loudly. Because the universe was against me, and Eliza's expression looked pissed, I already knew who it was before I turned around. Gerard Spinelli stood there with a triumphant look on his face. Suddenly, I felt the urge to punch him right in the nose, but I knew it wouldn't help anything.

"What do you want?" Eliza asked.

"Hey gorgeous. I'm not here for you. I'm here to talk to Crawford and his wife," he said.

"Why are you stalking me?" I asked through gritted teeth.

"Because I knew this marriage was fake. Your wife is hot, but you're not dumb, Crawford. You wouldn't get married. Not right now, at least," he said.

"They are married," Jason said.

"Right, on paper, but Nicole hasn't worn her ring in days. You two even slept in separate rooms." Gerard snorted.

"If you just wanted to make a point about their marriage, why did you try to kill us? Isn't that a bunch of unnecessary shit?" Eliza asked.

"I knew a security scare would get you all into the house. It was easier to listen that way." Spinelli shrugged.

"What do you want?" Rachel asked.

"Why don't we all go sit somewhere and have a chat?" He smiled deviously.

Chapter 24

We crowded around a round table at a bar five minutes away. None of us wanted to be next to the guy, for obvious reasons. We all sat on the other side of the table, leaving Spinelli with a lot of extra elbow room. It was silent until Gerard took a swig of his beer. None of us dared to breathe.

"I want The Table," he said.

"You can't have it," I said.

"Well, I'll eventually get it. Your mother's stand-in term is almost up," he said.

"Trust me, she does not play by the rules. She'll find a way to stay." I snorted.

"Not if my parents have anything to do with it."

"I'm not giving in, Spinelli," I said dryly.

"Fine. You have a couple weeks to make a decision. Can't wait to hear how your semester is going when you meet me to step down," he said, pushing his chair back as he stood.

"And then what?" Josh asked.

"Let's see how smart you are. Wouldn't want anything like the last time you made the wrong decision to happen again." Gerard laughed.

I balled my hands into fists as I tried to silently breathe and not make a scene. Nicole put a hand over one of my fists and looked at me questioningly. I shook my head. I wasn't in the mood to explain.

***

It was going to be alright. No one brought it up, and, therefore, I had nothing to worry about. I wasn't sure what my mother had told the board about why I went away for a while. It didn't matter. I just had to keep reminding myself that I didn't have to be ashamed of getting help.

"Noah Crawford, it's great to see you. I haven't seen you around," Gerard said, walking over with his hands in the pockets of his tailored suit. A group of some other assholes followed behind him.

"Great to see you, Gerard." I nodded curtly.

"Where were you?" he asked.

"I just went away. No worries, you won't have to miss me anymore. I do have to admit that the feelings are not mutual. I'm more of a ladies' man," I said coolly, even though I could feel myself warming up. The guy behind him chuckled.

"I heard you had to go to rehab. Something about you not being able to handle your shit," he said, causing the group to laugh more. What a load of idiots. Just a bunch of idiots bred from rich idiots.

I was silent while I tried to think of something to say back. I couldn't, so I turned to walk away. That's when

I felt a hand on my shoulder. I turned to see Gerard laughing while holding a glass of wine to his lips with the other hand. My arm swung, and the glass flew before it hit a nearby table.

"Oh, Crawford, bad choice. What are you going to do with all that glass? Try to kill yourself again?" he said, and the room went silent.

"What? I thought you had a drinking problem, man," a voice in the room said.

"G, leave him alone," another said.

"I'm sure everyone is wondering how you're going to do the job when you're crazy. I mean, what would Daddy say?" Gerard mocked.

"Hey! Enough," Greg's voice boomed, making both of us jump.

"Your keeper is here," Gerard said, "Gotta keep an eye on you and all."

I didn't blink because if I did, tears would come out, and I sure as hell was not going to let that happen. Gerard laughed when he realized I wasn't going to do anything else and sauntered away.

***

"So now what?" Rachel asked, pulling me from the depths of my memories.

"Well, I stole the USB in his pocket, so we should probably look at that," Josh said, leaning into the table.

We all looked at the small, silver stick between his fingers. Only someone in my bloodline could be so brilliant. My shoulders eased in relief, and he flashed me a *you're welcome* nod as a response.

"When did you do that?" Nicole asked.

"While he was going on about him being great because he's a rich white guy." He shrugged.

"I don't remember that part." Eliza chuckled.

"You probably zoned out. I did." Rachel snorted.

"Let's get a look at it," I said.

I leaned in to look at Nicole's laptop as Josh looked through the files. Whenever something was locked, Rachel would shout out some instructions, and it would work.

"You're brilliant, Rachel," Josh said, not looking up from the screen.

"That's my middle name." Rachel winked.

"It's Lauryn last time I checked," Nicole teased.

"Aw sorry Coco, did you think you were the only smart one here?" Rachel retorted.

"No, I always knew. Before you did." Nicole put her arm around her sister and smiled. Rachel laughed before kissing her forehead.

My eyes shifted from the sisterly love fest going on in the middle of the kitchen to the clock in the corner. It was eleven, and I was sure Mrs. Smith was sleeping. I assumed Mr. Smith was working at the hospital since his car wasn't in the driveway.

"We should probably keep it down. I don't want your mom to wake up and be mad," I said.

"Noah, you used to sneak up to Coco's room and almost break her headboard with both my parents in the house. Now you're scared?" Rachel gave me an incredulous look.

"Rach, *please*." Nicole hugged herself uncomfortably.

"Well, hearing that took a few years off my life, but anyway, what's on this USB, Josh?" Jason shivered on the island stool.

"I know what's not on it, your envy," Josh deadpanned.

Eliza chuckled loudly, and Jason shot her a look. She raised an eyebrow at him to dare him and, like stupid people do, he took the bait.

"I don't know what's so funny, Elizabeth. You're the one still boasting about sleeping with a man who has moved on," Jason said.

"At least I'm not still holding on to hope for a girl who is married to a billionaire," Eliza quipped.

"It's fake," Jason said.

"Is it?" She tilted her chin.

"Is it?" Jason looked over at Nicole.

"Yes," Nicole sighed, but there was something in her voice that made the rate of my heart quicken.

She noticed me looking at her and pushed a few braids off her shoulder before she looked down at her toes on the floor tile. I nudged her with my elbow, and she gave me a look that said we probably needed to talk later. I gave a small nod as I wondered how one person, how this small woman, could heal me and destroy me all at once.

"So, the recordings of the house are now deleted, and there's nothing on our phones," Josh said.

"Thanks, Josh. We owe you one," I said.

"You did good," Rachel said.

"Well, I had some help," he said, patting her shoulder.

Just then, my phone vibrated in my back pocket. I slipped it out and looked at the screen to see Greg's name on the screen.

"Hey," I said.

"Why are you all at Nicole's house?" Greg asked.

Nicole looked up at me slowly with narrowed eyes. She was standing so close that she heard him. I sighed inwardly and kissed her forehead before I left to take the call in the living room.

"Well, now she knows you track our phones like a helicopter mom," I sighed.

"*Oh, I'm sorry*, did your wife forget that you were almost killed last week? I keep an eye on you for a reason," Greg said.

"Anyway, what's up?" I asked.

"How did the party go?" Greg asked.

"Let's see… My best friend is probably banging Nicole's best friend, Gerard Spinelli is the asshole ruining our lives, and Josh single-handedly stopped him, for now," I said.

"Sounds like an eventful night. Well, we can sort that out tomorrow. I called to let you know that the official decision on your position will be made in a few weeks on February 8th," Greg said.

"What about Eliza and Jason?" I asked.

"They decided to spare him, and Eliza has her position back," he said.

"So why do they have to take so long for my decision?" I asked.

"It's your mother," Greg deadpanned.

"I'm so blessed."

"Well, it's three more weeks of… you know. Enjoy it."

"Good night," I grumbled before I hung up.

I sighed before I slid my phone back in my pocket. I fell back on the couch and ran a hand down my face. Nicole was going to have a lot to say about this extending into school time. Greg did say Valentine's Day, but I figured it was an overestimate. The longer this went on, the worse having to be strangers with her again would be. Nicole Smith would go on and want absolutely nothing to do with me, and the thought made my chest hurt. I felt so selfish for my thoughts, but I still had them.

"Noah, wake up," Nicole's voice said. I didn't need to open my eyes to know who it was.

"I'm not sleeping," I said with my eyes still shut.

"You've been sleeping for an hour. Everyone went to bed." She chuckled.

I opened my eyes and looked at my watch. How was it after midnight? I gave her a confused look as I looked around for a moment. She frowned and sighed.

"Let's go," she said as she made her way to the stairs with her shoes hanging from her hands.

"I got to drive home," I answered groggily.

"Not like that you're not. Let's go. My mom is going to wake up for work soon. We have to get blankets," she said.

This was not something I was going to argue. I was severely confused, but I sure as hell was not going to ask any questions. *Maybe I'm still dreaming*, I thought. I walked upstairs behind her quietly. I hardly breathed until I closed her bedroom door behind me. I leaned against her door and watched her. She threw her shoes to the floor of her closet before she sank onto her bed.

"Are you okay?" she asked.

"Okay? Maybe. Confused? Yes," I said, finally leaving the door behind me and taking a few steps forward.

"Why?" she asked.

"I'm here right now," I said.

"So?" she asked.

"Well, I just know that's not you. You don't do this," I said uneasily.

Why on Earth was I questioning this? I wanted to slap myself in the face. The girl of your dreams — this beautiful nymph — asked you to come up here, and you're talking her out of it. Maybe I needed to lay off the alcohol.

"What are you talking about? Give me a second. I'm tired of having this on," she said.

Nicole grabbed something from a drawer and excused herself before she went into the bathroom. Her absence was immediately felt, and I found myself watching the doorway where she once stood. The door was closed now. I took my jacket off and placed it on her chair. As I took my shoes off, I exposed my feet to the plush carpet. The air was warm and smelled like vanilla. I remembered Nicole's room like I knew my name. There was something about it, about this house in general that felt so welcoming. I always preferred it over my own. I remembered going home at night and feeling the immediate absence of whatever it was. Maybe it was just the lack of love.

She walked back out in matching pajamas. She almost walked toward me, but then stopped, like she had forgotten something, and silently went out into the dark hallway. She came back with a blanket, a pillow, and a smile on her face.

"Here we go. I think you're too tall for my window seat, so you'll have to use the floor. I can give you my yoga mat," she said.

The floor. Abort mission. I took the pillow and blanket from her hands. Trying not to look disappointed took a lot of effort as I set up on her floor. I went over to the bathroom and fixed the scowl I had been sporting on my face. I took my shirt off and used some mouthwash before I came back out to the room. Nicole had her legs folded as she scrolled on her phone.

"Why do you insist on not wearing clothes?" she asked without looking up.

"I don't sleep with clothes on. At least I kept my pants on… unless you have an objection," I said.

"It's time for bed," she said, ignoring my statement and finally looking up at me.

"You don't look tired," I said, sitting down on my blanket.

"I'm not, but you are."

"I'm awake now."

"Don't look at me like that, Noah."

"Why?"

"You know why."

I chuckled as I laid on my back. She rolled her eyes and got under her covers too. She turned the knob on her lamp, and the room got dimmer. She never liked the dark. I laughed at that too.

"What's so funny?" she asked.

"You're still scared of the dark," I said.

"I just don't like it," she said.

"Some good things have happened for me in the dark," I reasoned.

"Ew," she said.

I looked over at her bed and smiled. I couldn't see her face from down where I was, but I knew she smiled too.

"Truth or dare?" I asked, not ready for the conversation to be over yet.

"Truth," she said after a moment.

"Did you... Did you feel anything when we kissed in the court?" I asked because it was something that consumed my thoughts whenever danger wasn't. I wanted to know.

"I felt everything," she said softly.

I sat up and looked over at her. She had her back turned to me.

"Me too," I said.

"Noah… no, you didn't," she warned.

"Why do you do that? Everytime I tell you I love you, or that I feel something, you tell me I don't. *You don't know* what I'm feeling," I said, standing up.

She turned around and looked at me with a pained look. I sat next to her, and we just stared in silence.

"I do it because you're not supposed to like me," she said.

"That's not going to change my mind," I said.

"I know," she whispered.

I leaned in and kissed her. She didn't push me away.

Chapter 25

Something hit my face hard. Whatever it was wasn't hard itself, but the amount of force it hit me with stung my nose just a bit. Another attack was made, making me open my eyes to the dim light of the sunrise.

"What?" I yawned.

"Noah," Nicole said sternly.

I looked over to my side and immediately remembered what happened a few hours ago. She hugged the covers close to her chest as she miserably looked up to the ceiling.

"Are you okay?" I asked.

"No."

I sat up and gave her a questioning look.

"This shouldn't have happened. This isn't right," she said.

"Nikki, I'm sorry. You said yes and—" I began.

I stopped when I realized she was starting to cry. I sat up fully and pulled her to my chest. It only made her sob more. *Yikes*, the second time in a row you got laid and you made a girl cry the next morning. This is not a good look.

"I know what I said, Noah. I was learning how to live without you, and then all of this had to happen. I can't do this right now," she sobbed before grabbing her robe and running to the bathroom.

I didn't know how to respond to that. All I could do was stay silent as I thought about what I had been afraid of this whole time. I was Iqarus, she was the sun, and I flew too close this time. My chest hurt at the thought as I finally stood up and collected my clothes from the floor. When I got decent, I knocked on the bathroom door.

"Noah, please, leave me alone," she said from the other side of the door.

"I can't do that," I answered.

"You've done quite a bit already," she said dryly.

"I'm sorry," I said in almost a whisper.

After a moment of agony, she opened the door and leaned against the counter. Her eyes refused to look at mine. I eventually gave up trying to dare her to look at me and looked straight at the shower curtain in front of us.

"That can never happen again," she said.

"Yeah, I know," I said, not even trying to mask my disappointment. There was no use.

"I can't wait for all of this to be over. I need my life to go back to normal," she sighed.

"I guess I'll go back to doing what I've always done," I said.

"What's that?" she asked.

"Wishing you were still around," I said.

"You're so dramatic. You were living your life without me for two years." She chuckled before she left me alone in the bathroom.

***

Doing normal things after spending six months at The Valley Rehab Center felt strange. That included going to school. Dr. Franklin insisted that it was best I "continued my studies with my peers" because "college would be a shock to my system" if I finished high school online. I didn't know about all of that, but what I did know was that I had no interest in starting at a new school in my junior year. I promised I would attend our bi-weekly sessions — one on video call and one in person. He said he was proud of me for all of the progress I had made. What he didn't know was that in that time, I had also learned how to live in a state of being numb to most of the things life had thrown at me. I knew I would need it. He probably wouldn't be thrilled if he knew that.

He also would not be so thrilled with what I did with my buddy, Alexander Ramos, the day after my first Christmas back from being away. We sat on his roof with a few beers and passed a blunt back and forth between us.

"I'm surprised you wanted to smoke. You always say no." Alex snorted.

"I need something to take the load off," I said.

"School is going to be fine. You're going to charm the ladies like you always do. You're The Don," he said.

I took a long drag before I looked over at him with an incredulous look. More than anyone, Alex knew that I was not over Nicole. Most of the time, she was the only person I could think of. When things were difficult, I thought of how she would've wanted me to get better.

I wasn't allowed to use my phone the majority of the time at Valley. It wasn't allowed. When I was allowed, I couldn't get myself to actually dial her number. I had gotten a new phone and new number after the investigation, so if we were going to speak to each other, it was going to be because of me.

"You can always call her. She'll speak to you," he said.

"What makes you so sure about that?" I asked.

"She's one of the nice ones. Dude, Nikki Smith is pretty much a saint. She's just as kind as she is beautiful. That's a lot," he drawled.

I shut my eyes and sighed silently. He didn't understand, but how could I expect him to? Alex was just the nice kid, whose parents loved him, and took life one step at a time because he could. I loved my best friend. I knew he cared. The fact that he didn't press me when I called him from Valley, nor avoided me after the trial, I knew he was the truest of friends. I also knew he would never understand me as much as he tried.

"And that's exactly why I should leave her alone," I sighed.

"There she is walking with Michelle," Alex said.

"Where?" I asked, sitting up so fast that I almost took flight.

"Walking right there," he said, pointing across the street.

He was right. There, walking with her arms locked with her best friend, Michelle Solomon, was Nicole Smith laughing happily. She looked as perfect as she always did. I was so glad to see her happy. Maybe she had gotten over what had happened. She had moved forward, and it would be unfair to pull her back.

"Hey ladies," Alex hollered.

"What the actual fuck are you doing, Ramos?" I asked as I sank down behind his chimney. I sobered up so fast.

"What? She's right there," he said.

"No, I just told you I wasn't going to speak to her," I said through my teeth.

"Are you really going to go through with never speaking to the girl of your dreams ever again?" he asked.

***

I walked downstairs ahead of Nicole after she told me that both her mother and father were not home. Sitting around the kitchen island, as if they were waiting for our arrival, were Rachel, Eliza, Jason, and Josh. When we appeared through the entrance of the kitchen, they all froze as if they were almost afraid of what they would see.

"What?" I asked as Nicole made her way around me to go to the refrigerator.

No one answered. Instead, they alternated looking between the both of us as we made our way around the kitchen. I grabbed a waffle with my bare hand and decided to stare back at them with as much passion as they looked at us. Josh finally gave me a disgusted look.

"Why must you grab a waffle with your bare hands? Be better," he scoffed.

"Why must you all look at me like that?" I asked in response.

"Why must you answer questions with another question?" Eliza asked dryly.

Nicole sat at the empty seat on the island, and the attention went from me to her. She purposely did not look up as she tackled the waffles on her plate. Rachel reached for her hand, and Nicole exhaled visibly.

"Okay, I've had enough of this game. So you guys screwed," Eliza said before taking an amused sip from her mug.

"What is it with you announcing who Noah sleeps with?" Josh asked.

"Don't start with me, pretty boy. You're currently on my good list." Eliza narrowed her eyes.

Jason sat his mug down hard on the counter, making a loud clang that resonated throughout the kitchen. He hopped off the stool he was sitting on and stormed off into the living room. Nicole looked at me with tired eyes. I put a hand up to show that I got it before I followed in Westbrook's direction. Out in the living room, I found Jason pacing back and forth. He stopped when he saw me, and, by the looks of it, wished I would drop dead right there.

"Are you alright?" I asked softly.

"Yeah, I just wanted exercise," he deadpanned.

"Look, Jason, I don't know what you're going through. You pressed on because of your brother, but this ended up happening. I'm sorry that things ended the way they did with you and Nicole. I know it's hard for you," I said.

"You know *nothing* about how I feel. You're constantly getting whatever you want. There's never any consequences for what you do," he said.

"I wish that were the case. In fact, I have to pay for things other people do. I know you hate what's happening. I lost Nicole in a way very different from this, and yet, I'm certain any version of losing her would destroy one's heart just the same," I said.

"Look Shakespeare, I know it's over. I just need time to get over it," he said.

"Understandable," I said.

"Promise me you'll take care of her," he said softly.

"Always, but this will all be over in a few weeks," I said.

Jason snorted and put his hands in his pockets before he took a step in my direction. He laughed to himself as he shook his head.

"You might not realize it, but she's still into you. I knew it the day we ran into you for the first time in that lunch room. I knew it the day you guys kissed at the courts. I was not going to win her heart because there was nothing left to win. You already had it," he sighed.

Chapter 26

I moved into an apartment just a short walk away from campus. Living among a bunch of freshmen, who never took anything in life seriously and thought it was merely a bed of roses, pissed me off. They were wasting away as they drank and smoked themselves into oblivion. They were never quiet either.

I didn't think Nicole would think me living in her building would be that big of a deal, but when she saw Greg and me with boxes in our arms, she was silent before she granted us with the most eloquent string of profanity that either of us had heard in our lives. Seriously, I was impressed that after all Greg and myself had seen, she was still able to instill fear into us. I didn't decide to visit her until the second week of the semester. She answered the door and hardly acknowledged me when she left it open for me to walk in.

Everything was pretty much the same. Her apartment was neat and cozy. No wonder Jason always wanted to hang out there. I looked over at the windows and saw that they were locked. I couldn't blame her. Greg had a wild security system installed in my apartment. I was pretty sure he had planned to install one in Nicole's as well, but he was probably too afraid to bother her.

After I finished looking out at the busy street below, I turned to look at Nicole, who was standing by the stove with a mug in her hand. She was already staring at me and didn't look away when our eyes met. I couldn't read her expression, but at the same time, deep down, I felt like I understood it. I missed her.

"How have things been?" I asked.

"Good. Except for Thursdays," she said in between sips.

"What's on Thursdays?" I asked.

"Organic Chemistry. It's evil," she said.

"That sounds downright satanic," I deadpanned.

"I'm serious! It's even worse than it sounds," she laughed, "Alyssa and I already are losing sleep over it. I was up at the library until after ten last night."

"Ah yes, Alyssa, the girl who tried to hook up with Westbrook," I said, sitting down on the foot of her bed.

"Yeah, before you decided to punch him in the face," she said.

I narrowed my eyes at her, but Nikki gave me an "I dare you" look that made me crack a smile. She chuckled triumphantly before throwing her head back as she finished what most likely was tea and put the mug in the sink. It looked like she was about to walk in my direction, but changed her mind and stayed by the counter.

"What's wrong?" I asked.

"Um, nothing," she said, quickly looking over at the refrigerator and then disappearing behind the door.

I got up and walked over to her. When she stood up from the door, she jumped. I raised an eyebrow at her but stayed silent. I closed the door gently, and she didn't stop it. She looked down at her hands before she sighed.

"I wish we didn't do what we did," she said.

"I don't regret what we did," I said.

"Because you can just sleep around without it meaning anything," she said before she walked over to her bed.

"It meant a lot to me too, Nikki. Why wouldn't it? My feelings haven't changed," I said.

She fell back on her bed and put a pillow over her head before she sighed dramatically. A smirk formed at the side of my lips. It was nice to know she wasn't the only person who had what happened on their mind. She was right, we shouldn't have slept together. It would make saying goodbye much worse, and unfortunately, the clock was ticking.

"What made you come here?" she asked, finally sitting up.

"There's an event next Friday, and we're supposed to be there together," I said.

"What event?" she asked.

"Some gala for something we're supposed to care about." I shrugged.

"I don't have a gala dress," she said, rubbing her temples.

"Greg figured you wouldn't have the time. He'll send you a few to choose from," I said.

She nodded and didn't say anything. I walked over and sat next to her.

"Are you hungry?" I finally asked after a long silence.

"I could eat. It's dinner time." She shrugged.

"Would you like to go somewhere for dinner?" I asked.

"No," she said.

"Oh."

"It's cold. We can order something," she said.

"I could make something," I said.

Nikki chuckled to herself and tried to hide it. I rolled my eyes and nudged her, which made her laugh louder.

"The last time you made something, you almost burned your house down," she said.

It was not that bad. I tried to bake cookies, and somehow, they caused the house to be filled with smoke. It's a mistake any of us could have made.

"Josh got the chef gene. Not you," she said.

"Thanks," I said, tossing a throw pillow in her direction.

She threw one back purposely hard. She quickly got up and rushed to escape to her bathroom, but she was too slow, and I caught her right before she could close the door. Her fight was in vain. She was not going to move unless I let her. I wanted to kiss her so badly, but I knew my job was to stay away.

I was forgetting something. I let most things leave my mind unless Greg brought it to my attention, but whatever was supposed to happen that day left some type of imprint in my memory. I finally let her go, and she gave me a small kiss on the cheek before giving us some distance.

"What's that for?" I asked.

"Well, I spoke to Rachel," she sighed.

"And she told you to kiss me? Remind me to get her a really nice birthday gift." I chuckled.

"She said… 'Look, you are in this weird circumstance. Maybe you should just enjoy having your prince while you have him'," she said.

I didn't say anything. Her prince. When was the last time she had called me that? I tried to suppress the stupid smile that was creeping up on my face.

"You're not going to lose me after this, Nikki. I'll still be around," I said.

"Not like this," she said softly.

I looked over at the dry-erase calendar on her wall and saw the circled date. *What was supposed to happen today*, I thought. Then it hit me.

"I have to go," I said.

"Oh, okay," she said, and disappointment was laced in her voice.

"I'm sorry," I said before I shut the door behind me.

I didn't wait for the elevator as I ran up the stairs, two by two, making my way to the fifth floor. When I got there, I noticed my door was already open. I walked through the doorway slowly. There was no one in the living room or kitchen. I looked in my bedroom. Still nothing, but the air felt charged, like someone was just there. I walked to the small room that might as well have been a closet, but Greg turned into an office slash crash spot for when he was around. I pushed the door open and heard the sound of a gunshot. I felt a chill settle over my body before everything went in slow motion. Gerard Spinelli was holding a gun at Greg, and Greg was holding one back at him. Another shot went through a silencer, and Gerard fell to the ground. I looked at Greg with wide eyes.

"What the hell happened!" I shouted.

"He came here looking for you," Greg said.

"How did he even know I'd be here?" I asked.

"I don't know, " Greg sighed.

We both looked at Gerard, who was holding his leg in pain on the floor. There was blood on the carpet, and his gun had slid a few inches from my feet. I picked it up to make sure he couldn't get it again.

"You're going to pay for this," he said in a strained voice.

"For a new carpet? Yes," I sighed, showing him I didn't care.

"Hi, I need you to come up to the new apartment and deliver something to its parents," Greg said tiredly on the phone.

Within minutes, two men came upstairs and carried Gerard out. Another woman came in to clean the blood stain on the carpet. I watched it all silently. My life was an utter mess, and all these people cleaned it up for me without question. It seemed like everyone except me could handle what was going on.

"What happened here," Jason said, walking through the open apartment doorway.

He had his glasses on for the first time in a while. He looked so different with them, I almost didn't recognize him behind the large black frames.

"None of your concern," I said.

"I saw them pulling Gerard out. Luckily, no one else was in the hallway," he said.

"You what?" I asked, shocked that they would do such a messy job.

"No, I asked Greg," he said, chuckling.

"Why are you here?" I asked.

"I live on this floor, remember?" he asked.

"Oh, yeah. My brain blocks out traumatic details," I deadpanned.

Jason shook his head before he sat on the arm of the couch in front of me. He looked around slowly. It was the first time he had been here. We weren't necessarily the best of neighbors.

"How's Nicole?" he finally asked.

"You don't know?" I asked.

"No," he said.

He didn't add any more details after that. I watched as Westbrook looked down at his shoes. I hated that I felt bad. He had done this to himself, and I felt bad for him. Nicole was hurt, and I knew she had kept him at a distance. I just didn't know how much.

"She's doing good. She's Nicole. That's all she knows how to do." I smiled.

"Yeah," he said softly.

"It'll work out. If she can forgive me, you two can rebuild your friendship," I said.

He didn't answer. I sighed at the pity I felt for him. I got up and grabbed a couple beers from the refrigerator, popped them open, and handed one to him. He gave me an odd look, but accepted it after giving me a questioning look.

An hour and three beers later and things had gotten a lot funnier than they were before. I told Jason about the time I got on the school bus without pants because my mother didn't care enough to look at me before I left the house. He shared about his father, who could be very cold and checked out whenever he brought up Josh. Apparently, every year around the anniversary of Josh's disappearance, Mr. Westbrook would blame every mindless mistake he made on his son or his wife. Once, he burned dinner and found a way to blame Mrs. Westbrook, who was at a convention on the other side of the country. It all was pretty depressing to think about, but everything was funnier with some liquid courage.

"Do you ever wonder what type of parent you'll be? I mean, dude, your mother does not seem like…" he trailed off.

"Are you trying to tell me she's a witch?" I snorted.

"At least we're keeping it clean," he deadpanned.

I laughed as I put my third bottle down on the coffee table. I tried my best to keep it down since Greg had retreated to his office after everything was in order, but volume control and beer rarely went together.

"You didn't answer my question," he said.

"Oh, what was it?" I dragged out.

"Do you think you'll be a good parent?" he asked.

"I'm not going to have kids," I said.

Jason sat up in a completely sober fashion and looked at me with a bewildered look. He ran some fingers through his hair, and then rubbed his eyes as if he was trying to wake up. I raised an eyebrow at him, still laying down with my feet up in the recliner.

"Why not?" he asked.

I had only planned to have children with one girl, and we were about to be divorced. It probably wouldn't be fair to bring a child into whatever unhappy relationship they would be the result of. I was living evidence of how that could be problematic.

"I don't know." I shrugged.

"Nicole wants kids," he said.

"Great, tell husband number two that," I deadpanned.

"Imagine you two don't get divorced." He chuckled.

"I think it's time you drink some water," I sighed.

Chapter 27

I woke up to a phone call at seven in the morning. It was a school day, but there was no reason for me to be up. I was the farthest thing from a morning person. It had been this way since middle school, and I was finally able to live the schedule I was meant to live once high school was over. The pillow over my head was not blocking out the sound, and it was clear the fool thought it couldn't wait when I realized they were calling for a second time. A few curses left my mouth as I finally sat up to look at my phone screen. Tracey Crawford.

"Mother dearest," I said dryly.

"My son, it's so nice to hear your voice," she said.

"It's early," I responded, not interested in exchanging pleasantries.

"I got a call from Mrs. Spinelli last night . She wanted to express her sincerest
apologies about what happened with her son in your apartment some days ago. Why am I just hearing about it now?"

I snorted loudly. There was so much wrong with what she had just said. Not only had my mother failed to show an ounce of concern for my well-being in the past few months, she wasn't that great with doing so when I was growing up either. In fact, she was pretty fucking bad at it.

***

The summer after eighth grade was supposed to be fun. Ramos and I made plans to fix his dad's old ATVs and ride them in the woods. We also had plans for a concert. I had a smile on my face as I walked through my front door on the last day of school. Graduation would happen, and then we would have the best summer of our lives. I dropped my backpack by the door and walked over to the kitchen to grab a snack, but stopped when I saw my mother sitting by the island. She had a small smile on her face. It was the smile she always wore whenever she thought she had a good idea, so of course, that was never good.

"Hey, Mom," I said wearily, walking over to the refrigerator.

"Guess what I have planned for you this summer," she said enthusiastically, but it wasn't convincing. It was her.

"Oh no," I groaned.

"You're going to a sports camp," she said.

My lips tried to form words as I tried to sort through this new information. Why the actual hell would I need to go to a sports camp? I wasn't training to become an athlete.

"So, you're sending me to a bougie bootcamp. Did I do something to piss you off or something?" I asked, wracking my brain as I thought about the last time she had even cared enough to ground me for something.

"No, but I spoke to your uncle, and we thought it would be a great idea for you to learn how to defend yourself." She shrugged.

I rolled my eyes when I realized what this was really about. Reginald Crawford, my Dad's little brother and my uncle, was cool, but also insane. He would always tell me how I needed to bulk up, or that certain things I liked doing, like existing, would have to stop once I got older. That's dramatic, but it was still annoying. For example, whenever he would come to visit, and I would play the piano or film random stuff with the kids at school, he would tell me that I should spend more time learning about business and the stock market. I wondered if he knew about some weird breed of middle schooler that gave a shit about that stuff.

My latest offense was that I was not able to fight him off when we were roughhousing over spring break. Mind you, he was thirty-five and twice my size, which was fine because I was only a kid. After almost crushing my ribs, he repeatedly brought up for the rest of his visit that I needed to bulk up. "Little punks aren't in the family business," he would say. Got to love toxic masculinity.

"Can't you just enroll me in some classes here, or maybe just not at all," I begged.

"I think it'll be better if you could be immersed in the experience," my mother said, adjusting the sleeves of her blazer.

Let me translate that for any of you who may be confused: she didn't want to worry about having to parent me for a whole summer. She was miserable last summer when I would occasionally ask her to do something with me. I knew she would do anything to avoid having to go through it again.

"Plus, I have a two week spa retreat. I can't leave you home alone." She shrugged.

There it was. I scoffed because her leaving me home alone had been a thing since I was nine, and it wasn't even illegal anymore.

"When is this happening?" I asked.

"You leave in four days," she said, glancing at the screen of her phone.

"Mom! Why am I just hearing about this now? I had plans," I said.

"What plans? Running around with Alex and *those girls*?" she questioned.

"Michelle and Nicole," I sighed because I was too tired to discuss her ignorance at that moment.

"Yes, well, it would be nice for you to have some structure this summer. Sometimes it seems like you're just sitting around wasting your time," she said.

Translation: I wasn't doing what she and Reggie wanted me to do. At this point, we had argued so much that I knew there was no way to get out of this.

"This sucks. Well, if you ever want us to bust you out, let me know," Alex said.

"Um, when did I agree to this?" Nicole asked.

"We're ride or dies," Alex said.

"Okay, relax Clyde." I shook my head.

I hugged my friends before I got in the car. I was not interested in hearing my mother honk her horn again. Six weeks wouldn't be that bad. Would it?

It was. It was bad. It was hell. I thought about different ways of getting sick so I could go home. I yearned to sit in the office of CCT, the telecommunications investment company my father started, with my mother all day. Anything that was not Sergeant Asshole screaming in my face every second he got the chance to or waking up to the incessant sound of a bull horn. Yeah, it was structured, and I pushed myself, but I just wanted to be with my friends. We had just moved a few months ago, and I was glad I made any friends to begin with. I needed to be with them, not training like I was getting ready for war.

I got back home to Alex sitting on my front porch waiting for me like I was Santa Claus. I hopped out before Mom even came to a full stop and hugged him.

"Dude, you bulked up. You're going to get all the chicks. You're hot. You're a Don," he hollered.

"Thanks so much, Ramos. I love when my guy friends objectify me," I deadpanned.

"What did they do to you there?" he asked in a whisper as my mother walked by.

"Mainly strength training and playing sports. I worked out about four hours every day," I said.

"That sounds pretty horrible, honestly." Ramos frowned.

"Yeah, but I'm back now." I shrugged as I heard the fluttering of bike wheels spinning quickly. Nicole and Michelle came riding down the street. They came to a stop when they got to my front lawn.

"Hey guys. I'll see you later, Nicole," Michelle said before she took off.

"It's good to see you back, Noah," she said as she steadied her bike with a foot on the sidewalk.

"It's good to be back." I shrugged.

"What'd you do?" she asked.

"A lot of sports and working out," I said.

"Oh. Well, I guess I'll see you around," she said.

She rode off, and Alex and I were quiet for a moment. I thought about how I didn't realize how much I missed seeing her around, riding bikes and just talking with her.

"You got jacked and she got a rack," he said.

"We're going to stop objectifying our friends right now." I hit the back of his head.

"Ouch, that hurt a lot more than it used to," he whined.

"Sorry, dude." I chuckled.

***

"So, now that you know what happened in the apartment, why are you calling?" I yawned.

"I'm supposed to know. It's my right to know. I'm Head," she said.

"You want to know so you can spin things in your favor," I said.

"Fine, Noah. Be that way. I'll see you at the hearing on Thursday night," she said.

I opened my eyes again and looked at the digital calendar on my nightstand, courtesy of Greg, who was always finding new ways to organize my life. I tapped on the glass screen. It was supposed to be Saturday, not Thursday.

"It's supposed to be Saturday, not Thursday," I said.

"Saturday didn't work for us. You and your wife can make it, can't you?" she asked.

I sighed inwardly. She knew that was our busiest day of the week. She found out and decided to screw with us. I punched the pillow next to me.

"Why would you schedule this on a day you know we're busy?" I asked.

"If you want it, you'll make it work. If you can't make it, it must not be that important for the two of you," she said.

My mother never appreciated my goal to get a degree in psychology. She thought I should get something in business. I'd rather stick pins in my eyes. With everything that had happened to me in the past few years, I always thought maybe learning about the mind would help me understand myself.

"What time?" I asked.

"Seven sharp," she said, and I could hear the dark amusement in her voice.

Chapter 28

Nicole Smith is one of the best women I know. She's beyond nice and very understanding. That was what I always liked about her. But, I knew there were certain things that she would not be very chill about. Anything that would get in the way of school was one of them. Once, I asked her to cut last period with me since they wouldn't take attendance, and she looked at me like I had just told her the cruelest thing in existence.

To butter her up, I ordered her a huge bouquet of periwinkle hydrangeas and brought it to her apartment that afternoon. When she opened the door, her jaw dropped a little before I handed her the bouquet.

"Aw, Noah, what's this?" she asked.

"Just thought I'd bring you something that would make you smile," I said.

"I love these," she said with a quick kiss on my cheek.

I felt a smile creep up on my cheeks as I watched her get a vase from underneath the kitchen sink and fill it with water. It had been some time since it had been like this, me bringing her flowers and her smiling from something so simple. Nicole never wanted my money or anything. She was way deeper than that. I almost didn't want to tell her what would be happening that afternoon.

This saga of my position in The Table being in question would end, and eventually, so would we.

"Well, thank you. I really love hydrangeas. They're just so… complete," she beamed.

"Complete?" I asked.

"Yeah, they're so full and undoubtedly beautiful. All they need is some sun and water. They're pretty complete," she said softly as she put the vase on the table near her bed.

"Isn't that like most flowers?" I chuckled.

"Yeah, you're right, but I know I need a little more than just some water and sun." She shrugged.

"Like what?" I joked.

She didn't answer me at first. The expression on her face seemed whimsical, like she had a fun comeback. I hung on as I waited for what she would say next.

"Love, patience, maybe a little food," she said with a smile that went straight to my heart.

I smiled and sat next to her on the foot of the bed. Our hands were so close, and I wanted to grab hers, but I didn't. I didn't know where our boundaries were anymore, but I didn't want to push it.

"So, I have some news," I said.

"Okay, what is it?" she asked.

"They rescheduled the hearing," I said.

"Oh, so when is it?

"Tonight at seven," I said.

"*What?!* I have class until 5:45. How is that going to work?"

"We don't have a choice," I sighed.

When it came to hearings, an individual had to be present, or the opposing side would immediately win. It was an absolutely ludicrous rule, but it had been that way for the past two decades.

"I have a test today, so I can't cut," she sighed.

"Do you trust me?" I asked.

She gave me an apologetic look before laughing. *Thanks, wifey.* I rolled my eyes before I rolled up my sleeves and told her my plan.

It would've made more sense to skip class, because I could not pay attention for the life of me. My fingers typed away as Professor Lockhart spoke about Freud, but nothing sank in. My mind was already in that dark room, thinking about what my fate would be. It was weird, all of it. Regardless of what would happen that evening, there was no telling what would happen after that. If I was going to be the new Head of The Table, I had no idea how I would handle it. My training came to an end after I had to go to Valley.

If I was going to lose my title, what would happen to me and the rest of my friends? It was weird calling them that, but they were my friends. We were almost like a family. Would I be on my own? I guess I would have to officially move out of Tracey's house and find somewhere to live. I knew Dad had set some money aside for me, but I would still work. What else would I do without the world working against me? It's all I had ever known for the past seven years. Either way, my life was up in the air and hearing about Freud's unethical experiments was just not enough to get my mind off of it.

I looked up from the slide on the screen to the clock above it. There were only five minutes left. I felt the knots in my stomach tighten. I switched over to the texting app on my laptop and confirmed with Greg that he was outside. He was waiting with the car running. We would hop in and jet to Queens, in New York rush hour traffic. It would be fine. That's what I had to keep telling myself, despite the huge amount of doubt that was weighing on me.

I texted Nicole. There was no answer. She must've still been taking her test. I cursed under my breath. It would take her forever to make it to our building. I texted Greg and told him to get a head start to her building. I would run or something.

When we were let out, I walked out into the hallway to see Nicole standing there out of breath. She had her heels in her hand and her sneakers on her feet. I groaned at her before I picked the phone up to my ear.

"She's here with me," I said.

"Shit. I'm almost at her building. Start making your way to the building and we'll meet on Fourth and Green," Greg sighed.

"Let's go," I said, pulling Nicole's arm as I started to make my way to the nearest stairwell.

She pulled her arm out of my grasp and I stopped in my tracks. She put her hands on her hips and shook her head at me.

"I just ran here. Where are we going now?" she asked in between her breaths.

"Fourth and Green," I said.

"I just came from there. I'm tired. What happened?" she asked through her teeth.

I picked her up and put her over my shoulder before I ran toward the stairs that read "exit" over them. She punched my backpack, but I kept shuffling down the stairs, my feet barely touching a step.

"I'm going to kill you," she protested.

"We'll both be dead if we don't get there on time," I said as I carried her outside into the crisp air.

"Can you please make sure my ass isn't showing?" she asked.

"You're all good." I tapped her bottom that was covered by her black skirt. She kicked my stomach in response. It actually hurt, but I laughed to save face.

I briskly walked on the sidewalk as people gave us questioning looks. There wasn't enough time to pay them any real attention. I started to look for Greg's car. We were already losing time and there were many black cars. I grabbed my phone and tightened my arm around her thighs.

"Where are you?" I asked.

"Holding up traffic by the food cart. Hurry up," Greg answered.

"Wave a hand or something," I said.

That's when I saw him. His frantic wave faltered when he saw that I had Nicole over my shoulder. I ran across the street the last two possible seconds I could before yellow cabs would start charging towards us and put Nicole down by the car. She gave me an annoyed look before she slid in the back. I slid in next to her. I was out of breath. Greg started driving and we were off, just very slowly.

"Dear God, is there any other way we can take?" I asked after ten minutes of nauseating inching.

"We have to take the tunnel," Greg said.

Nicole looked up at that and started typing furiously on her phone. I tiredly looked over at her. Her face started to light up, and I felt a glimmer of hope in my chest. *Maybe we could make it there in the next hour*, I thought.

"Let's take the bridge. We can figure the rest out when we get to Queens," she said.

"Yeah, let's do it. I was just following the GPS," Greg said.

"Trust me," she said confidently.

"I can do that," he said. I could see his smile in the mirror.

I spent the majority of the ride looking at my phone as I begged time to move just a little slower for me. When it hit six-thirty, I felt my heart rate quicken. We had made it to Queens, but the traffic was still moving slow. My leg started to bop until Nicole put her hand on my knee to stop me.

"We're ten minutes away. It'll be fine. Put your tie on," she soothed.

If I wasn't having a crisis, I would have kissed her in that moment. She was so confident and calm while I was a mess. I never let people see me like this. Cool and collected — that was supposed to be me. Freaking out was not me, except for when it was, and there was no telling when I would go back to normal. I hated that she had to see me like this, but I wasn't embarrassed like I was when anyone else got a glimpse of me not having it together.

I put my tie on slowly and tried to focus on everything else but the time. *Chill out, dude. We were close, which meant that I was close to finding out how the rest of my life would turn out. I was only nineteen. That's, hopefully or unfortunately, a lot more life to live. Okay, it wasn't working,* I thought. I took a risk and grabbed Nicole's hand that was resting on her thigh as she scrolled on her phone with the other. She almost jumped. It was unexpected, but she didn't pull away. She caressed my knuckles with her thumb, and I tried to suppress my smile in the shadows in the car.

"Um," Greg said uneasily, ending the moment.

"What?" I asked.

"The road's closed," he said.

Nicole and I leaned forward to look out the windshield at the barricades a few yards in front of us. I immediately knew it was my mother's doing and I sighed deeply. There wasn't any other way to drive to the office. I looked over at Nicole, who was typing on her phone at a mile a minute.

"We can walk. Well, really, it would be running, but we could still make it on time," she said, sliding her coat on her shoulders.

I sighed and glanced out the window as Greg drove up as close to the barricades as possible.

"Do you trust me?" she asked.

"More than anyone," I said.

"Gee, thanks," Greg joked from the driver's seat.

"We got this far. We can't let them win now. Let's go. We have fourteen minutes," she said. I grabbed her hand and opened the door before we leapt out for our lives.

Chapter 29

We had three blocks to go when Nicole asked me to carry her. I was shocked. So shocked that I actually stopped for a moment to look at her. She rolled her eyes before she jumped into my arms and demanded I keep running. At this point, I knew I was five minutes from sweating through my suit, but that didn't matter. The office was in sight, and it gave me the will to run even faster.

When we got there, I used my ID to get in and was surprised that my mother didn't do something to knock my name off the system to give me a hard time getting in. It was definitely an oversight. We ran across the large white room and punched the elevator button until it came. Two minutes. I rubbed my sweaty palms on my pants, which prompted Nicole to caress my arm with one hand while she straightened her clothes with the other.

The elevator doors opened into the long white hallway that I had dreaded for the last few years. We held hands as we briskly walked into the room. Tracey sat there with a look of shock on her face. Our grasps tightened as she stood up, making the rest of the members around The Table follow. I nodded cooly and Nicole gave a polite smile.

"My son, you made it. I was worried," my mother said, and even she couldn't make such a lie sound convincing enough.

"Well, we're here," I said, sitting down after Nicole.

"Right, well, it's time to vote," Daniel said, glancing at Eliza, who sat behind him against the wall.

Our eyes met and she gave me a sly smile. I raised an eyebrow, but she looked away as a response. I turned to Nicole, but she was looking at everyone else. I could see the fear in her eyes, even though she stood up straight with a stoic front. I patted her knee under the table.

"To ensure privacy, this will be a silent vote," Daniel said.

Nicole looked over at me and I back at her. We were thinking the same thing at the same time. This could be rigged. I looked over at Eliza, who still had a cool expression on her face. She widened her eyes as if she was telling me to stop worrying. Nicole was looking at her this time, too.

"Stop worrying," she mouthed silently.

After five minutes, everyone had voted and slid their pieces of paper to the middle of the table. It was silent for a moment while everyone looked at it. The future of everything laid right there. I fought to keep my breaths steady.

"My daughter, Eliza, will count the votes aloud," Daniel said with a tinge of annoyance.

Eliza sauntered over to the pile of papers in between her father and Jen Spinelli. She opened the first piece of paper.

"One for Ms. Crawford," she said.

Nicole sighed and reached for my hand under the table. I was sure some of her worry was for me, but I couldn't forget this had to do with her too. Eliza picked up another piece of paper and smiled.

"One for Noah," she said.

She picked up some more and read off the names. I pulled into myself and focused on my thoughts instead. I would figure out what would be thrown at me in the next few moments no matter what. I heard Eliza say my name again, and that's when Nicole yelped. I snapped out of my thoughts and looked at her with a confused look. She nodded and hugged me so tight that her strength surprised me. I pulled away and kissed her.

"Order, please," Daniel said.

"Sorry, so sorry," Nicole said, pulling away from my lips, but letting me still hold her.

"The last vote is for Noah, making the vote a landslide victory for Noah Crawford. Congratulations," she said.

Everyone golf-clapped. My mother stood and reached out to shake my hand. I took it and shook firmly. She had a look in her eyes that made my stomach flip, but I got distracted when Daniel's hand reached out to shake mine. I shook it, and he even granted me a small smile. Eliza ran up and hugged Nicole first before she hugged me.

"Thank God. I thought I would have to switch some votes. I was worried about you guys," Eliza said.

"I was worried about us too." Nicole nodded.

"Why do you smell like ass?" Eliza asked.

"I ran two miles total today. Cut me some slack," I said.

Daniel cleared his throat and the three of us stood at attention as the room became quiet again.

"I now declare Noah Carter Crawford Head of The Table," he said as he slammed his gavel down. The sound in the room echoed.

"Yes, just as Carter wanted," Tracey said cheerfully, but I could hear the bitterness in her voice.

Tracey took a step away from her seat at the head of the table and put her hand out to guide me. I grabbed Nicole's hand and walked her over to my new spot. She gave me a confused look as we both stood at the head.

"Thank you," I said. Everyone recited the pledge with their four fingers raised, one for each pillar or leg of our organization.

I looked straight across at the portrait of Dad on the wall. He was standing right where I was now, and, for a moment, I felt him. He was there. I had a lot of work ahead of me, but it would all be worth it, for him.

I thought it was completely warranted for me to sleep in the next morning. My bed and I were one, and, for the first time in a long time, I felt like I deserved to rest. I woke up and emptied my bladder for the first time in twelve hours when I heard a knock on my door. I walked over to the door and looked through the peephole. I saw Greg and Nicole chatting. I opened the door and looked at them questionably.

"Why aren't you both sleeping?" I asked.

"Because it's two-thirty in the afternoon and we have an event to go to in a few hours," Nicole said.

"He probably forgot," Greg sighed with multiple suit bags on his arms.

"I did. It takes me thirty minutes to get ready. Why must I get up now?" I groaned.

"Because you're helping me figure out what dress I'm wearing, and then, we'll pick the suit that goes best with it," she sighed.

"Oh joy," I said.

"I knew we'd be on the same page," she said as she walked past me to go to the bathroom with one of the bags.

We decided on a dress that was a dark red, or *maroon*, like what Nicole had called it. It looked magnificent against her skin. The stylists soon came and they used Greg's office to do her hair and makeup. He told me to shower, shave, and do something for my hair because I looked like I just rolled out of bed — which I had done right before they took over my apartment.

When I decided that my appearance would be deemed acceptable by Gregory and *my wife*, I walked out to pick from one of the three suits that would go with her dress. I decided on a dark grey suit with black velvet lapels. I walked out to the living area to see Greg typing on his laptop. I cleared my throat and turned around smugly, which got a chuckle out of him. Then he went back to typing again.

"What are you doing?" I asked.

"Well, I know you don't meet with your mother until Monday to officially transfer over responsibilities, but I'm doing some paperwork that you might need. That also reminds me. I have a question. There's no pressure," he said.

"What's up?" I asked, sitting across from him.

"Are you taking your mother's assistant? I should probably contact them if you are."

"Why would I do that?"

"Because she has been doing the job for the past seven years."

"But you're my guy. Do you not want to be my assistant?" I asked, sounding more sad than I wanted to.

"I want nothing more than to take care of my favorite hot-mess teenager, but legally, I have to give you your options," he said.

"Then I want you to do it. I want you to be my right-hand man," I said.

"Sounds good to me. Anything you want me to do before Monday? It'll get pretty busy," he said.

I didn't answer immediately. He already knew what had to be done. I took a deep breath before I jolted myself back to a standing position. It wasn't time to be upset about what I knew would happen all along.

"The divorce papers… draft them up, please," I said.

Greg didn't say anything. He nodded slowly with a sympathetic expression that made me turn away. I didn't want to think about it that night. I was going to have the best night possible with my favorite person. I started to make my way to Greg's office to find her.

"Greg," I said, stopping in my tracks. "After you do that, take the weekend off. Spend it with your girlfriend. At least one of us will get to."

Inside Greg's office were Nicole and two stylists fussing around her. They both laughed while some low music played in the background. The stylists froze when they saw me and stood to the side. Nicole finally turned around and whistled at me with a quick once over. I smirked and shook my head at her.

"Hey handsome," she said.

"Hey beautiful," I said softly.

"Am I done guys?" she asked the two stylists, who were watching us with curious eyes.

"Yes baby, you're done. Call me anytime. I would love to work with you again. Your skin and hair are perfect," one of the men gushed as he picked up his bag.

"Thank you," she said as they walked out the room.

"You ready?" I asked.

She stood up and ran a hand over the smooth material that fell perfectly over her body. I had to remind myself to lift my jaw back from the ground.

"What do you think?" she asked.

"You look amazing," I said softly.

She smiled and brushed at the lapel of my jacket. That's when I saw her wrist and I tried to find the words.

"You look pretty amazing, too," she said.

"Is that the bracelet?" I asked.

"Oh, yeah." She smiled before she walked out the room to let me revel in thoughts.

It was the bracelet I had gotten her before we had started dating. It was in some thrift shop for cheap, but she loved it. She would wear it all the time when we were dating, but it was the first time I had seen her wear it in years. I smiled with a hand over my chest and followed her out.

I never knew what these ridiculously large events were ever for, but what I did know was that there would be a lot more of them in my future. I smiled and had small talk with people I recognized, as well as those who were strangers. Nicole stayed by my side for most of the evening. Eliza would occasionally steal her away, but she would come back to be on my arm again. The world was a lot less scary when she was at my side, and I basked in the last night it would be like this.

Daniel asked me to do a toast when the event was coming to an end. I wished I had thought about this being a possibility. I sheepishly asked him what the point of the event was, and he rolled his eyes before he told me it was a charity event for art. I couldn't suppress the chuckle that left my lips. It was the most natural emotion he had shown in forever. I looked around and saw that we were in a museum, and it did make sense.

I stood up on the little stage that was in front of the vast room and people started to lower their voices. People who were quadruple my age wanted to know what I had to say, and the thought was scary. I took a deep breath and looked over at Nicole, who was sitting at one of the front tables.

"Good evening, everybody," I said.

"Good evening," the room greeted back.

"It's an honor to be here tonight. So... *art*," I trailed off.

I could see Eliza sink in her seat, bracing herself for embarrassment. I had to force myself not to laugh at my words. Nicole kept a smile on her face and waited patiently. This was for her. I had to do this for her.

"It's so easily overlooked. Someone releases their heart and soul into something, and we consume it many times without much thought about it. It's quite sad, actually, so I guess I'm glad we have times like these, when we get to honor that work; we get to honor the work that we will never fully understand. Let's toast to that," I said.

Nicole's smile widened, and she clapped, cueing the rest of the room to clap with her. I nodded at her. I had to say something else.

"Furthermore, let's toast to those whose work will never be seen physically, but are felt just the same. They, themselves, are works of art in their own right. My wife, Nicole, makes the hurdles life throws at me — *us* so much more bearable. I believe that's what makes her so damn remarkable. Many of us carry a lot of pain, pain that time makes you numb to, but never goes away. Some of us are lucky enough to find someone that makes everything… better. It's all that heart and soul. They have so much, they are willing to share some with the rest of us losers."

The room laughed, but the only person who I could focus on was the one staring at me with wide eyes.

"For me, that's my wife. Nicole, you're it for me and that's for certain…So, let's toast to those who have brought the heart and soul back into our lives. Whether they are those who create art or embody it themselves, we cannot do without them," I said, raising my glass of champagne.

The room clapped and cheered ferociously. I nodded as I raised my glass one more time before I stepped down from the platform. Daniel nodded in surprised approval as he patted my shoulder. I made my way to the crowd that was still clapping. I wanted to find Nicole. I didn't know what she would say, but I wanted to see her, regardless of what it was. That was until my mother stepped out in front of me.

"Mother." I nodded before I attempted to walk around her.

"Noah," she said, grabbing my arm.

"Yes?"

"I hope you enjoy the moment. It won't last forever."

"Mother, you're threatening me? It's so beneath you," I deadpanned.

"I know you think you won, but you didn't," she said.

"Look, I knew you would not be pleased if I got the position, but it was a fair vote. It's time to let go of whatever anger you are holding inside. It's like you blame me for whatever happened between you and Dad. He wouldn't want this," I said quietly so only she could hear.

"You think *I miss* your father? I hate that I still have to look at his face every day when I see you," she said through her teeth.

"Love that," I said, trying to hide how much that hurt me.

"Then you have the audacity to love him and hate me. I was always the bad one. Well, you know what? You're just like me. Carter may have gotten you on the outside, but I got the inside. The way you speak, the essence of who you are — that's me," she said.

"Alright, and you're my mother. Am I supposed to shudder at the thought that I may resemble you?" I asked before taking a long sip of champagne.

"You'll never be like your father. I know you plan to make things right. You won't, because you would've done exactly what I did," she said.

I knew she was trying to get in my head, but it wasn't going to work. Not this time. There was too much on the line. I had worked too hard for this.

"I might be like you, Mother, but you forgot one thing," I said.

"And what's that?"

"I'm better. I've always been the bigger person. Dad knew that, too." I shrugged.

"Just watch your back. Be kind and pass the message along to your *wife* as well. She will need it," she said.

"Enjoy your retirement, Mother," I said before I walked away.

Chapter 30

I couldn't find Nicole anywhere. When I finally found Eliza, she frowned at the sight of me. She excused herself from the conversation she was holding with a guy and girl our age. She walked me to a quiet hallway. I already knew the truth before she finally decided to speak.

"She left," Eliza said softly.

"I figured," I said, sinking down onto a soft bench next to us.

She sat down next to me and put her head on my shoulder.

"I'm sorry. What you said, it was spectacular," she said.

"I knew it was supposed to end," I sighed, letting tears run down my face.

"Noah, don't do that. You don't cry. That's me," she said.

"Can't help it." I chucked.

"I wish I could change this," she said.

"You do?" I asked.

Eliza sighed as she pulled away from me to lean on the carved wood wall. We had a weird past. I didn't expect her to provide me with any sympathy, and that was okay. She didn't owe me anything after what I had done.

"Because you're the Noah I knew you could be with her. Yeah, I wish it could be me, but it's not. She makes you better. Just like what you said." She shrugged.

"I don't do the same for her," I said.

"You love her. You were willing to risk your whole world for her. Not everyone can say that. You deserve each other," she said.

I sighed as I tried to not cry more. Her words didn't really help in that department. I leaned on her shoulder this time, and she rested her head on top of mine. When she wanted to be, she could be so kind.

"Liz, you're going to find a man who deserves you. That's one thing I do know," I said softly.

"Hmm, maybe. If not, I'll just have to play this game on my own," she said.

"Me too." I chuckled.

"Well, at least you got the chance to know what it was like to love someone so infinitely. It's better to miss something than to yearn for it because you never had it," she said.

I went up that weekend to visit Josh. I figured escaping reality even for a couple days would help with the pain I felt. When I turned up that Friday night looking like a hot mess, Josh gave me a questioning look. He looked right past me, as if he was looking for someone else.

"Sorry, expecting someone else?" I asked dryly.

"Oh, I was just hoping you brought the gang." He shrugged.

"No," I said.

"What's wrong?" he asked.

"I'm getting a divorce," I sighed.

"I forgot about that. I'm sorry, man. I know you love her." He frowned before he pulled me into a full hug. I was a little surprised by it.

"What's all of this?" I asked, patting his back.

"I think we both need a hug right now," he said.

After a moment, I pulled away from him and gave a questioning look. He snorted and rolled his eyes before he rubbed at them from under his glasses.

"Don't ask," he snorted, "I'm just an idiot."

I almost screamed when I saw Greg in the kitchen a couple mornings later. I was dressed and packed, ready for the drive back home. The cook was in front of the stove, flipping the perfect omelette. Greg wagged his eyebrows at me, and I slowly sat down as I looked at him quizzically.

"Morning, Crawford." He smiled.

"Morning. I thought you were taking the weekend off," I said.

"I have great news. Your divorce papers are ready," he said.

"Did you have Nicole sign them? Is she okay with everything? I'll just sign whatever she wants," I sighed.

"Yeah, she looked at it! Smile, it's the beginning of the rest of your life," he said, dropping the manilla envelope in front of me before grabbing his plate to leave.

I rolled my eyes at his lack of sympathy as I opened the envelope. I flipped through the papers and stopped when I noticed she hadn't signed anything. I walked out of the kitchen, confused, and walked over to Greg's office. That's when I saw her standing there with a nervous smile on her face.

"What are you doing here?" I asked.

"To talk," Nicole said.

"You didn't sign the papers."

"I know."

I frowned in confusion.

"Why didn't you? Do you want something changed?" I asked.

"Yeah," she said.

"Which part? I'll tell Greg," I said, grabbing a pen.

"The part where we get divorced," she said softly.

I looked up at her as the pen and pack of paper fell to the ground. Her eyes looked at the floor before she slowly looked up at me again. I shook my head at her because I couldn't believe what she was saying. Was it possible that I dreamt it?

"What?" I asked, taking a step in her direction.

"When we were younger, I always dreamt about us getting married. Actually, to me, it was based in law and facts. Protons are positive. Electrons are negative. New York has the best pizza. We were going to get married. We drew that line in the sand, or I guess, concrete, a long time ago. It feels like we've lived a lifetime since then, but the questions still remain. What if we are really meant to end up together? These are by far the worst circumstances, but I don't know. I don't want us to be over. Unless you want that, and I totally understand. We're so young, but I thought it was worth saying," she said with tears in her eyes.

I took a few steps toward her before I dropped to my knees and wrapped my arms around her thighs. She gasped in surprise before I felt a sob leave her lips. I pulled away and grabbed her hand.

"Nicole Aaliyah Smith, will you marry me, again?" I asked.

"If I *must* do it again, yes," she teased as she tried to fight back her tears.

"Absolutely. One day, when we're ready, we're going to have the biggest wedding," I said, standing up and pulling her to me.

She laughed, and I smiled before I kissed her. I exhaled as I thanked whoever was up there. Life wasn't perfect, and there was a long road ahead of us, but without even trying, she made it worth it. She was all I needed.

Once the excitement of the fact that Nicole and I were not going to get divorced was over, Josh and I decided it was time to meet Erica, my Dad's ex-girlfriend and Josh's mother. I had told Josh that I would go with him whenever he was ready. He was hesitant in every sense, but I think him seeing how terrible having a mother who didn't care hurt me, in the most slow and painful way possible, made him want to know if he was holding on to false hope. I knew he wasn't. I didn't trust Jason when it came to many things, but I knew he was right about one thing: Erica would want to see her son.

Josh fidgeted anxiously as I rang the doorbell. Nicole locked her arm around his to try to soothe him. I patted his shoulder. Jason answered the door with a smile and let us in. He led us to a cozy living room before he left to get his mother. The room was filled with family photos. My eyes stopped when I got to one of Josh and Jason together. Josh had Jason on his lap, the two had expressions that were of pure bliss. I thought about what it must've been like to live thinking your family was gone and you had no one. Josh handled it all well, but I wish I could get in his head sometimes. He was the only person that successfully hid their feelings better than I could. I wore a scowl, and he wore a smile.

"What if she doesn't like me?" Josh asked.

"That won't happen," Nicole said.

A woman with golden brown skin walked in and dropped the magazine in her hand. She looked at me and then back to Josh, and then back to me. It was like she was deciding who to speak to first. I pushed Josh forward.

"Hi, Mommy," he said softly.

"Joshua?" she asked.

"Yeah," he said with a small chuckle.

She hugged him so hard that he almost fell backwards. It was heartwarming to see that despite sixteen years passing, she still knew her baby. I guess a mother always knew. Nicole and I held hands as we watched the two sob in each other's arms. I could feel the tears in my eyes fighting their way out, but I didn't dare let them fall.

"And you must be Noah. You look just like your dad when I met him," she said, pulling me into an embrace just as warm as the one she gave Josh.

"Yeah, that's me." I chuckled as I hugged her back.

"I have to say, I'm surprised you're here. I thought you wouldn't want to meet me. I made things complicated for your mom and dad," she said.

"Eh, I think my mom made things complicated for my mom and dad." I shrugged.

She gave me a wary look, but didn't say anything further about it. When she finished hugging me so tight that my ribs hurt, she took a step toward Nicole. Nicole smiled shyly.

"What's your name, sweetie?" she asked.

"Nicole," Nikki answered.

"My wife," I added.

"Wife? Oh my goodness! You're so young," she said, pulling her into a warm, more gentle hug.

"Yeah, it's a long story." She laughed.

"I wish I could have you here longer, but you all really shouldn't be here," Erica said.

"Why not?" I asked.

"She knows about you, Josh," she said.

"Who knows about me?" Josh asked.

"Tracey Crawford. She's looking for you," Erica said.

Acknowledgements

I would like to thank:

- God for the endless amount of strength He granted me to write this book during one of the most challenging years of my life.

-My parents, Carol and Ian. I am forever grateful for your support.

-My brother Ahmed and sister Khadija. I truly treasure the hours of discussing the world of this series at great lengths. Your insight and support are invaluable.

-My grandmother Laurel whose frequent words of encouragement and prayers kept me moving forward.

-My godmother Roseanne, for her endless love as well as for being one of my first readers.

-My editor, Landri, who is absolutely amazing and helped make the words of Noah flourish.

-Sarah, my cover designer, who created such a beautiful cover and was so patient with me during the process.

-All of my friends who are so supportive, but also inspire me to be better by being the amazing people that they are.

-To all my readers who have sent nothing, but love and support this past year. It brought me absolute joy hearing your thoughts and theories about Focus.

-To everyone I forgot because let's face it, I definitely did and you're most definitely awesome too.